BRAVE
WATER

Xoxoxoxo
Sarah

Brave Water

Copyright © 2022 by Sarah Johnson

All rights reserved.

Cover design by Lan Gao
Hand-drawn map by Cadence Purdy
Hand-written letters by Sarah Robsdottir
Interior illustrations by Sarah Robsdottir

ISBN: 979-8-9857719-3-0

Voyage Comics & Publishing
PO Box 721, Wisconsin Rapids, WI 54495

BRAVE WATER

SARAH ROBSDOTTIR

VOYAGE COMICS & PUBLISHING
WISCONSIN RAPIDS, WISCONSIN

"Young girl, I say to you, arise."

—Mark 5:41

TABLE OF CONTENTS

✦≣✦

*This story is dedicated to
Mother Josephine Bakhita,
a survivor of human trafficking.*

*A portion of the proceeds will be donated
to drill wells, fight human trafficking
and help those in need around the world
(see appendix for details).*

Great Red Valley
eastern
AFRICA

Northwest Edge of the Great Red Valley

N

KORIN VILLAGE Pop:30

5TH DAY MARKET

Hand-Watered Farmland

DEKADENTE MANSION

Ketasi River

Azasumi Pop:60K

Spirit Tree

Weeping Rock

Spring

KILOKIE VILLAGE POP:50

GREAT MOUNTAIN

Spring-Fed Swamp

Vacant Shafts

ROAD:
TRAIL:
HUTS:

EDITOR'S NOTE

Although Talitha and the Great Red Valley are a work of fiction, the customs, wildlife, and social issues presented in this book are based on many cultural heritages and realities present in eastern Africa. Talitha's story blends these elements into a narrative that aims to respectfully introduce readers to the beauties and difficulties present in this part of the world without singling out any particular nation or group of people. Please see the appendices for more information and further resources on *Brave Water*'s real-life connections.

*See the glossary in the back of the book for definitions of unfamiliar words.

WHAT THE BIRDS
AND FLOWERS SAW

A PROLOGUE

The angry red sun
hangs only mid-high
steam rises off the cracked ground in plumes

A leopard of a man
hunts the girl we love most
you know her, the silent one
she scatters crumbs
and shares her precious water

Legs pumping high
eyes white and wide
his with hunger, hers terrified

And everywhere, the air is electric

Eagerly,
we watch, we wilt, we wonder…
Will she get away?

MORNING

CHAPTER 1

Talitha
before dawn

MAMA WAKES ME IN THE SHADOWS. Her breath muggy as midday in my ear, "Up, baby, up," she says. "Time to get the water."

I turn over, slow and tired. A fly circles the hut, slow and tired.

Mama hops, a round-bellied ripe gazelle, between aunties and babies swathed in mosquito netting. At rest, we're a sea of brown arms and legs and the pale undersides of feet, as our hut has many belly sleepers.

A baby cries. His mama scoops his fat body to her side— a lovely swish, like a dance. A single swoop of her arm to keep the magic of so many bodies sound asleep. That baby nurses loudly. Smacking his lips, rubbing his mama's ear. His foot pops up over her waist. Pebble toes curl. Squeaky, sucky sounds mix with the snores of open-mouthed aunties. This is morning time in my hut. Soft and warm and making me want to sleep some more.

But Mama's fast like the light flicking in through the ripped green curtain—the tattered cloth that hangs as a door on our hut, the widest in our village. All the other huts are built the same way as ours: a circle with thick clay walls that stay cool to the touch, even damp, sweating like a man in the field on the hottest of days. Other huts, though, are smaller than ours. Made for a mama, a papa, and their children. The one we live in is for us *Others*. Wives without husbands. Children with dead papas, sometimes dead mamas too. Anyone with no close family to belong to. I'm lucky because I've got Mama and my brother Peter. He's twelve—three years younger than me, even though I have to stand on my tippy-toes to reach his shoulder. Sometimes I think about how if he had just been a few years older, enough to be counted as a man instead of a child, maybe we wouldn't have had to leave our hut. If *he* had been the older one instead of me…

But he wasn't, so we moved in with the *Others* right after Papa's accident six months ago, just before Mama's belly started to show the baby.

※　※　※

The horrible news came midday. The sun was orange as a well-fed chicken's yolk. One of the miners—he ran back to the village. Out of breath and black with soot. Sitting on the stump, he fell forward on his knees.

"There's been a collapse," he sputtered, covering his head with dirty hands that trembled like leaves on the wind.

All we could do for the rest the day was wait and pray, pray and wait. And so we did.

Eventually, a few filthy papas shuffled back with haunted eyes. They were greeted with screams and cries. Wives and grannies fell to the dust, weeping at their feet. Little ones screamed the same happy way they did every night when their papas came home. I remember watching them, thinking their dances fit the fact that these papas didn't die. Even though the babies—they knew nothing about it.

Mama sat at the end of the trail all afternoon, through dusk and late into the night. She wouldn't eat, take a sip of water, or even turn her head a bit to the right or a bit to the left. Peter and I held back, side by side, under the shade of the crooked waterberry tree, running our fingers along its rough bark.

We watched her watch the trail, holding hands even though that's not something we do. And mostly, we just kept quiet. Aunties tried to hug Mama's shoulders, tried to guide her back to the fire, but she'd smack them away like they were a mess of stinging wasps.

Mama watched all day. Never once taking her eyes from the grassy patch down the way where Papa would stop every night and run to jump and swing on the low branch of the marula tree. He'd bounce a little bit and knock a few leathery fruits to the ground, thud-thud-thud. He'd whistle up to us, his smile white and wide. Peeling off the outside rind of a ripe one, he'd suck the honey-colored flesh, then crack the seeds between his teeth. And by the time he got home, his hands swirled scented clouds through the sky, tingling our noses with a smell like fresh-ripped field grass and lemons.

That night Mama sat waiting was a bright one. The moon cast her shadow in a long straight line all the way to our family's small hut. Peter and I leaned into each other and, slowly, we walked to her within the path of this dark shadow.

Ever…so…carefully, we stopped just a few steps behind her, not knowing what to say, not knowing what to do. She must have sensed us because she—a strong-backed stone pillar—suddenly crumbled to the ground and, pressing her face to the clay, finally made a sound.

At first it was a moan, a muffled whimper, the sound a child makes when stepped on in the night. But then her groan grew until nothing, no crying pleas from Peter or me, could quiet her. So we stopped trying. Instead, we stood back, weeping soundlessly into each other's salty, wet necks.

And every living thing—every man, woman, and child, every cricket and lonely wood owl joined us. Standing back, the world fell silent. Reverent. Mama's sounds were the only ones heard, as she beat her heart with her fist, again and again, crying out to the night, crying out to the light of the bright full moon.

CHAPTER 2

Talitha

an overripe orange

WHEN WE FIRST MOVED IN with the Others, I lived and breathed despair. Nothing anyone did helped. Not Peter with his smile just like Papa's, or his easy way—just like Papa's.

Even with Peter's lifted chin and all the times he'd whisper things like "We'll see Papa again in heaven," and his "I'm-the-man-now" puffed-out chest, he didn't really mean any of it. Because one day I found him all alone in our hut. I ran in because it sounded like a windstorm in there with him kicking our stuff and breaking bowls and punching walls. He even had a reed clenched between his teeth to hide his screams. And when I stepped into the dark room, we locked eyes. There was a fire in his that I'd never seen before. A fury like Mama's. A sadness like mine.

It was around that time—the day I found Peter surrounded by broken spoons—that my tears ran dry. For a long time, I'd been an overripe orange after a hard rain, tears flowing in sudden spurts *and streams constantly, sprinkling my food with clear, salty drops and dripping into my ears while I slept. But all of a sudden, I was completely squeezed out, with nothing left but ashy, dry pulp. It was around this time that Mama brought me Nala.*

☀ ☀ ☀

Nala's papa was with mine the day the shaft collapsed, and her mama…we don't know what happened to her. We only know Shani walked to the spring soon after the mine accident and never came back. That was five months ago. Since then, it's like Nala's become my baby. But I don't want to think about what happened to Shani right now. I just want to sleep some more. So I dig my nose into Nala's hair. I breathe her in. And oh, it's the best smell ever—baby sweat, dirt, and the sun shining off the river.

I peek up from behind her curls to see Mama in front of our foggy mirror. She ties up her hair in a blue *netela*, then slyly dips her hand into the metal cistern. A few precious drops to smooth my hair. "*Waste of drink,*" aunties would tisk. But Mama has to make me pretty. I can see it in her eyes as she leans over to brush away my mosquito net and fix my frizzy hair. She's sorry I'm so skinny with no curves on the top or the bottom. And my hair. It's wild. More like a weaverbird's nest than a crown.

"Come on, baby girl."

Her face is upside down. She smiles, but dimly. Her hands twist a few quick braids. Droplets fall cool on my cheeks. I rub them into my eyes, sit up, and stretch in the darkness.

"Time to go!" she yell-whispers the fast way she does when she's about to get mad. Her teeth show on the sides in sharp white points. Her hands are on her hips, and her slanted eyes make her look like a fox.

But I'm so tired, I flop back down. I almost wish I'd injured my leg the way Peter did a few weeks ago so that I could sleep a little longer. Ever since he slipped coming down the hill into the village and twisted his knee, he's been staying back to help with the *Others* instead of going to the fields. Auntie Eshe says he should be able to take his splint off soon. But for now, he gets to stay on his mat a little longer.

Mama has no pity for me, though. She exhales and swats my bottom. Finally, she tickles my side and I scurry to my *mtungi*— the large plastic container we use to carry water—like a chameleon to the sun.

ᳵ ᳵ ᳵ

I give thanks Mama walked beside me this day—this terrible day, this magical day. This day you may find more like a dream or even a nightmare. Mama walked so I would not walk alone. But she didn't carry a mtungi, *for her belly had grown too ripe. None of the* Others *could have taken her place. She wouldn't let them.*

"Too old," she scowled when I'd reach for an auntie, "too sick," "too tired," "too weak."

So Mama was at my side. My witness. And I'm glad, because this day…

This day that darkness and light fought a battle around and inside of me…I bless it.

It's a day engraved in the fleshiest part of my memory. Carved in blood. A landmark, a pillar stuck in the middle of my life so far. Time leading up to it is the before. *Life following is the* after.

23

No one was safe from the battle. Light and night touched every-one, hit everything, with splatters of paint—black, white, and gray. But this day, you'll see… it began in such an ordinary way.

☀ ☀ ☀

Outside in the dark she straps the empty, twenty-kilo *mtungi* to my back. And once again, it's just Mama, me, and the morning. On a narrow path, high on the top of our ridge, all is soft and damp. Our feet pat-pat the clay worn down well by our aunties and mamas, walking in a rhythm, gathering water.

The breeze is cool and clean. Brush grass splits before our feet in whispers. To my right lies a green and yellow valley cut by our black river. Its corn and *teff* fields are already spotted with farmers hauling water. These men work from sunup until dark, balancing buckets on either end of huge sticks laid across their shoulders. They're the biggest, strongest men from the villages. The ones whose backs are too broad to squeeze into the emerald mines where most of the men in our valley work. But from way up here, these farmers look like tiny toy soldiers. I know because Peter had a few of these little green toy men once. He found them rattling around in the bottom of an aid package. He'd take them everywhere, line them up on the flat rock outside our hut, and splash them in puddles by the river. He'd give them names and make them talk to each other with serious voices.

I stop to yawn as the farmers pass a bucket in a line. Man-to-man, they move hauled water from the river all the way to the far edge of a soybean plot.

What ever happened to those little toy warriors?

The thought comes to mind with a smile. I remember Papa sneaking up to dump water on the little green men at their "outpost"—the wide rock we use to grind cornmeal.

"*Here comes the flood!*" he yelled.

Soldiers washed off the rock onto the clay. Peter chased him around. Mama and I laughed. The memory gives me a feeling like daisies blooming open in my heart. But then, the truth of what's happened is never far away.

And I want to rip those daisies up from their roots. I want to trample them down like weeds.

"Whatcha' thinkin', daughter?"

Mama glances at me, tugging her flapping green *kitenge* closed against the breeze. Her voice is air, but her eyes are glass.

I try to answer, but I can't find the words. It's like they're stuck, hiding behind my heart. Just as my tears are stuck, hiding behind my eyes. So I fake a smile and click my tongue. She clicks back, and we walk on.

Mama's heavy hips swing low and wide. We've only walked a bit, but the new baby—no matter how she denies it—weighs her down. She spreads her fingers beneath her enormous belly, hoisting him up tenderly. She pulls out her knotted rope and quietly sings her prayers. Climbing up the hill, her voice climbs as well.

"*Lord have mercy, Lord have mercy, Lord have mercy…*"

Then, her song descends with the slope.

"*Lord have mercy, Lord have mercy, Lord have mercy…*"

And even though her prayers are barely a whisper, fear grips my heart. I search for the painted faces of our people behind the bushes, hoping they don't hear her. Of course no one's there, but still—I'm relieved when she's quiet again. Before Papa died, we only prayed in secret, as it would anger the chief and the elders and most of the villagers even though they're not angry people, not at all. Most of them are sweet and good like Auntie Eshe. But they don't like how we don't pay reverence to the gods of our tribe and the chief and his ancestors, the way our people have done for generations. They don't like that our priest is an outsider who doesn't come from the Kilokie or any of the neighboring tribes. So each morning, Mama and Papa would lie on their mat quietly mouthing the Our Father. They'd hold hands with the sun streaming in through the cracks in the clay walls. Their lips shaped the words, but they barely made a sound.

"They just…don't understand," Mama would sigh when I asked why our Shepherd God had to be a secret. But ever since the accident, it's like Mama doesn't care who hears her anymore. I worry, though. With the baby growing in her belly and the disapproving looks the aunties give her whenever she speaks against the old ways…I worry.

Auntie Eshe is one of our tribe's elders, the one who speaks for the *Others.* She knows Mama better than anyone, but even she shakes her head whenever she sees Mama coming into the village without bowing her head toward Great Mountain first. "This mountain is sacred to our people," Auntie insists. *"If your God is really everywhere as you claim, why can you not pay your respects to him there, too?"* But Mama never looks toward Great Mountain when she prays. So I don't either.

We shuffle on. To the left of our ridge, on the opposite side of the fields, the treetops of a spring-fed forest swoosh against each other. And behind these dark trees a swamp buzzes to life. It's a place I visited often with Papa to spear frogs on moonlit nights; a place I can't imagine ever facing again all alone, or with anyone else to keep me company. Papa and I would hunt turtles too, which we'd always turn into *wat*—a stew that's especially tasty if there's an onion or some cassava leaves. Also, there are gigantic crocodiles with scales hard as granite down there, so hard that if the creature slides under a log, its rippled back makes a sound like a stick along a fence. I hear one now, and even though it's far away, the rattle sends a spider up my spine.

Shepherd boys pass us on the way to their flocks with *"hi, there's"* and sleepy eyes. These boys, some as young as seven or eight years old, graze their sheep in the sweetgrass by the river. There's a meadow down below, watered by runoff from the swamp. Most days, it's a murky place, leaving the boys to breathe through cloths tied around their faces because the tiny black flies swarm thick as ghosts no matter how you burn leaves to keep them away. But there's a nice breeze today. No bugs.

We stop at the cliff's edge—the most dangerous spot on our path. Sweat dots my neck as I look out over the drop.

"Mama, wait here for me"—but she's already halfway down, reaching her hands wide, grabbing loose roots, pointing her toe toward a jutting rock.

I face the crumbling wall and cough on the dust. My fingers and feet grip familiar grooves when he calls my name.

"Talitha!"

I freeze. Below me, Mama turns to the voice that's making my heart speed to a trot. I swing from a dangling root, drop to a short ledge, then slide the last meter. My feet slap the ground, but I won't turn around. Instead, hidden by a chalky red cloud, my hands fly to my face *searching, searching, searching* my cheeks for crumbs from the small breakfast of fried banana patties Mama and I just shared. I slide a thumbnail between my teeth, brush off my chest, and tuck back a screaming curl.

He calls to me again and a flock of invisible baby birds take flight from their perch in my stomach. They flit and flutter up and down and all around my chest, my thighs, and my neck. These tiny birds finally land, pricking the tips of my most tender parts purple with their itty-bitty claws, snatching my breath, spelling his name—

Moses.

CHAPTER 3

Talitha
the enormous egg

THE FIRST TIME I SAW MOSES, I was waist high in mud. It was the middle of the dry season and there had been no rain for weeks. All was dusty and thick—the air, our dried-out tongues, what should have been our river split mucky around my waist. Its water, like our legs, ran swampy and slow, much like how time passes now when I'm waiting—always waiting—to see Moses again.

❋   ❋   ❋

"Hey girl," he called. "What are you doing? Come back, or you'll be swept away."

I laughed without turning around and moved out farther. My arms hovered above the water, lifting my kitenge *like a pair of dragonfly wings. I stepped slowly, carefully, through a long-drowned* riverbed. Pebbles rolled beneath my calloused feet. Most of them smooth, but there's always the odd one with a point or an edge, jagged as a blade.

"You do not know my river," I called back, carefully pressing on to my prize. A goose egg, big as the moon, tucked inside a brambled nest in the center of the sandbar. Lady bird leaves some almost every day, and how Nala squeals when her mash glows yellow with yolk.

"Please, girl," he called again. "I cannot swim. How will I save you?"

I shook my head as I went farther out, soaking myself up to my armpits. Reaching into the nest, I found the egg. Smooth and round. Hot and white. With a weight in my hands like a sopping wet rag.

Only then did I turn to the handsome voice. And with perfectly outstretched arms, I presented to him the enormous, bone-white pearl.

He laughed. The sound was honey in my cup.

And this is Moses. This is the picture I return to again and again on my dusty red path when my mtungi is too heavy, when life is too heavy. His playful smile, his broad shoulders, and those sweet brown eyes.

His gaze met mine. I sank beneath it, my knees bending under the weight of his fascinated stare. Holding the egg with my fingertips, I balanced it on my head to keep it clean. He laughed again. I did too.

I waded up from the river to the pebbled shore just beneath him. My drenched kitenge clung to my skin. And all at once, I was keenly aware of my hungry ribs, my narrow hips, and my path-worn feet. But as I looked into his eyes, I could tell—he saw only the egg.

"Oh," he gasped, "I've never seen one of those! May I tou—"

He stumbled toward me, his feet in floppy Western shoes. The good kind with thickness on the bottom and strings to tie them on. They were too small for him, so he cut holes in the front to let his big, hairy toes stick out. And the sight of those toes—for some reason—felt sunny, even funny. Suddenly, Moses was familiar to me, like Peter or Nala or another version of myself. The shy way I usually am with new people wasn't there. It just wasn't.

I knew right away this was the one I had heard the aunties talk about. The strong one from Great Mountain, which separates us from the cities and the rest of the world. He'd come for the spring hunt.

I dropped the warm egg into his open hands. He gasped. I giggled again, even though I'm not much of a giggler. Just as I passed him the egg, a breeze washed over us, licking the tiny hairs on the back of my neck cool. He looked at me. I looked at him. He seemed to see me the same way he saw the egg…with wonder. And so we stood there, looking at the egg, smiling at each other, looking back at the egg and back at each other some more. Time seemed to disappear, standing silently together so much longer than strangers typically would.

"Don't tell anyone my secret," he finally whispered, his face flushed with heat.

"What's that?" I asked, my eyes following his wrist up to the crease where his bicep began. I had the urge to trace the line with my finger, but I didn't. I would never.

"That I cannot swim," he replied as he cupped the back of my hands and refilled them with the heavy egg. His touch on my knuckles shot lightning up my arms.

Without thinking, without choosing my words…"I'll teach you," flew from my mouth like three meerkats spooked from their den.

The words hung between us in the parched white sky for a moment until his eyes met mine—wide brown eyes, shining with fascination. But there was something else besides fascination in his gaze. And it was that something else that made me drop the egg back into his hands and dash up the slope.

"Thank you, thank you…girl, wait—tell me your name…" His laughter followed me as I ran, fluttering over my skin like so many baby birds.

❋　❋　❋

Mama shuffles ahead to greet Moses, the heel of her palm pressed into her lower back. I hang behind at the base of our ridge, slapping dust from my *kitenge* and gathering the yeheb nuts that collect here. I'll nibble a few of these sour yehebs that fill you up as good as meat, but save the rest for Deaf Man, Papa's oldest friend who is hunched over even though he is not old. He's just different, or "special," as Papa would say. We'll pass him soon. He used to be Kilokie, like us, but for as long as I can remember he's chosen to live out here all by himself, never straying from the path to the spring. Often, giving Deaf Man my yeheb nuts or fried banana patties leaves my stomach growling, as most days—like today—Mama and I only have the tiniest scrap to share between us. But now, the shock of seeing Moses has made my hunger pains disappear like the morning mist.

I walk toward them as they talk, but I focus on the towering jackalberry trees behind them. This trick of staring at something besides Moses when he's around keeps me from feeling nervous and shy. I've gotten good at it. I'll watch the clouds or follow a stream of smoke from a distant fire. Now, I keep my eyes on the swishing treetops, watching their waxy balls of sour fruit—the size of Nala's fist—dip and sway, looking like they're about to fall from the branches. Mama and Moses talk about the weather, about crops. But I keep my eyes on the branches where a squirrel leaps from tree to tree then attacks a fallen pod smashed all over a rock. The pod's bright yellow flesh is mixed with the tiny black seeds that jackals eat and poop all over this valley, spreading trees that hardly need water but that—thankfully—give us some shade.

Mama suddenly drops to the ground between us, wincing over a streak of blood across her foot.

"*Oh*," I gasp, shocked but relieved when I hear her laughing. A thorn is lodged under her toenail. She smiles at my concern. I kneel beside her, pull it out, and press the cut with the corner of my *kitenge.*

"*Talitha,*" Moses grabs my arm suddenly and pulls me away. Mama looks at us with a stitch in her brow. I know what she's thinking—Moses shouldn't be touching me that way; he should help her up. Instead, he leaves her on the ground and...

"I must speak with you," his breath is hot in my ear. "*Alone.*"

I search for his eyes as he nudges me off the path.

"Moses?" I gasp at the gentle soul who once got tears in his eyes when he found a drowned puppy, this boy-man who never visits Nala without a sprig of white flowers.

But he won't look at me. He stalks away, and I notice his shirt is soaked through. Black soot stains cover his skin and he smells like copper—the odor of the mines. He kicks a stump. He paces back and forth. The blue cloth he uses to wrap fresh kills is knotted around his fist. He wrings it mercilessly. Any other day, the idea of Moses asking to speak with me alone would be …*wonderful*. But this isn't wonderful at all.

The wind rushes hot through the trees, shaking off more jackalberries with thumping *bump bump bumps*. The squirrel flies frantically from broken fruit to broken fruit, chittering loudly, its fluffy tail high to the sky.

Finally, Moses lets out a strangled moan. The knotted cloth sails from his fist and thwacks Mama on the chest where she's shuffled to meet us. She startles. And finally, his bloodshot eyes meet mine.

"Oh!" he gasps, pointing at Mama and covering his face, "I didn't mean to—I'm sorry! I'm so sorry!"

Mama tisks, clicking her tongue in a soothing way. It's obvious he didn't mean to hit her. It's also obvious she's fine. The twisted rag could do no harm.

"Come on, you two," she smiles as she drops a handful of yeheb nuts into Moses' hand, "we got to go. Deaf Man will be getting hungry."

Mama lays the twisted rag by his feet and guides me away. There's a look in her eye, but she doesn't speak. We walk on a few steps when Moses stops us with a strange question. His curiosity is simple, but his words ricochet through the sky, shocking me, cutting into my skin like so many shards of shattered glass.

"Will Desta be at the spring today?"

CHAPTER 4

Talitha
Moses' cutting question

"WILL DESTA BE AT THE SPRING TODAY?" he yells a second time as he picks up his twisted rag and lopes toward us, his eyes to the ground.

I don't answer. It's not like him to ask after my pretty cousin. Closing the space between us, he trips over his own feet and almost falls. And if it weren't for the dark look in his eyes, I'd giggle at his clumsy way—a manner of moving that is like an elephant pretending to be a cheetah.

His awkwardness is so much worse today, and I know it has to do with whatever is making his eyes so red and his skin so sweaty. Closer now, the smell of the mines is even worse, making me sick and also a little embarrassed for him. This Moses is very different from the one I know. Finally, I answer—

"I think she will be…Why?"

Mama leaves us, returning to the path. He doesn't say a thing. Instead, he covers his face with his hands. There's a rasping sound behind them.

"Are you *crying*?"

I reach for him as his arms fling out, knocking me off balance.

He grabs my shoulder to steady me. Our eyes meet. His are mapped with squiggly red lines.

☀ ☀ ☀

During one of our swimming lessons, Moses shyly explained his clumsiness. He'd grown out of his boyhood body in the short time it took his goat to kid. For this, for his new manly build, he gets a lot of looks. Uncles are eager to fill his meaty hands with spears and loads of firewood. Aunties and grannies titter when he walks by, always serving him an extra scoop of wat. *Girls or the girls who are almost women—they turn into a flock of cuckoo birds when he comes around. It's "Hi, Moses" this and "Hi, Moses" that and "Oh, just look at me in my curvy red* kitenge." *My cousin Desta is the worst. And even though she's always been to me what light is to day, when she cuts between me and Moses with her sparkling eyes and her quick, snappy mouth—oh, I just want to pull her stupid braids.*

But for hating Desta in these moments, I feel horrible. For hating her, I'd love to find my lost tears and cry them for days.

☀ ☀ ☀

I look over my shoulder to see Mama with a hand on her hip. She's eyeing us the way she does when Moses brings his bowl to our side of the fire at night. I don't understand why she worries. I talk to Moses the same way I talk to my brother, and he to me. Moses is always flicking me with pebbles or calling me *Birdy*, a name I might like if he wasn't talking about my skinny arms and legs. It also means—secretly—he's talking about the day we met. And the goose egg. *And* my skinny arms and legs. Which I hate, even though I kinda' *love* that he teases me about them. For some reason, though, the worry in Mama's eyes is more intense than usual. For some reason, Moses' is too.

I know he'd tell me what's wrong if we were completely alone, but that would never be allowed. As it is, our time swimming is something we keep quiet. We never made a promise not to tell, even though teaching a man-child to float like a leaf and jump off the high rocks is hardly something to hide. Still, we don't talk about it. Boys and girls, men and women, aren't usually left alone in our village unless they're brother and sister or married.

"What's wrong?" I try again.

His whole body trembles as he grabs my hands. His palms feel like cold, wet meat.

"I just need to know..." he sighs, "are you *sure* Desta will be at the spring?"

My thoughts are a sleepwalker, trying hard to catch up. *Desta? My pretty cousin? The strange look in his eyes...*

I add up the facts just as Mama taught me when we did math with a stick in the clay—Moses, this odd behavior, and now him asking after my beautiful cousin that every boy in the valley adores.

"Of course." My answer is clipped. "Unless she's sick, but she's never..."

Without another word, he darts away and slides on his heels down the slope. His head disappears under a cloud of dust, which still hovers long after we hear him splash across a shallow spot in the river. When we see him again, he's leaping over the dirt road before the farmland and heading in the direction of the mines. In spite of his distance, I can hear his "sneakers," as he calls them, *squeak squeak squeaking* across the clay.

Mama returns to my side.

"What was that all about?" she asks as we watch him run.

But I have nothing to say. So she pulls me back to the trail, muttering something about *boys his age* and how they can be *confused and confusing*. I don't really hear her because my mind's a whirl. The throbbing pulse in Moses' neck, his clammy hands, and the stench of him. It hangs in the air like a troubling dream.

We watch him shrink in the distance. He's covered the ground quickly, loping like a lion on the trail of fresh blood.

Mama seems to know to keep quiet. And I'm relieved. Thankful for this typical way of hers, so much more in this moment than ever before.

My stomach's a knot. My thoughts are a blur, thinking of Desta…of her laughing with Moses the last time we all went swimming. Soaking wet, she did her silly weaverbird dance. Her tiny waist, her round bottom swaying. She looked like a plum, ripe for the picking. And, as always, everyone else seemed to notice except her.

Does Moses want Desta the same way all the other boys do?

CHAPTER 5

Talitha
the cruel answer

THE CRUEL ANSWER COMES QUICKLY. *He does.* The realization sinks me down onto the nearest rock. Tears evaporate from my eyes before I can cry them. Instead, the tiniest groan dies in my throat. Mama bends near. Her concern is too much, so I fake a laugh that sounds more like a cough.

Questions roll from her tongue.

"Did he smell like the mines? What was that all about?"

But it's all so much more than I can understand or explain, especially so early in the morning. My eyes are still heavy with sleep and the day's only just begun. So I grab Mama's hand.

Back on the trail, there's relief in our stride even though it's extra slow because of her baby. But still, it's just Mama, me, and the morning. We head up the next hill and scooch down its other side. Sliding on our bottoms, we cover our faces with the corners of our wraps, but grit sneaks in anyway, lining our ears, drying out our noses.

At the base of the slope, Mama smacks off the dirt while she hums the *Alleluia*. The song is always on her lips, even though the priest hasn't come for our secret liturgy in months. And even though I miss it, I'm relieved. Sneaking off to the woods at dusk, worrying about the chief finding out, worrying about the crocodiles—I don't know what's worse. Still, Mama hums and my sour taste buds swirl, remembering the wine-soaked bread, remembering Papa.

I glance over at her. Is she thinking about those nights too? With *Abba* Yosef and his voice hushed to a whisper? I have so many questions for her, questions like this one, but I can't seem to say them aloud.

"What is it, Talitha?"

I look away. Because even when she asks, I can't answer. I just stare over her shoulder at the broken trees in front of the swamp. The sun is peeking through them, sending skinny lines of light through the mossy branches. Mosquitoes dot puddles. A low-moving creature appears as my eyes drift away. I snap my head back, but it's gone.

"Just thinking about Nala," I say, looking up to note the sun's position. "She'll be waking up now."

We rest at the cliff's peak as we always do. It's a place where, from far away, the red clay below is speckled with browns, yellows, and every shade of green. A place where the wind spins up fast from below, where our huts from such a distance are tucked in the valley like eggs in a nest: the chief's hut in the center near the main fire pit, surrounded by the huts of his wives and their families. Other aunties and uncles' huts radiate out in a circle, with us *Others* on the far edge. And this village is our home, on the Kilokie side of the Great Red Valley. It's a special place where desert doesn't rule, but where Great Mountain casts shade on dark, winding rivers.

"Nala will be up if Brave has his way," Mama laughs at the thought of the three-year-old who, like Nala, has stolen our hearts. Brave's a bit older, but the two of them are a pair, spending most of the day in trouble, rolling around in the dirt like a couple of pups. "They remind me of you and Peter—only *you* were the naughty one."

Talk of baby Brave always puts a smile on my face. He was Papa's favorite too. The little boy would sit beside him in front of the fire every evening. Brave would cover his face with his dimpled hands and say, "*I hide.*"

"*Oh no!*" Papa would play along. "*Where's my Brave? Oh, please come back!*" And the boy would hop on Papa's back with a squeal. They'd go on like that late into the night, and there was always a twinkle in Papa's eye, an understanding that this was a game he first played with me.

So many memories of Papa make me sad, but remembering him with Brave is so wonderful it's like magic. Maybe I should *only* remember Papa with Brave. That way it won't matter if I've forgotten how to cry. But the thought of Nala waving her tiny pink mug brings my daydream to a halt because *we've got to get on to the spring.* Between stopping for Moses and Mama's big belly, we're taking forever. But as I look down at her—she's leaning back on her hands and trying to hide it—she's panting. So I don't say a thing. I just watch her watch the child within her, twisting and stretching, pressing his limbs through her tightly stretched tunic that's already soaked with blooming sweat stains.

She smiles, wipes her brow, and again—*I just know*—she's going to have a boy.

"I can hear Brave from here," Mama cups her ear and leans out over the valley. She laughs because from this windy spot, our hut of *Others* is just a tiny brown speck. Still, it's funny to think of Brave and Nala down there, driving all the aunties crazy. Up here, our hut, like everything else in the valley, looks so peaceful and quiet.

From this high point, you can even see the reeds of our roof, laid out in a perfect circle. You'd never know from the outside just how stuffy and crowded it is in there right now—full of crying babies where *everything is always dirty all the time* as Mama often moans, the red dust from the valley finding its way through every crack. Always under her breath and always with a sigh if she sees that I hear her. She knows I carry as much water as I possibly can. Still, during the dry season, it's only just enough to keep us from withering away. All our lips are cracked. All our dreams are of rain.

When it does rain, we rejoice and run outside with the tiny bars of soap the *wazungu*—or white—missionary women bring us on their visits. We make our own soap too, out of the ashes of certain barks and leaves, but that has to set for weeks. It saves the aunties a lot of time when we can use the missionaries' gifts. I lather up Nala, then sit smelling her fluffy hair for days. In the rainy season, during the long rains, it pours for hours every day. In those months, we hardly ever have to walk to the spring. We just sit under a thick swath of branches and watch and listen as the wide metal cistern *plunk plunk plunks* full of water. Filling so fast, it steams and froths and bubbles with heavy waves lapping over the edges. Everyone happily dips their cups so many extra times. But during the dry season, it's a different story, especially when a drought comes. I think now the greedy sky must share my problem—it hasn't cried in months.

Lucky for us, the soap-giving missionaries have been more generous than the clouds, and they did pay us a visit the other day. There are two of them. They dress like Moses and come from a city on the other side of Great Mountain, just like Mama—even though she won't talk about that. These kind *wazungu,* white ladies, bring us what they can. And it's always exciting when they arrive, with their heavy bags of rice and dried corn, with every child crowding in, squealing, their tiny hands fighting for a touch of their skin. One time, the women left a little green Bible. Mama grabbed it. She angrily fanned open the pages in front of the lady with yellow hair.

"Tell your man," she said, leaning in to her face, *"these papers are good for nothing out here except kindling a fire! What we need,"* she said, sweeping her arm in the direction of our village, *"is* water!"

The woman's cheeks flared pink. Her mouth hung wide as she looked at Mama the way city people do when they hear her speak like them. It's as if they realize right away where she's from and are confused to see her out here with us Kilokie. I guess it's like finding an emerald in the darkest rubble. Even though Mama wouldn't want me to see it that way. For how angry Mama was when she was waving the Bible, I was surprised to hear her reading it softly by the kerosene lamp that night. She called me over. Her eyes were damp. We read our psalm together, her finger guiding me over the strange-sounding words just as she had long ago. It had been ages since I'd heard her read, or since I'd even seen Papa's thick black Bible, the one all marked

up with ink, the one with pages like onion skin, crinkly and
soft as powder.

What's become of Papa's Bible?

The verses Mama read that night took me back to our family's little hut—to the days when we all had each other. And again,
I wanted to cry so badly I lay on my mat rubbing my eyes raw,
forcing myself to think about the most horrible parts of Papa
dying in the mine—about him moaning and begging for help
and nobody hearing him. Thoughts that used to make me weep
until I couldn't breathe. But it was so awful because all this pain
I stirred up had nowhere to go. Because no matter how I tried,
my eyes stayed dry, refusing to shed even one single tear.

I gave up and sat by the window, reading our psalm by the
light of the moon. That line about *leading me beside still waters*
made me mad. Now it always comes to mind whenever we walk
by our river. The reason we *can't* drink its water is because it *is* so
still, at least at this time of the year. We can cool off in it, rinse
our pots *if* they're quickly laid on the fire. But we do this with
our mouths sealed tight. Because even just a teensy-tiny gulp of
our river could be the spark that spreads disease throughout the
entire village, killing off grandmas and babies with the red-dotted
rash and a burning hot fever. In the least, a sip will put the devil's
grip on your tummy for days—and send you behind the trees
pooping fire until that fire turns to blood.

I always wish Mama's Shepherd God would lead us beside
rushing waters. Those are the kind that stay clean.

CHAPTER 6

Talitha
stealing from trees

EVEN THOUGH I'M DYING TO GO, I let Mama rest a little more as I rub the sun's heat into my arms. Finally, she stands up slowly and walks to the cliff's edge as if she's spotted something in the distance.

The story is that when Papa brought Mama back from the city he had nothing to give her for a wedding gift, so he brought her to this spot, opened his arms wide, and gave her the valley. I used to tease her about this. I'd say, *"May I join you at your peak, Mama?"* or *"May I gaze at your herd of zebras, Mama?"* But I never say things like that anymore.

She shields her eyes and looks toward the mine owners' compound.

"Yup. They're turnin' on those sprinklers."

Scowling, she squints in the direction of Dekadente, the white marble mansion on the far side of the valley. Rumor has it the mine owners who live there had coconut trees shipped in from some Asian island. But the trees kept dying until they began watering them most of the day.

Mama spots a branch on the ground by her feet. It would make a good walking stick but instead she picks it up and bangs it again and again on the rock barrier between us and the steep drop below. Clay clods patter down. Mama coughs on the dust cloud she's created. Someone passing by would think this very pregnant woman was crazy. But I know Mama. Papa used to call her his little firecracker. *"She's tiny, but watch out!"* he'd say with a wink. And then he'd back off, just as I'm giving her space right now. Because I know that even the idea of the mine owners and their sprinklers makes Mama beat things with sticks.

※　※　※

"They drilled a well for the trees!" Mama pounded cassava with her machete. White specks of root flew everywhere, along with flecks of spit from her mouth that came at moments like these. Moments when she was boiling mad at Papa's bosses—so, pretty much all the time. Papa was used to hearing her rant. He sat there, rubbing his sore shoulder and smiling at me tiredly.

"Then they set up guards to protect the sprinklers so our children can't steal water from their trees!" The whites of her eyes matched the cassava, which matched her teeth and her white-hot anger.

Papa scratched his head. When he realized I was hanging on to her words, he pulled me close. He was resting on the upside-down cast-iron bucket and was using a blackened rag to wash up as best he could. Ordinarily, he'd have cleaned himself in the river, but everybody had been spreading word about glowing fish and underwater rainbow ghosts because the mine owners dumped their chemicals that morning—chemicals that would burn your skin clean off. So we all stayed away and slept dirty for a few days.

Sounds of children playing and other papas coming home floated in through our hut's open window. The end of the day hadn't cooled the air a bit. Rather, a vapor hung in the sky, smothering us, slathering our foreheads and cheeks with a glossy sheen, as always seems to be the weather's way on days we can't swim. I rubbed Papa's rough cheek against mine and settled in to play with the tarnished bronze cross hanging from his neck. I'd long learned to ignore Mama when she was chopping like that, extra loud with the machete and her words. Peter didn't hear her anymore either. He played with his toy soldiers as I turned Papa's braided metal cross over again and again in my hand.

Papa's cross… just the thought of it makes me sigh. During the daytime, he kept it hidden inside his tunic. Made up of pounded bronze strips, six each way—side to side and up and down, all of them wound through one another in the center. A cross the size of my hand. I'd press its top point into the pad of my middle finger and cup its base on the flesh of my palm. Its weight in my hand was like resting in the shade.

Following a routine, I dropped the cross and moved over to Papa's side to rub my fingertips along the lumpy lines on the tops of his arms—three on each side, rope-like scars made on purpose. I'd asked him about these marks so many times.

"Tell you later," was all he'd say. Or with a shadow in his eyes, "Don't ask me now." He used to brush my hands away. But finally, he gave up, as my fingertips always found their way back. Those scars told a story, even though I never found out what it was.

Tiring of the heat, I kissed his cheek and went outside to play mancala. *I remember licking my lips as I stepped out into the evening air. They burned with the salt of Papa's sweat, from his hours in the mine where he'd just gotten off a long shift.*

Lately, his back hurt from being crouched down in a damp corner all day, digging for emeralds. His hands oozed with sores from the constant moisture and his eyes were turning into slits from working by a dim headlamp. Mama was always burning mad about his aches and pains, so she'd beat her fists into piles of floury dough, ignoring us, cursing about Papa's bosses, using words like "evil" and "injustice" and "oppression." She did this so often back then, I had to get super creative to think about something else. I'd go over math figures in my mind or press on my closed eyelids until I saw black and yellow stars.

Outside, the evening air had finally cooled. I sat there for hours with Peter, drawing flowers and diamonds and waterfalls in the clay with a stick. Papa joined us, praying in secret on his mequeteria— *the beads dangling on the inside of his robe. But Mama stayed inside the hut, chop chop chopping. The sounds of her swear words and the swinging machete floated out through the open window and mixed with Papa's prayers.*

☀ ☀ ☀

Now, she heaves her stick over the cliff. It hits rocks and sideways-growing trees all the way down to the valley. Mama's back is to me, but I can tell she's wiping her eyes with the backs of her hands, because she *found* her tears right around the time mine disappeared. But hers always appear at the oddest moments. When nothing sad is going on, like now. They never arrive when someone mentions Papa's name or when Peter whistles a tune as he paints his skin with white chalk to protect it from the sun—looking so much like Papa even Auntie Eshe's eyes shine like they were hit with smoke. But Mama cries at the sight of coconut trees and sprinklers. I know she doesn't want me to notice, so I point to the corn stalks beyond the river, their flowery tops shaking in the breeze.

"Lots of corn this year," I say, "enough to eat fresh, and even more to store away."

I squeeze her arm to nudge her on, as we really must go. Her head falls forward. She clicks her tongue. We turn to leave when something in the distance—something big and fast enough to kick up a billowing cloud of red dust—catches my eye. I dart back to the edge, lean out, and squint hard. Still, I can't tell what this swirling red funnel is…

But it's heading straight for us.

CHAPTER 7

Talitha
too quick to be a zebra

"**W**HAT IS THAT?" Mama asks sharply.
She holds on to her round belly like whatever's coming
is gonna' snatch her baby away. Squinting and pointing, we try
to make out the creature that's dipping and bobbing, racing
closer and closer.

"It's definitely not a zebra." The words slip out, and I regret
them right away.

"Are you sure?" Mama winces, and I imagine how Auntie
Eshe would tease, calling her "city girl," making fun, lifting her
nose up to the sky.

❋ ❋ ❋

*Mama hasn't always gathered water, you see—not the way we
do now. She grew up on the other side of Great Mountain in a place*

*where pipes run underground and then come up in the middle of
your hut, splashing a clean flow right into your pot. The thought
of walking somewhere to carry water for your family in a* mtungi
*would be silly. But I think the idea of having water spit into a pot
that's already in my hut is silly. Wonderful—but silly.*

*Also, a hut is called a "house" where Mama's from. And it's
much bigger. Its floors aren't made of cold, packed mud. You can't
lie down on your bare back on a hot day to cool off. But Mama says
that's the only bad part about living in a house.*

*Mama met Papa when her brother Ibrahim went to university
and joined up with the church people who bring us rice and soap.
He helped them speak to us Kilokie, as he knew both languages.
I once asked Mama why she wouldn't teach me anymore, especially
about the Shepherd God. She got real quiet, so I left her alone.*

*Because for a short time, she and Papa did teach me and Peter.
We had such fun in the dark of night in our tiny hut. Papa lit a candle. He took a stick and wrote in the clay. We learned math—lots
of math—from Mama. But then we'd hold hands and pray. We'd
learn Bible words like "Lord" and "Shepherd" and "pasture." They
taught us hymns. Some Desta and I sing now, but only when we're
all alone.*

*"Why didn't your Shepherd God save Papa?" I wept one day
shortly after the accident. "Why didn't He pull him out with the
hook of His staff?"*

*The question popped from my mouth, and I was certain Mama
would cry too. But instead, she tilted her head to the side. Then
she looked around to make sure we were all alone, and carefully
she lifted her woven sleeping mat. There, tucked inside her hiding
spot, was a folded paper. She opened it up to reveal a painting of
a Shepherd with a lamb draped around His shoulders. I'd seen*

this glossy, dirt-smudged picture before. Papa was so enamored with it as a young man that Ibrahim had ripped the page from his Bible and gave it to him (since there was no Scripture written on the back).

Years later, Mama's thumb grazed the glossy paper, touching the Shepherd's pierced hands, His precious lamb, "I don't know why He didn't save Papa, Talitha," her voice was peaceful but sad, "Yet..." She turned her head away, staring into the darkness of our hut as if she were contemplating a vista, "Yet...for many things, we never know why. But it's okay...because we know Him." She kissed the Shepherd, folded the paper and put it back.

I sat staring at her as she rifled through her hiding spot, my mind aching, trying to make sense of what she said. I couldn't, so I peeked over her shoulder at her other treasures. They were similar to the ones Auntie Eshe and all the rest of us have under our mats. We scrape these secret hiding places out with the side of a flat stone. I glimpsed Mama's two copper coins, an emerald the size of her front tooth, and a faded photo of her sister, who has dimples just like hers. She touched these precious objects then returned them, topping her hiding spot the way we all do, with a flat rock, a sleeping mat, and—sometimes—a sleeping body.

Mama once said if we searched under all the villagers' mats, we'd have enough emeralds to dig our own well. I also heard her say that the aid station deep in the desert was supposed to drill us one with money from Ibrahim's church group, but the money was stolen.

I think that's why Mama yelled at the missionaries that day they gave her the Bible, even though I don't think the girls knew Ibrahim or his church group. Still, their faces looked like consti-pated babies, and I think about them whenever I need to laugh.

The first time I told Moses that story while scrunching up my face, he spit his water into the fire. It hissed on the flames, and the thought—he laughs at me the way everyone laughs at Desta—floated up in glowing red sparks.

☀ ☀ ☀

The long swirling cloud is closer now, just beyond the river and the cornfield.

"It's probably a herd of gazelles," I say, trying to pull Mama away, but she won't budge. The speck has grown quickly into a dark, bouncing truck, but I'm hoping Mama's weak eyes won't be able to make it out. My heart hammers in my chest. I try to stay calm for her and the baby, especially with her suddenly looking so pale.

"Please," I say, trying to force her to sit down again. She refuses. Instead, she grips the pointed boulder and whispers, "That's too quick to be a zebra, too quick…"

The bouncing truck is so close that even Mama can see it's a black jeep. It hits bumps and ruts, carving out giant circles in a patch of dried clay.

"Miners," she scowls, and even though Papa was a miner the word leaves her mouth like she's swearing. Because these kinds of miners are different. They're the ones who get to use the company trucks, the ones who sell and smoke what the aunties call "demon weed"—the junat plant. These miners and the fact that girls keep disappearing from the trail are the reasons Mama won't let me walk to the spring alone anymore.

The jeep squeaks as it hits the road, heading in the direction of the spring. I can't make out the miners' faces, but I imagine a lot of them—at least five or six packed in tight. Shovels and pickaxes stand up straight out the back window like spears. The faint hum of their music travels up the cliff's wall.

Eyes the color of crushed berries flash to mind as a fresh curl of dust swirls up in the sky above them. Announcing them, trailing them.

Like a serpent's tail.

CHAPTER 8

Lucian
a gorilla with a yellow smile

Lucian holds the bottle close to his face, studying its golden label. Ten years managing the mine and he still can't get used to the dark. He's tried special glasses and LED lanterns. He even strung his underground headquarters full of white Christmas lights, much to his brother Nelson's amusement. But no matter what he does, the darkness seeps in. It follows him everywhere, like a pair of insidious, smoky claws.

The darkness. The dampness. These and his many worries drive Lucian to chew his fingernails down to bloody nubs. This habit gives Nelson another reason to poke fun at him, since constantly chewing mine-blackened nails leaves stains on Lucian's teeth. Nelson calls him "Rot," implying that his teeth are rotten. Lucian tries to ignore him. He's been involved with his family's emerald holdings in one way or another for the past thirty-five years, literally cutting his baby teeth on unpolished emeralds, as local mothers believe gnawing on a string of the gems takes away the pain of teething.

The incessant cold of the cave fifty feet under the earth. The dripping. The slipping. The sleeping and waking to the same purgatorial *tap, tap, taps* of men digging minerals that hold up the very walls around them. The ceilings that graze his head at even the highest spots.

Claustrophobia is a gorilla with a yellow smile—toying, taunting, ever eager to smother Lucian. So he drinks to forget. And when drinking doesn't work, he smokes junat.

"Rot, get in here," Nelson calls. "We've got another one lined up. We're getting a girl today."

Lucian's stomach tightens.

"Rot, where are you?" Nelson calls again. "I've gotta' tell you about this one."

Lucian rises from a card table and rounds the corner into the other half of the mine's cramped office. The same single light bulb hangs from a cord over the desk that had been there when their father was overseer. Back then, though, times were good. Every emerald pulled out of the ground went right into marble to pave the floors of their family's estate Dekadente, the mansion where Lucian and Nelson still live. But since the price of emeralds dropped and the amount they've been able to mine keeps decreasing, the bank now owns everything— all of Dekadente's marble and even the mines themselves.

The real problems began when the business came under Lucian's management ten years ago, after their father died. Lucian was forced to take out loans to cover "everything but the dirt." For this, he spends most of his time stressed red, as Lucian's fair skin and hair, a mixture of his British father and African mother, easily takes on the glow of the clay flats around him. He seeks out junat because it numbs his worries and gives his chewed-up cuticles a break. Unfortunately, junat costs about the same price as emeralds per ounce.

"What do you mean *you've got another girl*?" Lucian grabs on to the desk so hard he threatens to topple it. His head throbs from junat withdrawal. He can't think straight.

"The first time you said—you said—*that you'd never do it again!*" Lucian's voice catches in his throat. "No, no, no—this has got to stop!"

Lucian's amber eyes are wide and watery. Nelson ignores him and instead strikes a match against the rocky wall. He brings the sulfuric flame to a small glass pipe at his lips and inhales deeply. He lets the sweet-smelling smoke curl up around his face as he slumps down in the squeaky chair. He kicks out his heels, and the chair rolls back against the wall that's reinforced above them with a few metal supports. The supports creak and a wave of panic ripples through Lucian. Because the fear of being buried alive is always there, filling his nights with tangled, sweaty sheets and his days with trembling hands. But since the "accident" that caused a mine collapse a few months ago, his claustrophobia has heightened to the point of a rubber band stretched totally and completely taut, ready at any second— *to snap.* Lucian flails his hand over the desk toward the pipe, but can't reach. He comes around, grabs it from his brother, and takes a hard draw.

The effect is immediate. A heavy fog creeps in on cottoned feet. Washing over him, numbing his mind, tingling the length of his body from his earlobes to the very tips of his toes. The contempt he felt just a second ago at the thought of kidnapping a teenage girl to sell for profit rinses away, like soot off an emerald in a pan. He feels shiny and new. He laughs with Nelson. And for a moment, he's no longer *Rot*. He's Lucian. He and his brother are simply *Lucian and Nelson* again. He relaxes his heavy head into his hands.

CHAPTER 9

Talitha
the sharpest sting

"**S**IT, MAMA, PLEASE!" I finally force her down. The jeep's music is even louder now, blasting up the sides of the wall. Mama's pale as a ghost and shaking all over. Her hands cover her enormous belly protectively, and all of a sudden I can't bear to look at her. So I turn away, swallowing down the dust and the pain, thinking—as always—of Papa. Because if he were here, he'd have a fit. I can just hear him, hushing Mama, trying to keep her calm. He couldn't stand it when she got worked up like this when she was pregnant—even though none of the other babies "stuck" this long before, as Auntie Eshe would say, other than me and my brother Peter.

※ ※ ※

"Hush," Papa always begged, cupping her face, insisting Mama lie down. He'd scrub out the dinner pot too, all by himself each and every night if her smile gave away a hint of a new brother or sister. None of the other Kilokie papas would ever scrub a pot. But then again, Papa was different.

Papa met Mama when he journeyed back with Ibrahim to their city on the other side of Great Mountain. Ibrahim had told Papa about the miraculous healings that happened at a church in the town where he, Mama, and their sister Jane had been raised. Papa came to see the shrine for himself.

Papa grew up Kilokie, and, like so many of his people, he never wanted to leave the life of the red clay. He didn't care that there were tall buildings and fine foods and fast cars on the other side of the mountain. But he did want to find a cure. No one ever asked Papa what he wanted to be healed of when he happily repeated the story of meeting Mama for the first time—he had brought a goat into her house as a gift for their family. Mama walked in wearing her pressed school uniform to find the goat eating a bottle of dish soap. She shrieked, but the goat carried on, bleating like a drunk man and burping up bubbles that floated through the air all clear and shiny and catching color like a rainbow.

Silently, we knew Papa wanted a cure for his stutter, but shhh—no one said it. Words got stuck in his mouth, bumping and bucking, not wanting to come out. It happened all the time. He'd shake his head and rub his fist in his hand. Auntie Eshe said as a child he was teased mercilessly, and it wasn't always better for him as a grown up.

I'll never forget the day, one of the mine owners, named Mr. Lucian, came around. He was all red-faced, stomping and storming through the huts, accusing the men of stealing his pickaxes. The chief was by his side, silently watching—we all knew he had to stay on the mine owners' good sides.

"Go, go, go," Papa said, his eyes desperate, his empty hands held out in front of him. "Fl-fli-flip over our, our th-th-things...We ha, ha, have n-n-no-th-thing."

Mr. Lucian stopped, stared at Papa with amusement in his eyes. He then repeated back what Papa said, only loudly and copycatting his stutter. Then Mr. Lucian bent over, put his hands on his knees, and let out a long, wheezing laugh. With a glow in his cheeks, that sick man imitated Papa in front of everyone, "We haa-haa-haaave na-na-nothing."

Our chief was quiet as the mine owner laughed again, louder and longer. I could tell the chief was embarrassed for Papa too, but he knew better than to cross someone as powerful as Mr. Lucian. Mama's jaw clenched tight. Papa tried to stand tall, but humiliation shone in his slumped shoulders.

That was the first time I understood just why Papa had travelled to the shrine years ago. At least visiting the holy site healed Papa's mouth some of the time—his words flowed like honey when we were alone at night in our little hut. We'd lie on our backs with the roof thatched open to the stars. Mama and Papa would hold hands. I'd curl up to the side of Mama, and Peter would lie beside Papa. Mama and Papa would talk long into the night, thinking Peter and I were asleep. Sometimes we were. But lots of times we listened.

Papa's voice was silk.

᙭ ᙭ ᙭

The jeep's noisy horn snaps me to the present. *Honk honk honking* again and again, the driver seems to be harassing a farmer on the side of the road. The little old man looks confused, even from this far away. He stands there, his head tilted to the side as if he's asking a question.

"You should have stayed back!" I whisper to Mama, wondering what kind of men would give a little old farmer a hard time.

"I couldn't," she sighs. White strings stretch between her tongue and the roof of her mouth as she adds in a heated whisper, "I will not have you stolen like Adia and Shani!"

Our stolen girls—their names spoken aloud are the sharpest sting.

"Also, I need to drink my fill at the spring," she touches her hard belly gently. "You've left me thirsty, haven't you? *Ever so thirsty...*"

CHAPTER 10

□

Lucian
their treehouse

LUCIAN TAKES ANOTHER HIT of the pipe and closes his eyes…
Their kite swirls above him. It's the purple and green one
they flew behind Dekadente when he and Nelson were boys.
Its fluttering white tail spins, trailing them like a guardian angel.

They run, their bare feet slapping the hot, packed clay. They
are fleeing from their father, who hardly ever came home, but
when he did his very presence stiffened the air. The furniture and
the flowers would stand at attention. Even houseflies exhaled
when he'd head back to the mine.

The brothers also ran from tutors, nannies, and most especially from their mother. On the rare occasion she left her bedroom, she'd smell stale and say strange things. She'd try to hug
them or ask what they'd learned in their lessons, but her gaze
was always somewhere else. Also, her slippery green robe felt

like snakes, so they avoided her. And together on the clay flats behind their white mansion, they ran.

Lucian exhales again and a floating puddle of sweet-smelling vapor fills the air, filling the shadows of the mine's headquarters and spilling out into its dark tunnels. He tips back his head to look at the crushing, wet ceiling. And as always, something about smoking junat makes his office feel less like a coffin and more like anywhere else he'd rather be. He takes another hit and he's covered with a warmth so real he's clamoring up the treehouse ladder he and Nelson made by nailing boards to the jackalberry tree.

Their hideout. A few foothills behind Dekadente, tucked snugly inside a row of thick brambles that snap when you step on them and ooze with a white, sticky paste smelling of mint. The ladder leads to a trapdoor they'd push open, climb up, and drop back into place. And what lay on the other side was their whole mysterious boyhood world—binoculars, comic books, and a towering pile of sweets pilfered from their maid Clara's bedroom…

Nelson holds in his puff as long as he can, then slowly exhales. His snarky smile lights the headquarters as dimly as the match he uses to strike the pipe. Lucian, however, still feels a wave of relief when his brother comes around. But just in the sense that he wouldn't die alone if the mine were to collapse on him. Nelson's company ceased to be any sort of true camaraderie long ago. Lucian, nevertheless, continues to reach for his brother even if he receives only a junat pipe, taking whatever solace he can get from the one with whom he was once so close.

Nelson pushes a handful of black curls off his milked-coffee brow. All the nannies said he was lucky to favor their mother

with her thick hair, wide eyes, and full lips. Lucky, but still…
of a mixed race, not belonging with the white-skinned cousins
he and Lucian were sent to spend the summer with—the ones
whose flesh looked like heavy cream and who spoke with words
so crisp Lucian imagined bullets shooting from their mouths.

☀ ☀ ☀

*While the brothers never met the African cousins on their
mother's side, they assumed any such reunion would be as chilly
as the welcome they received from the few locals with whom they
had contact. These neighbors had skin black as the darkest night, so
black the whites of their eyes and teeth contrasted from the canvas
of their chiseled faces like carefully placed stars. When these neighbors—all of whom their father employed in one way or another—
were alone together, they'd joke around, their voices full of mirth,
their eyes smiling.*

*A few of these men guarded Dekadente. They'd share cigarettes
and jokes. But the second Lucian or Nelson stepped out by the pool,
they'd cross their arms across their broad chests and lower their
eyes to the ground. They'd stare ahead with a look on their faces
that spoke of a foul wind. Even when the brothers were toddlers,
the guards and other laborers—maids, cooks, and delivery boys—
treated Lucian and Nelson with disdain, ignoring their outstretched
arms when they'd reach up to be carried, as if they were diseased or
even something worse—unwanted, unloved children of the white
man who exploited their lands and people.*

*But there was one place Lucian and Nelson were each wanted
and loved perfectly, at least as children. And that was together,
alone in the treehouse they had built themselves.*

☀ ☀ ☀

Lucian's pipe burns out. Nelson relights it and Lucian wonders—a fleeting thought—if his brother ever thinks of their old hideout too.

CHAPTER 11

Talitha
the part that terrified me most

THE JEEP VEERS AWAY FROM US, crossing over a shallow spot in the river and slowing to a prowling crawl. Mama digs her fingernails into my shoulder as she whispers their names, the girls we've lost, again and again.

"Adia…Shani…Adia…Shani…"

Just the thought of them makes me scared and frustrated—though not as frustrated as I am now that I realize Mama's been thirsty all these weeks. Because Mama's thirst—I can do something about that!

"Why didn't you tell me I wasn't bringing enough water?" I demand, wishing I had a few small drops in a skin. She hushes me, but I continue, "That's it! I'm making two trips a day 'til that baby comes! And from now on you're staying back with Auntie Eshe!"

Suddenly, the jeep bounces over a ripe field, zig-zagging back and forth, crushing food that could have filled us for weeks.

"Adia, oh, Adia…" Mama mutters her name, as she knew her best—the girl who disappeared first, about five months ago. And we all know it's miners like these who steal girls to sell for junat. We weren't there to see it happen. But still, what we imagine fuels our nightmares. A squeaky truck. A sudden stop. Leering men with appetites dark and strange. The grabbing. The kicking and scratching and her full *mtungi* spilling. A wet blossom spreading out on the clay, taking its color from sun-bleached orange to the darkest ember. The truck revving off, hitting roots and rocks, popping the girl around like a ragdoll.

This is why no one walks to the spring alone anymore. It's also why Mama always carries Papa's folding knife inside her *kitenge* when we leave the village.

✷ ✷ ✷

Adia was only fourteen, but like my cousin Desta, she looked much older. With her light skin, high cheekbones, and curvy body, men paid extra attention when she passed. But Adia just stomped by with a smile, like Nala running to the river, splashing through puddles, catching frogs.

What made Adia most tender to us was her silence, as she had no tongue. That's what people said, anyway. Actually, she had a funny-looking, injured tongue that she'd gladly show off to anyone who asked. No one knows exactly what happened to her, but aunties say she was injured as a baby. Most agree it was an accident. Auntie Eshe once whispered, "She was born with her baby teeth" (a bad omen), "and the mama wanted to protect her. The knife must have slipped, and she panicked." Auntie Eshe found Adia as a newborn choking on her own blood in a bundle of dirty rags by the river.

"That's rare—a baby born with teeth?" Mama wondered aloud once while she and Auntie Eshe were weaving a mat together, "What's wrong with that?" she scowled, shaking her head at this long-held superstition. "Why would her mama try to cut them out?"

Adia was working on a basket that day too, but had stepped out to soak her dry, grassy strands in the cistern. She dipped and swished the reedy bundle, then splashed the bare-bottomed babies at her feet.

An auntie yelled over the ruckus, "You keep wasting that water, girl, and you won't know what smacked you!"

Adia flushed pink, pulled out her long, dripping strands, and got back to work. Her creation, when she finished it, had a base round as a fat lady's bottom and was completely even on all sides. We still use it to store wooden spoons. And whenever we pass the finger-stained basket at mealtime, I think of that day—Adia standing beside the tall cistern with unwoven strands streaming down to her ankles, babies begging for rain, Adia hiding a smile. I'm probably the only one who remembers Adia wove the basket that holds our spoons. Not that it matters now.

"Shame Flora, shame," Auntie Eshe hissed under her breath as she cut a string with her teeth. "You should know better—after all these years!"

"After all these years—what?" Mama demanded, tying off her own end, her elbows and teeth and eyes flashing with anger and the afternoon's sunlight.

Auntie Eshe didn't answer right away. She exhaled loudly, shook her head, and looked toward Great Mountain. She then kissed a tiny satchel of wheat hanging on a cord around her neck, honoring the gods of harvest. She chanted a prayer under her breath, bent over, scraped up a handful of clay, spit in it, and slapped it back and forth between her hands. She then drew a single red line down the middle of her forehead, signifying every type of grain. She drew one on each baby's face as well. Then, with a wide sweep of her arm, Auntie Eshe threw the wet mess across the hut at Mama. The clay smacked her chest with sound like a kiss. Mama tucked her chin, frowning down at the smudge.

"Adia's mama was smart enough to appease the gods." Auntie Eshe spoke soft but quick. "You—you, with your educated ways— should be this wise too."

Mama's face contorted all crazy, but she just let out a humph and didn't say anything else.

Fortunately for the baby Auntie Eshe found by the river, our medicine woman and wet-nurse, Jaia, welcomed her warmly. But then, Jaia welcomes all the Others who find themselves swept up in the folds of her kitenge. With a lot of work, Jaia nursed the girl like she was her own—slowly dripping pressed breast milk into Adia's mouth with a clean rag, as newborns need their tongues to suckle. And in time, Adia simply belonged to the village.

※ ※ ※

The jeep slams to a stop. Skinny lines of smoke sneak up from beneath its hood, disappearing into the sky much like the memory of Shani—my little Nala's mama. I feel so guilty I've been thinking of Adia, missing Adia, without lifting a prayer for Shani. But Adia was our cinnamon stick, with her golden skin and her warbly laugh. Also, she was the first one taken, so there was the newness of it all.

But with Shani—just one girl later—the shock was softer. The outrage, barely a whisper. And in a way, our mild anger... well, that was the part that terrified me most.

CHAPTER 12

Talitha
the sweetest sound

AT THE BOTTOM OF THE HILL, a man hops out of the jeep. Mama's hand goes to her hip, reaching for the folding knife she keeps tied to a cord. But it's not there. Her hand slips to her thigh, then to her other side to find nothing.

"The knife!" she says, searching the ground. "Where's Papa's knife!"

She waddle-runs back down the slope, searching all over, panting and talking to herself under her breath.

"It's gone!"

Her eyes meet mine. I try to look calm, but my mind is *screaming, screaming, screaming* my friend's name—

Adia…

Her silence made her hard to know. For this reason, I have a thorn of guilt scratching at my side. Also, for this reason— a vapid scream—she was most certainly stolen.

☀ ☀ ☀

Sometimes Adia and I would walk together to the spring. One day, she hurried ahead of me back to the village, excited because her goat was ready to kid. I'll never forget the last time I saw her. Rushing along the top of the ridge, one hand to steady her mtungi *on the top of her head, the other holding her yellow* netela, *unwound on the breeze, stretching out forever behind her, waving like a flag.*

She never made it home. The uncles found her mtungi *turned over on its side. A pool of water surrounded it, wide enough to wash a dozen baby goats. Even though Adia wouldn't have wasted clean water on a goat. Goats can drink the river's water—it won't make them sick.*

I was there to see the slimy kid come out straight and walk right over to nurse its mama. I was also there when Azizi, one of the men who refuses to wear clothes from the aid packages, limped back to the village, out of breath. His burgundy robe was soaked in sweat.

"I followed tire tracks for many kilometers," he huffed, his strong frame leaning defeated on his staff. It's the weapon he uses to keep jackals away from our goats and to hold up his body, a body strong in every way except for a foot twisted on its side.

I stared at the seething face of the god of the herds, carved at the top of Azizi's wooden staff. My eyes then traced the length of his weapon down to where his crooked foot rested nimbly, balanced on top of his good one. I saw the odd, bulging spot at his ankle and remembered the day I poked it with my thumb, when I was not much older than Nala. He let me do it as we all sat around sharing a meal, amused at my childlike curiosity. When I asked, "Why did the Shepherd God make your foot crooked?" Mama shushed me, but he laughed that off too.

Azizi was a few years older than Adia, but they understood each other better than anyone. No one had spoken of this, but his care for her was evident and we all guessed they'd get married someday. He used to light up when she trekked home from the swamp with giant frogs, their legs splaying wildly from her hands.

Unlike the rest of us, Azizi made an effort to talk to Adia. He'd hand her sticks and ask her to draw pictures in the clay. They'd even come up with a sort of grunting and pointing method for speaking. He used this as well, which didn't make sense—that he'd grunt and point when his mouth worked just fine. But it made her glad. And so, Azizi would bring Adia a newborn kid. She'd smile and motion her hand in thanks as she knelt down to greet the little one. He'd motion back. They both knew he meant "you're welcome," because so much of talking is nonsense anyway—a filling up of an empty space in the mouth or the mind or the sky.

A few nights before Papa died, well after the evening meal, the huts were full of trapped heat. So we sat outside longer than usual. Crickets chirped. Locusts drummed. Mama and Papa were holding hands as they always did. I sat on Papa's other side, and we watched as Azizi and Adia scratched out their words in the clay with a stick. They were sitting with their backs against the wall of the Others' hut. Adia laughed aloud. Her voice caught our attention as it had a clumsy, quivering way about it. But still, it was the sweetest sound.

"Wa-wa-watching them, I wo-wonder," Papa whispered as he squeezed Mama's hand, "d-did the Great Potter slip when He made them...or d-did He create a ma-masterpiece?"

Mama rested her head on his shoulder just as baby Brave toddled over to us on wobbly feet. The boy's round belly led the way, knocking him off balance. Jaia trailed him like a mother hen. Papa clapped for Brave, and the fuzzy-headed boy stopped to ponder *his own tiny hands. Then, quite decidedly, he clapped back at us. Delighted, Papa let out the whooping sound he saved just for play, when he'd chase Peter and me through the village or toss us into the river.*

"If you only had such grace for yourself," Mama smiled, her eyes roving from Adia to Azizi, then back to the side of Papa's strong face. By then, Brave was bouncing on his lap.

I knew Mama was talking about the Potter and how she thought Papa was a masterpiece—stutter and all—but I don't think Papa heard her. I often wonder if he did.

I hope he did.

☀ ☀ ☀

"Don't worry about the knife!" I say, wishing she'd calm down. "We'll be fine without it!"

Mama won't even look at me, because the knife wasn't just about keeping us safe. It was about keeping a reminder, a piece of Papa, with her. His hand held that weighty handle every day, gutting fish and slicing twine with its sharp folding blade. And at every meal he'd cut up our portions, popping bits of food in his mouth with its shiny point. Mama probably just forgot it in the rush of the morning, though. It's probably where it always is—wedged inside a high skinny crack in the wall beside the door.

Still, she's such a mess. Pale and sweaty. Weary. I can't stand seeing my strong Mama like this, but we've got to get on. That's the best thing for her, anyway—to make her sit her tired self down beside our spring and drink and drink and drink until she's had her fill.

CHAPTER 13

⊡

Talitha
*dead dandelion
wisps on the wind*

THE JEEP'S DRIVER OPENS THE HOOD. A black cloud billows up in his face.

"Look Mama," I point over the cliff. "Their truck doesn't even work. Let's go."

The sun's position tells me Nala would have just gotten her first and only sip of water for the day until I come back with my *mtungi*. Auntie Eshe lines up all the babies right about now and ladles the tiniest gulp into each of their mouths. So often I worry Nala's water is spilled down her chest or soaked into the ground, especially because Auntie Eshe's so grumpy with the babies and I'm not there to help.

Mama sees the jeep's smoke but doesn't budge.

"I don't recognize these ones," she says, squinting her eyes at the men.

They're far away, but I sniff the exhaust from their vehicle and shudder at the thought of being stolen away like Adia and Shani.

What would happen to me if I were taken? The horrible idea clenches my stomach.

☀ ☀ ☀

The night we searched for Adia, the pot hissed yellow with a boring, meatless mash, as no one had time to make anything else. We knew we had to find her soon if we were going to find her at all—her trail would go cold, and then even our chief would be powerless to get her back.

Azizi trembled under the care of so many hushed voices while the elders met with the chief to discuss what to do next. "The tracks ran from her mtungi all the way to City Road," he explained, referring to the winding dirt trail that crosses Great Mountain and connects us to life on the other side—to Mama's city as well as a few others. His face was still flushed, his lungs gasping for breath. His staff slipped under his weight and clacked away. Azizi went down with it, collapsing beneath himself, dropping his head forward over his knees.

"She's gone," he whispered, his broad shoulders wilting.

Someone fed the fire. Logs cracked, snapping and popping in the heat. Gray smoke twisted up, around Azizi's defeated face and out into the night. Gentle arms reached to console him, only to return to their owners' sides limp—drained from touching such sadness. Uncles staggered back from the search, looking hollow-eyed, skinny, and exhausted.

Crushed.

How can we win against those with guns, steel trucks, and hatred in their hearts?

Sometimes we can. When we sing together. When we laugh and celebrate a good harvest or a new birth. When we dance around the fire in a rhythm all our own, a rhythm so deep it runs from our souls down to our feet and into the ground that holds us. We are Kilokie, the People of the Red Clay. We know we could cross Great Mountain. Some have, but Adia was stolen. And we all knew, in the silence of our hearts, that she was being driven over that City Road as we sat helpless, all of us crippled in a way so much worse than Azizi's twisted foot. No one said it, but the fire showed anguish in our eyes.

There had been stories of girls from other tribes winding up in the cities, their lips painted red, their bodies used for a price. Sometimes, it was strangers who took them. Other times, it was the offer of a well-paying job or a chance at education from someone they thought they could trust, except then the girls disappeared without a trace. Neighboring villages passed on warnings to keep the pretty ones close. But still, we never thought this would happen to us, to one of our own. To Adia.

We all knew who was responsible. Badru's men and the mine owners—Lucian and Nelson—were the only ones in the valley who could have left those tire tracks. They were also the only ones who would treat a person as a thing to be stolen. But no one would risk a visit to Badru and his gang, seeking them out in the abandoned mine where everyone knows they do horrible things to their victims. Not even the bravest uncle, not even Azizi with his tender feelings for Adia, was crazy enough to face a beating, even death, at the hands of Badru or Dekadente's attack dogs when deep down we all knew it—Adia was already beyond our reach.

Mama had just lost Papa. Her grief was raw.

"Are we going to just sit here?" she paced, once the elders finished meeting and the chief told us there was nothing more to be done. Mama's hands were down at her sides, her fingers splayed straight. "We have to do something! Mosi? Zuberi?" She looked to the exhausted men who were sheepishly accepting their steaming bowls of wat. They hadn't eaten for hours, yet they didn't touch their food.

"Come on! Please! We've got to do something!" Mama cried with tears carving clean lines down her smudged cheeks. She lunged at the men sitting on the ground, her eyes lit by the flames. When no one responded, she grabbed the pot by its handle and flung it out of the pit. Golden mash spilled like lava. Auntie Eshe's skinny dog hopped up to sniff it.

"Now you just stop there!" Auntie Eshe yelled with a clap. We all thought she was talking to her dog, but her glare narrowed in on Mama. She had been at the discussion with the elders, so she knew how futile our situation was. And even though her voice was pained at the grief of losing Adia, it was sharp too.

"What do you say we do, Flora? Follow the tire tracks on foot for three days to your people in the city? We could ask them if they've seen, or rather—heard—a silent girl. Or perhaps Azizi should go to Badru and see how his words hold up against bullets or his thumbs to a hunter's blade? What do you say we do, Flora? What do you say we do?"

Mama dropped to her knees, crumpled over her mango bump of a belly, and cried quietly. I went to her with Peter. We clung to each other. As she shook, I imagined myself running to Great Mountain and leaping over it with one graceful jump. I imagined returning hand in hand to the village with Adia. Everyone would cheer. We'd roast a goat to celebrate.

But I never did search for Adia. Then, right away, Shani was stolen too—and again, we had to give up on the search far too soon. I felt so guilty for letting their trails go cold, for not screaming their names, but I had Nala on my hip. I had too much to do for the living to help those who were lost. And it seemed everyone else did too. I had to work hard each day, then settle a crying Nala down for the night, only to wake before dawn and do it all over again.

At least, that's what I told myself when I tried to sleep on my mat only to stare at Adia's and Shani's empty spots against the mud-packed wall. I've told myself these things over and over—"You had to comfort Nala; you had to get the water; you had to bring in the wheat"—even though I know they're not completely true. You see, it isn't just Nala or my chores that's kept me from searching for, screaming for Adia and Shani…it's my fear.

But not just the normal kind everyone has—of ghosts, or being cursed, or wandering lost and alone at night. No, my fear is more than that. It's the reason I won't dance in a circle stomp even when I want to, or talk to someone new, or sing in front of everyone when our tribe is celebrating the end of the planting. I wasn't born with Mama's fire. I inherited Papa's stutter instead. Only it isn't in my voice, but in my soul.

And in the past few months, it was as if Adia and Shani had simply vanished. There was a shameful sadness among us, a shared guilt. That we didn't fight for them. That we didn't even search beyond the trees. That we didn't cry out their names for days on end. That we gave up at the sight of a spilled mtungi on the side of the trail.

Often, I saw Azizi pacing with his limp, leaning into his staff, staring off at Great Mountain before he took the herd out to graze each morning. His hair quickly took on the look of his clay-spotted face. Run through, speckled gray, like the wispy top of a dead dandelion—one that had been snapped up and held for a moment, until a wish sent its strands out on the breeze.

☀ ☀ ☀

There are two of them now, looking under the jeep's hood. And even though we're far away, I can tell they're fighting. After a few minutes, though, they slam the hood and drive on in the direction of our spring.

"Moses can't be far," I whisper, knowing that whatever was on his mind this morning, whatever made him act so strange—even if it *is* a crush on my cousin—it won't keep him from protecting us so we can get our water.

"We'll find him," I say, wrapping my arm around Mama's shoulders. "Don't worry. Moses will keep us safe."

CHAPTER 14

Moses
two matching red lines

HE SITS IN THE BACKSEAT of the smoking black jeep, shaking and praying. Just as Moses gets up the courage to run, Badru's men return. With the engine fixed, they drive on. The jeep dips as it enters a dark spot between two trees. Swaths of branches scratch the metal doors like fingernails on hands clawing for help.

"*Please,*" Moses begs the men up front, "I can't do this!"

They ignore him. They're in from the city and are short and muscle-bound. They speak with funny accents and smell of strong cologne. Moses coughs on the car exhaust still streaming from the hood. His sour stomach keeps lurching up with dry heaves. Sweat pours from his armpits. He stinks. He pulls his knees in tightly, but the shaking and the sweating won't stop. It only gets worse the closer they creep to the spring.

"What, man?" the driver yells over his shoulder. "Relax, we're almost done with you."

The engine sputters, sounding like it will fall apart. Moses peeks out the window, praying they'll break down again.

Only this time, I'll jump out, he thinks. But then a glance at the black guns on the dashboard makes him lose his nerve. The jeep swerves around a shady bend and, once again, Talitha's trail is in sight. The spot he glimpses—a giant boulder called Weeping Rock—is a place Moses knows well. For months he's found countless reasons to sit and wait at this enormous flat boulder at this exact moment of the day, always hoping to catch even the quickest glance of the girl who's captured his imagination. But the thought of seeing her now—with her delicate neck and knowing brown eyes—even the idea of her makes him want to jump out of the jeep in spite of the guns, running and screaming a warning.

"*Get away!*" he'd cry. "*Go, go, go!!!*"

And that's exactly what he'd do if a hunting knife the size of his forearm was not presently fixed at his uncle's throat. That terrifying sight was how Moses started his morning— the stout mercenary Badru's surly smile, his gold tooth glinting.

☀ ☀ ☀

"I won't do it." Moses stood his ground just before dawn, at first refusing to help Badru kidnap a girl. He fought to wrench his arms away from the men who wrestled him from his mat. They dragged him down into a dormant mine shaft where the mercenary had taken over one of the offices. Moses found himself in a dimly lit, wet cave, surrounded by men with guns; all of them wearing sunglasses—even though there was hardly any light. The men wore combat boots and carried antennaed radios, leaning back against

the black, carved-out walls. One of them also carried a machete and the rest had knives attached to their belts. Their leader, Badru, had a pistol stuck in the back of his pants at his waist. Moses saw it when this man, a faithless mercenary who'd long ago fled his Korin tribe to develop an underground market, turned away to open a metal locker on the wall.

Pulling out a spool of blue wire, Badru smiled. "I thought you might need some incentive," he said as he turned to his men. "Bring him in."

Two of Badru's guys left and returned with Moses' uncle, Tebaho. The small man's mouth was gagged with a dirty rag. The men walked quickly but Tebaho's legs dragged behind them, struggling to keep up. They dropped him at the table. He wore a stained T-shirt with no sleeves. His skinny arms shivered, the dampness of the mine showing on his goose-pimpled flesh.

"Uncle!" Moses yelled, reaching for him. Badru's men pulled the teenager back.

Tebaho gasped when Badru grabbed his hands, stretched them out, and bound them to the rough wooden table, winding the wire so tight that what little flesh the skinny man had on his wrists bulged on either side.

"Uncle!" Moses cried again, looking side to side, imploring the men "Let him go! Your problem is with me!"

"That's true," Badru laughed, leaning into Moses' face. "But you borrowed money to pay for your uncle's farm, and I've come to collect."

"We'll pay you," Moses begged. "I've sold pelts and…I'll have more money when our wheat comes in."

Moses' uncle nodded passionately, mumbling through his gag. Badru held up his hands to silence them.

"You said that last month and the month before that."

Tebaho's eyes were wide with fear. He pulled his wrists against the wires, but they wouldn't budge.

Badru laughed again and leaned down slowly, taking his time to look directly into the old man's eyes. "Oh, you think you're going to break free?" *The mercenary then slowly, tauntingly unfolded a hunting knife a centimeter in front of Tebaho's face. Without flinching, he nicked both of Tebaho's cheekbones just under his eyes.*

"No! Please! Stop!" Moses struggled harder to break free as two matching red lines appeared on either side of his uncle's face. Blood dripped down, splashing on his gray beard.

Badru straightened to his full height, held the knife in front of his own smiling face, and dropped it. The blade plunged through the air and deep into the table, missing the tip of Tebaho's finger by a hair.

The old man jumped, letting out a muffled yelp, and turned his face away from his nephew.

"Fine!" Moses gasped as he broke free from the men. "I'll do what you say! Just don't hurt him! Please don't hurt him!"

CHAPTER 15

Talitha
a high, curling ribbon

BACK ON THE TRAIL, Mama strains to see the black jeep through the trees.

"Come on," I say, "think about Nala and Brave—they'll be gettin' thirsty too."

We follow the river around the only spot where a sudden drop makes it run fast, where a misty spray cools the air and eases Mama's agitation just a bit.

I check the sun and realize Nala's eating her breakfast about now—*teff* mashed with a few quail eggs. The thought of Auntie Eshe cooking the tiny, speckled eggs up the way Nala likes them makes me smile. I snatch Mama's hand.

"We're fine," I say, sounding extra calm. "We don't need that knife, and look," I motion to the sun, "we haven't lost much time."

My efforts don't work. There's tension between us, expanding like a rain cloud. And even though the last thing I want to do is upset her more, a question I've been holding back forever suddenly flies from my mouth—

"Why didn't we ever go back to your city?"

Mama slows down and makes a face like she's searching the hut for something—something like a weaving hook or a scrap of string for my hair. And just when I think she might cry again, she hums a little tune.

My mouth starts to form another question, but I stop that rabbit before it darts out. Because I wish I could snatch back my words from where they're floating in the sky before us. I can tell by the look on her face that my question was too heavy to speak, to be *"given life"* as Auntie Eshe would say about talking.

I've upset her, but *my* mind is lighter. Relieved. For this question has been buzzing around inside my skull for such a long time. Mama's been so sad about Papa, about the dirty hut, about Dekadente's sprinklers, about everything. I imagine if I were her, I'd want to run away. I'd want to cross back over Great Mountain to where water ran up through a pipe and right into my pot.

Mama's eyes brim with tears. They don't spill down her cheeks, but I'm sure they blur everything she sees, from the lone monkey spying on us as he swings through the branches to the leaves spinning in the breeze.

Mama's sadness makes me so frustrated, I want to run on, but I'd never leave her behind like that. When—

"Ha ha ha!"

She laughs aloud, bursting the heaviness between us like a melon on a rock. Her voice sails, a high, curling ribbon, and my mind flashes to summer—the last time I heard such a sound.

☀ ☀ ☀

We were by the river, eating cantaloupe for dessert. I was soaked up to my waist. Papa and Peter were pushing each other down in the frothy waves, since the river was fast and high after a few days of rain. A pile of mossy green rinds was stacked up on the pebbles where Mama sat enjoying the scene. Two more uneaten melons sat on either side of her. Her hands rested on them softly, like the heads of sleeping children.

☀ ☀ ☀

"Come on, daughter," Mama smiles again just as she did that day, grabbing my wrist, veering me slightly off our path through a rocky shortcut. She pushes back a leafy branch with a wink that says, *All is well. I'll answer you in time.*

CHAPTER 16

Talitha
a long, squealing sigh

HIDDEN BEHIND THE TREES, Mama and I check on our weaverbird's nest, gasping at the things we find—hair, always lots of curly black hair, but today—

"An oryx's horn and a bead shaker!"

The enormous husband and wife creatures return, flapping and squawking with pointy beaks and beady black eyes. They kick up a cloud of flying feathers that sends us coughing as we struggle out the shortcut's other side, branches slapping our backs, birds screeching at us, and Mama laughing again like nothing in the world is wrong.

Still humming, still ignoring my question about why she never went back to the city, she walks on a few steps ahead of me. There's a dance in her step as if she's not carrying an enormous baby in her belly, as if she's completely forgotten our many troubles—this too is Mama's way.

Finally, Weeping Rock's in sight—the meeting spot between our tribe and Desta's. It's such a sad name for so happy a place, as it's where we meet our friends. They say this giant boulder's name was given after a battle where the women came to collect the bodies of their men. The dust around the great rock caked from their tears and gave us our patches of clay. We mix this clay with ground-up leaves to build our huts, to decorate our faces, and to protect our skin from the sun's rays.

Mama scowls, chicken-stepping over fresh goat waste. Smells hit her harder when she's pregnant. Just last night the steam from our mash made her look like she was about to throw up. She served us heaping bowls but didn't eat any herself. Instead, she walked alone in the dark, barefoot, under a starry sky.

My cousin Desta greets us in her usual way, lying facedown on the rock, her arms splayed out on the hot granite, her knees bent to let the bottoms of her feet feel the sun. Her wooden ankle bracelets *click-clack* together. If I didn't know her, I'd think she was strange or childish. But Desta always throws herself like this on Weeping Rock.

"Oh, Mama," she'll moan to Auntie Neema. *"Just give us a little rest."*

But Auntie Neema isn't with Desta today. Deaf Man sits on the ground below her in his usual spot, drinking from the tin cup she always fills. He squints up at me. I drop the rest of our shelled *yeheb* nuts in his hand. He stuffs them all in his mouth at once, and I feel bad I made him wait so long.

As always, Deaf Man presses his back against the granite, clutching its grooves in his hands from behind. Auntie Neema told us once that he'd been there since she was a little girl, "holding up the rock." He hardly opens his eyes and is said not to hear, yet he always holds out his hands when we pass. Both our tribe and Desta's tribe—the Korins—care for him as we can.

"Where's Neema?" Mama asks, then winces as if the baby's turning again and heavily sits herself on the rock. Desta offers her waterskin. While she'd typically refuse, Mama drinks thirstily. Water gushes from the skin and she coughs. It dribbles down her chin and onto her chest where she pats herself with a smile.

"Mama's got a headache," Desta replies. "Also, her bowels kept her *runnin'* last night."

Worry bands stretch across Mama's forehead; I imagine it's because she assumes Auntie Neema has gotten some dirty water. This happens a lot in our valley, no matter how careful we are. If you swipe your hand in the river to cool your neck then accidentally chew a scraggly fingernail, you pay.

But then Mama's face darkens even more. She leans over Weeping Rock awkwardly and seems to be stuck. I'm sure the granite feels warm on her cheek. Finally, she lets out a long, squealing sigh and pushes herself up.

"I'm going back to Eshe now," she says calmly. "You two are gonna' bring me water—lots of it. This baby's coming today after all." She talks to her belly, patting it affectionately, "Yes, yes, I know, you changed your mind. Just get me back to Eshe first; just get me back to Eshe."

CHAPTER 17

Moses
shrieking branches

THE REST OF THE RIDE out to the spring—where he now waits hidden, crouching behind a row of shrubby trees— was torture. Visions of his uncle shivering in the mine tormented him with the jeep's every shudder and squeak. He trembles as he remembers it once more. The sound of Badru's knife slicing the air, nicking his uncle's cheekbones. The drops of blood. His uncle's eyes—the shock and fear in the watery gloss of them.

❋ ❋ ❋

That moment replayed in the forefront of Moses' mind all morning. It was all he saw, all he felt, in what was his first vehicle ride ever. French rock music blasted through tinny speakers, taunting Moses like a quickly spreading rash, and he seemed to itch all over. *The sneering driver sped along wildly, cutting through ripe plot after plot, ruining sweet potatoes and soybeans and corn. People stopped to stare wherever they passed. Some wore tribal robes. Others, button-down shirts and pants purchased from the city or pulled from aid packages. A group of children ran alongside the jeep, keeping up with it for a bit, banging its sides with long sticks until the driver opened a can of hot mints with a laugh. "Let them eat fire," he said and threw the candy out the window.*

The jeep slowed when it neared the marketplace, a spot most clearly demonstrating life on the southeastern base of Great Mountain. A few teenage girls came in close, pointing at their reflections in the rearview mirrors. Imported blood oranges spilled from baskets next to stacked-up piles of bootlegged cassette tapes. Hunters, tall and sinewy, wearing loincloths and carrying spears still red from the morning's kill, rubbed elbows with cousins in T-shirts and jeans. A baby peeked out from her mama's sling to nurse a naked breast. A small Asian woman—obviously in for the day from the city— sat on a lawn chair beside her pickup truck full of shiny cooking wares. She sipped a can of diet cola.

"Here are a few pretty ones," the driver puckered his lips into a long string of kissy noises as the girls fought for a look in his tinted glass.

"No, man," Moses mumbled, unable to look up. "Drive on."

They couldn't steal a girl in the middle of the marketplace, where everyone could see. They needed to be sure no one would intervene, that she wouldn't be able to get away and that they wouldn't get caught. The isolated spring where the locals went to collect water was a better option, but the women often socialized there or came together in groups. That was the real reason they needed Moses. He knew the road to the spring well, well enough that they believed he could tell them the best place and moment to strike.

Unfortunately, the only girls whose habits Moses knows well enough to be of any use to these men are Talitha's and Desta's. And as he left his uncle in the mine, he rationalized that Desta has a miserable life now as it is, spending her days taking care of a mother who swears and screams as she rolls around their hut's floor, suffering from headaches. Moses naively hoped against hope that Badru wanted to sell a girl in the city so she'd be used as a laborer, keeping gardens, cleaning and cooking. He knew, however, that Badru's plans were much more sinister—he'd heard one of the men talking about prostitution. But he couldn't think about it, not with his uncle bound in the mine. Badru promised to sever both Tebaho's hands by sundown if Moses didn't get him what he wanted—a "full-bodied girl" to fetch a high price.

Badru's mocking voice still rang in his ears—"Help my boys pull this off, and I'll let your uncle go. I might even cut down on some of that interest you owe me, if she sells for enough money."

And so, Moses felt he must offer up Desta.

He couldn't stand the thought of the men taking Talitha. Because she's his…he doesn't know what to call her. The way he feels about her—he doesn't understand it, except to know the very thought of Talitha makes his heart swell to the point of pain. But it's a pain he likes, a pain that's sweet.

Moses didn't realize how full and confused his feelings were toward his little friend who weaves bright feathers in her hair in the most intricate patterns, thus earning her his nickname Birdy. It was as if those feelings had emerged slowly over the past few months, beginning with Adia's and Shani's disappearances. Moses heard the horrible stories one evening when Talitha sheepishly *dragged in a hedgehog she'd trapped. He helped her skin and dress it as she explained why she wasn't supposed to be checking the traps all by herself.*

"Your Mama's right!" Moses exclaimed, the thought of her being alone at dusk hitting him with alarm. "Please," he said, his hand accidentally brushing her knee, "take me with you next time—you must."

Talitha's eyes widened at his touch. Moses looked away, focusing on the carcass he struggled to pierce through with a stake. For the rest of the evening, they shared shy glances as they took turns rotating the hedgehog slowly, listening to its fat hiss in the flames. Their eager eyes reflected the firelight, their mouths watering for the impending taste of salty meat.

☀ ☀ ☀

And now, Moses waits behind a row of shrubby trees. Badru's men are beside him in their jeep, which idles in the glare of the sun. Moses trembles all over with defeat, as if he's already swallowed this bitter pill. He's taken the men to Desta out of desperation to save his uncle. But still, he sobs silently into his hands. Because no matter how many times he tells himself that Desta will be better off on the other side of Great Mountain, he can't find a way to believe his own lie.

CHAPTER 18

Talitha
women and goats

"**T**HE BABY!" DESTA SQUEALS, jumping up and down beside Deaf Man. He must sense her motion because he hugs his knees and rocks back and forth, making that happy whistling sound with his teeth.

But Mama's so calm—nothing like the frantic women and goats I've watched Auntie Eshe and Jaia help in labor countless times.

"You said he wouldn't arrive for another moon!"

"Yes, well, he's changed his mind," Mama nods. "And so— you two are gonna' go. The cistern is dry; you know how much water we need for a baby."

I beg to stay with her, but she shakes her head, not listening to a word I say. Also, Desta is pulling me away. But she doesn't have to pull hard because I know—all the water in the world isn't enough for the day of a birth—the extra washing, the thirsty mama, not to mention the rest of the *Others* who will be needing even more to drink from all the excitement.

So Desta and I take off at a sprint—shooting each other quick smiles—knowing we'll make this trip at least three more times before nightfall.

After crossing a bright, sunny field, we pick up the trail again where it cuts between two trees, sending us into a wooded patch. By the time I get to the dip where rustling branches smack us on either side, I've just about lost Desta.

"Slow down!" she calls, and though it pains me I stop to catch my breath.

Hurry up! I want to scream as I watch her through the branches, moving *ever…so…slowly…*daintily making her way around the trees, wearing that sulky face (her *"you left me behind"* pout that I've seen far too many times). When she's a little closer, I whip around, only to quickly lose her again because *Mama's in labor!* Auntie Eshe and Jaia will be there to help her, and maybe it's a blessing that Peter is home today too, but we have to get back with this water *soon*—Desta's feelings will have to wait!

We reach the end of the woods and thump down the last hill. The shady spot surrounding the spring comes into view from across the wide, red plain, looking like an oasis that might disappear—a *mirage,* I think it's called. This spring is the only green patch in the valley where water isn't stolen from the seeping swamp or painfully moved from the river with endless hauled buckets. The water here bubbles up clean and cold from a well deep inside the earth, encircled by a cluster of flat sandstones. Tall sweetgrass sways around the stones' edges like the women who gather here. I watch them from afar—leaning in, chatting happily, filling basins, buckets, and bins. Their naked babies crawl at their feet, splashing in the shallow spots.

"Mama's having her baby!" I call, and all the living creatures below—the babies, the mamas, even the birds and flowers rejoice, reaching for the sky, stretching out open arms to me. And I run to them, mimicking their joy, enjoying a break from the scowl I wear so often lately, especially around Desta.

CHAPTER 19

Moses
black masks

A FEW MINUTES LATER, HE PEEKS through the trees to see a line of women walking away in a row, their heads high, their water canisters even higher. Only Talitha and Desta remain at the spring. Desta is off by herself, while Talitha stands regal in the sunlight. She has the same serious expression she had during their secret swimming lessons. He thinks about how he loves to splash her, to be the one to make her smile.

"Hey," the driver calls, "is she there yet?"

Before Moses can answer, the two men slip on black masks. And the sight of these masks—the realization he's joined forces with Badru, the most hated man in the valley—sends his fists to rake his hair. He shakes his head back and forth, longing to scream a warning at the girls, while also dying inside to rescue his uncle. He can't do it; he can't stay to watch this happen.

Without thinking, he runs back toward the men. "Take the one in red," he says. "The other girl casts spells!"

And Moses is off. He hopes the line about Talitha casting spells, one that crystallized moments before when they passed through the market and saw a man selling potions, will protect her even though it's not true. While city thugs like these have no problem buying and selling tribal girls as property, he knows indigenous people with their pierced lips and body paint, with their rites and incantations, are mysterious to city dwellers. Moses even cashed in on some of this mystique when travelers would pass by his mountainside home situated right in the middle of the rocky peaks, midway between the cities and the valley often compared to the Garden of Eden.

☀ ☀ ☀

When these city folk traveled in noisy caravans or on foot with their white skin and even whiter socks, their plastic water bottles and cameras, Moses would set up a souvenir cart full of pendant-sized zebras, elephants, and cheetahs (these sold the best). It was obvious many of the tourists thought his trinkets held some sort of power, often asking things like, "Will this bring me good luck?" To which he'd smile and reply, "I hope…"

Moses' mother would throw her head back and laugh when her son came in at the end of the day with a stack of green bills. His family was very poor, his mother being young when she had him and his parents having never married.

Moses' father had actually belonged to one of the tribes in the valley, passing through on his way to the cities on the other side of Great Mountain. One day, he knocked on the door of their cliff-perched home and asked for food in exchange for work. *Moses' grandfather let him tend the goats that wandered the peaks of their hamlet—a spot tourists often stopped to photograph, as it offered both a view of the city and then, on the other side of Great Mountain, the ancient Red Valley. Also, the hamlet's lushness, its waterfalls and twisting tamboti trees, appeared otherworldly, with its tall grassy mounds dotted by goats and surrounded by clouds.*

"A taste of heaven," sighed the travelers, but to Moses the place was home.

Weeks after the pilgrim moved on, Moses' mother discovered she was pregnant. She was young and naive when it came to men. And even if she had a way to contact Moses' father, her own father was so furious she feared for the young man's life. In the end, Moses and his mother carved out a sweet existence. They raised each other, being so close in age people often mistook them for brother and sister. Moses also had the doting attention of many old men. His grandfather, great-grandfather, and Uncle Tebaho all let easy game slip away into the woods when Moses stepped, like a ray of light, into their presence.

"I never once had to whip him," his mother bragged. "Never even had to speak a harsh word."

☀ ☀ ☀

Moses runs as fast as he can, escaping Badru's masked men and sprinting toward the woods. His feet thump the clay, filling his funny shoes with powdery clods that rattle at the backs of his heels. Finally, an ancient forest, a quiet place that seems to call to him, is in sight.

Out of breath and looking over his shoulder again and again, he doesn't stop running until he's hidden deep within the woods. Waterberry trees surround him, cool and dark. Their soaring trunks drip mossy vines that hang like soft hammocks.

"*Talitha,*" he groans at the swishing treetops.

And without warning, flashes of this morning return—his skinny uncle, Badru's shiny blade. A sense of spinning; he closes his eyes to see Talitha and Desta walking to the spring, oblivious to what's going to happen—to what's happening *right now...*

"*Talitha,*" he sobs, only louder and with the abandonment of finally being alone. "Oh, Uncle, I'm sorry, I'm just so sorry," Moses weeps into his hands, imagining the worst for both of them.

✹ ✹ ✹

Having never known a father, Moses filled the void with a devotion to his Uncle Tebaho. And after years of begging, this was the first season he'd been allowed to help his uncle with his farm—work that had become nearly impossible since mortgaging his wheat plots with a city bank to help pay the loan on his brother's, Moses' grandfather's, mountainside ranch.

At first, city banks loaning money to rural people had seemed like a good idea. It used to be only the Badru types who would offer money on extremely high interest for supplies like seeds, balers, and feed. The farmers thought it was wonderful—until they came to find the city banks had the same usury principals as the mercenaries. Only instead of cutting off your hands when you couldn't repay, they'd collect your equipment. Instead of kidnapping your child, they'd seize your home—throwing you, your possessions, and your family out on the road as they changed the locks. The bank's form of punishment for not repaying a loan one couldn't afford, didn't understand, and shouldn't have been given in the first place was at first blush more humane. But one only had to take a closer look to see the banks were behaving like Badru, only dressed in pressed suits.

This was also Moses' first season apart from his mother. He'd been so proud when he packed his sack, gave her all the cash he'd earned from his souvenir cart, and headed down Great Mountain all alone. His mother and grandparents cried as they stood out on the road to bid him goodbye. Their colorful handkerchiefs flapped in the distance like the rainbow wings of a kambu taking flight.

"Don't be sad," he called to them through cupped hands. "The harvest will be a great one!"

As he walked down the mountain, Moses envisioned returning with a knapsack bursting with money. They'd celebrate, rejoicing that he'd saved both farms. Moses imagined looking into his mother's face—"Now you won't have to work so hard," he'd say. "Now you can be the girl you never got to be—because you were busy raising me."

He'd hand her the money and beg her to fulfill his lifelong dream: "Let's go to the city and find my papa! Just you and me. We can be happy together. We can be a family…"

❄ ❄ ❄

These daydreams taunt him now as Moses stands alone in the shadowy forest. He's not cold, but still, he shivers.

"Birdy," her nickname escapes, a sigh, a plaintive prayer.

Talitha fills his senses—her profile, the dip of her clavicle— as he steps off a log into the marsh. Cold soil fills his shoes, mounding in lumps between his toes. He winces, knowing how she'd tease him right now, pointing at his floppy sneakers, smirking in a way only she can. He pulls at his hair, he groans.

"How will I ever face you again?"

CHAPTER 20

Moses
those eyes

IZZY, HE LEANS HIS FOREHEAD into a tree only to find Talitha staring at him in his mind's eye. Her eyes sober and dark—the power they have over him, crushing him like a tidal wave. Only in this picture, those dark eyes are dancing.

❋ ❋ ❋

They were coming home from their swimming spot. Desta and Nala followed on their heels. The happy din came to a halt when Talitha asked about Uncle's harvest—

"If it's poor, are you going to work in the mines?"

Desta must have sensed the two needed to talk, so she tagged Nala and the girl ran ahead, her curls shaking with each step. Nala was naked except for a pair of boy's underpants Talitha had pulled from an aid bin. Nala loved the green trunks covered with tiny yellow puppies. She'd point to her hip and bark. Talitha tried to use them only for swimming, as Auntie Eshe prefers that all Kilokie wear the traditional clothes of their tribe.

Desta and Nala were meters ahead, jumping up to swing on the marula branch, when Moses cleared his throat.

"I think I must work in the mines," he said softly. "If Uncle is to keep his farm, I think I must."

Talitha stopped. She couldn't take another step. She couldn't look at him either, but stared ahead at Desta lifting Nala to the same low branch her father bounced her on when she was little. Desta held the child steady and gave a tap. Nala smiled, showing off her tiny white teeth.

Moses realized Talitha wasn't beside him anymore. He turned around and those dark eyes assailed him. Eyes that speak louder and with more frequency than the heart-shaped mouth beneath them. Eyes that burn into his soul and make his palms sweat.

So he forced a laugh.

"Oh, Birdy, don't look so serious. They've fixed the crawl spaces since the—"

"Please," she held up a hand. "Don't."

He stepped toward her, reaching for her shoulder, but instead he somehow tripped over nothing, absolutely nothing. He knew it was absolutely nothing because after he very awkwardly toppled her, splaying their bodies perpendicular on the trail with her laughing up at the pink-streaked sky like a hyena and him blazing brick red with embarrassment, Moses sat up and searched the ground.

A loose root? *he thought.* What tripped me? A jutting rock?

But there was nothing. *Only his huge hairy toes sticking out of the "sneakers" he so expertly cut, the ones attached to his enormous feet, which could be the only things—yet again—to blame for his* clumsiness. Instinctively, he pulled his limbs in tight. And the cumbersome, embarrassed feeling of himself that he usually forgot when he was with Talitha rushed in like a flood.

He couldn't look at her. She was lying on the trail, gasping and making that sighing sound people make when their laughing comes to an end.

"Moses, are you all right? Moses?" she exhaled. "What happened?"

But he was so ashamed he hid his face in his bent knees.

She hopped up and offered him a hand. He reached for her and finally, shyly smiled. Her hand in his felt so small—so delicate, like a tiny sack of bones.

They faced each other, not letting go, holding hands a little longer.

"Aw, Moses," she said, her eyes twinkling. "It's just me. You can be clumsy with me. I still know who you are."

※ ※ ※

"I still know who you are." The comforting words she spoke just a few weeks earlier are now his torment.

His own heavy breathing deafens his ears as he paces between the trees. Their branches smack at his skin, but he doesn't shield himself. His mind's a whirlwind; questions scream through his skull—

The masked men?

Talitha?

Desta?

Uncle?

The-masked-men-Talitha-Desta-Uncle?

What's happening to Talitha right now? What's happening to Desta and Uncle?

While Moses' terror is for them all, he continues to see only Talitha when he bangs his head, again and again, against a tree. She's holding out the egg. Steam rises off its smooth white sides.

He looks away—even from her memory, he looks away. Knowing this girl, with her beauty and her goodness and her brilliantly sharp mind, he could never behold her again.

CHAPTER 21

Talitha
night singing

SITTING BESIDE THE SPRING, I drink my fill. Moses' troubled eyes from earlier this morning come to mind between icy gulps, as do Mama's parched lips. Scooping handful after handful, I feel like a queen for not having to boil and cool my water first (like most other tribes must).

Laying a wet hand on the back of my neck, I feel like it's such a luxury to rest for a bit, to watch the long, underwater grasses plume and swirl. But I give in to the short break, because the more I drink now, the less I'll need later.

I press my *mtungi* down and giant bubbles *glug, glug, glug* to the surface. Then, with all my might, I hoist the heavy *mtungi* up on top of my head and walk away as fast as I can, careful—ever careful—not to spill one single drop. I'm barely across the flat when I hear—

"Talitha! Slow down!"

I turn around to see Desta turtling behind me. Her face is flushed, her ruby wrap clings to her skin, and precious water Mama needs at *this very instant* slops from her *mtungi*. She's making her sulky face again, only this time it's even more dramatic. Now, it's the face she makes whenever Auntie Neema forces her up from her nap on Weeping Rock—a tiny rest Desta would let go on and on until the sun's high and everyone else is dying of thirst.

So I stop to wait on Desta even though it feels like I'm *always* waiting on Desta while she suns on a rock or *waiting on Desta* while she chit-chats too long at the spring. The more I think about it, and the more I stand here *waiting on Desta*, especially with Mama and the baby needing this water, the more I realize—I'm sick and tired of *waiting on Desta!*

She struggles toward me with so much water dripping on her face I wonder if there's any left in her *mtungi*. Her cheeks are pink and sweat drenches her chest. Yet somehow, she still looks pretty.

"*Birdy*," she cries, stealing Moses' nickname for me. "Take my hand." Her voice is winded. "Don't you worry about Mama. I'll borrow a *mtungi* and carry one on my head *and* one in my arms the next trip. I've done it before."

My heart crumbles. I take her hand, but I can't look at her because jealousy is an itch you can't scratch, an oozing welt from a steel-jawed beetle. Its sharp fangs latch on and *gnaw and gnaw and gnaw* at the tender spot in the very center of your back, at that tiny spot you can't reach between your shoulder blades.

I've known sadness, but its storms are driving rains, leaving me cleaner and more kind. Jealousy, however, is eating the flesh off my bones, picking them clean like vultures at a corpse.

It's been going on too long now, and no matter how I try, I can't seem to escape it.

This jealousy first took root sometime in the past year when Desta, a cousin on Papa's side and my very oldest and closest friend, secretly wove a cocoon. She went inside when no one was looking. Then, in what felt like a breath, she unfolded from its shell, fluttering through the sky on brilliant wings. I assume she did this while I was busy caring for Nala or searching for my own cocoon—or at least some sort of change when I hold my tunic tight against my chest. But no, no change there. No cocoon either.

I turn back to walk on, not wanting to meet her eyes. Also, I haven't spilled a drop of my own water yet and I don't plan to.

"What's wrong, Talitha?"

What am I supposed to say? *I hate you because you're a fresh cluster of dates and I'm a dry, twiggy tree.* Or, *I'm mad because you always have funny things to say, while just the thought of talking to people makes me want to hide.*

Or the truth—*I wish I was you instead of me.*

I can't say any of that, so I force myself to smile.

"I'm just nervous for Mama," I sigh, which is partly true.

We walk on and my mind rushes ahead of my legs, carefully planning what to do with our water. First, I'll pour out a long drink for Mama. Then, I'll have to give at least a little bit to Peter and the aunties and babies as well. Nala will be having a fit by the time I get back, waving her pink mug in the air, crying for me. And as hard as it's going to be, I'm *not* filling her cup a second time. I can always give her my own portion if I must.

Next, I'll save a little for nighttime in the green glass jar with the wide mouth. I'll fill it to the top, tighten its lid, and hide it on the high shelf where we keep the sugar. I'll surprise everyone before bed with one tiny sip each.

But as Desta and I stumble on, a midmorning sun singes the tips of my ears. Heat waves blur before my eyes, making this patch of red clay look even more parched than ever. Suddenly, my plan for the water balanced on my head feels silly. And even though I just drank my fill at the spring, my throat is cotton. I imagine drinking down the whole *mtungi* all by myself—dumping it over my head, rubbing it into my dry, pasty eyes.

Desta trips. I shoot her a look, and she doesn't dare ask me to slow down. I couldn't even if I tried because my legs and my mind are *racing, racing, racing*—to what the rest of this day will bring.

After I hide a bit of water away for nighttime, we'll use every last drop for the birth. I'll have to boil and cool it first to make sure it's perfectly clean for the baby. Then we'll wash the squirming purple child, Mama, and any tools Jaia and Auntie Eshe may need in helping them.

My plan leaves nothing to mix into mash, which means if there's no time for another trip to the spring, we'll have to share a meal with the other families in the village. I know they won't mind, though—a new birth is a cause of celebration for the whole tribe, so they'll all want to help in whatever way they can. I'm wondering if a few of the aunties might help us carry more water from the spring as Desta—*once again*—interrupts my thoughts.

"Cheer up," she says. "Sing with me, *Birdy*!"

She hums the beginning of a favorite song, but I can't join in. So much of my life I've spent singing with Desta, but lately it feels like an act. Like something I'm faking, only badly. So I stay quiet. Again, this hurts. I see it in her eyes, hear it in her voice—it hurts her too.

※　※　※

Desta and I are really more like sisters than cousins. She used to live in our hut with Papa, Mama, Peter, and me when we were little. Her mama, Papa's cousin Neema, has no husband or other children and gets these bad headaches that force her to stay in their dark hut for days. She's tried all sorts of cures but finds no help except to lay on the packed mud, where she presses her head for hours, moaning and crying, with one of her eyes running a river of tears.

One day, Papa was called out to help her and came back with Desta. She was only supposed to stay for a few days, but those days stretched into years. Years in which we'd paint each other's faces with mud by the river, climb the highest trees for bright feathers to weave into our hair, and steal Auntie Eshe's cooking tools—replacing them with bones or funny-shaped sticks just to watch her waddle after us on flat feet, cursing and trying to smack our bottoms. And of course, we'd sing.

We'd sing all day and late into the night. Lying side by side, we'd look up through our hut's open thatch at the stars. We'd sing made-up songs, Kilokie rhythms, and hymns Mama and Papa taught us. We had to—and still have to—sing the hymns in secret, when we're alone in the woods or by the river. Auntie Eshe and lots of the elders who keep with the old ways—they want nothing of Mama and Papa's Shepherd God. They're suspicious of our hymns.

But Desta and I love them. Even though Desta doesn't believe in just one big Shepherd God like we do. Desta, like Auntie Eshe and most everybody else, pays respect to many gods. They fear them and keep them at bay by making many offerings. The chief will make a pilgrimage to Great Mountain, the Kilokie's sacred place, or offer a burnt bushel of teff or a slain hen at the center of the village before each new moon. Auntie Eshe and many others make the most offerings to the gods of the dig, but the gods of the hunt are carved—their eyes bulging, their teeth fierce—into the crown of many walking staffs. These gods are honored by our tribe's ancient ceremonies, which are led by the chief at planting time and harvest time, or whenever there's a special need: a sickness, a drought, a blight in the crops. Our people sing prayers, and an elder like Auntie Eshe or the chief's brother leads the song. There are certain dances that go with each ritual; and just about everyone who's old enough joins in.

Well, everyone except my family. Papa never stopped dressing the traditional Kilokie way, and he still used many of the tribe's prayers, but he'd address them to the Shepherd God instead of the gods of our people. He let Peter and me learn the dances that are just for celebrating a birth or a marriage, the circle stomps that are so much fun. But he and Mama didn't want us taking part in the other rituals, and they never offered the small sacrifices that most of the villagers do: mead, the blood of a goat before it's butchered, or honey poured over polished hunting blades, machetes, and threshing sickles.

I think that's the real reason Auntie Eshe and the others disapprove of our faith so much. They don't see why Papa couldn't keep the old ways along with his new prayers. They whispered of the curses he'd bring on his family and the tribe for refusing to pay tribute to his ancestors and their gods.

When we were younger, Peter and I used to be scared that the elders were right. Peter whispered to me once, "Maybe our wheat is taking so long to come up because Papa wouldn't let the chief bless his sickle."

But Papa overheard him and chased away our fears with his easy smile. "The wheat will come up in our Shepherd God's good time. We have His love and His blessing. That is more than enough." And it was. In the end, our wheat grew just fine. Papa gave the best of it to Abba Yosef and Ibrahim so they could share it with families poorer than ours.

Still, Mama and Papa's beliefs were a sore spot for many of the members of our tribe. "Who ever heard of a god who washed dirty feet?" Auntie Eshe laughed at Papa one night when he brought out his Bible.

Another Kilokie chimed in and soon they were all laughing, "Kings are mighty warriors, but your god came as a weak little baby! Nonsense!"

They laughed and Papa tried to answer them, but his voice bucked and bumped, only to be drowned out by their cackling. I remember sitting there, staring into the fire's red embers, which seethed as I did with embarrassment. My only consolation was Desta, her arm wrapped tightly around my shoulders.

But then one day, Auntie Neema took Desta back. It was in the middle of the hot season, and we'd just had a hard rain. Steam filled the air like a thick, misty blanket. Bugs swarmed everywhere—black dots blurring our eyes, burrowing into our ears, and floating into our throats only to come to a swift death upon a cough. Desta, Peter, and I were smacking the sky around our heads in a shady patch in front of our hut while we crushed tiny yellow blossoms to make a bright dye. Auntie Eshe was sweating over a pot of rock-hard cassava roots, cursing them, beating them down with a flat-bottomed paddle. The three of us snickered *at her silly words—I'm sure she makes them up—when Papa found us.*

"Your mama wa-wants you b-b-b-back," he said, touching Desta gently on her shoulder.

Without a word, we threw down the flowers, their weedy stalks scattering out wildly on the clay. Her hand smacked into mine and we turned to run. Peter followed us, but we were too fast.

Desta and I spent the rest of the day walking through wheat fields, nibbling ripe grains and talking about how we'd still be best friends even when she moved back to her mama, how we'd practice our singing apart, so we could still harmonize when we were together.

And we used to do just this, sing loud and in harmony, every morning as soon as we'd meet at Weeping Rock. Often, we'd simply find ourselves singing, neither one remembering who'd started the song.

CHAPTER 22

Talitha
no longer a secret

"**I** SAW MOSES LAST NIGHT." Desta catches up again, her braids dripping wet. "He asked after you," she says with a smile.

I stop in my tracks, feeling my face twist in anger. I look directly at her, even though that's something—at least lately— I try not to do.

"I saw him this morning," I snap back, remembering his troubled eyes. "He asked *me* about *you.*"

"Hmm," she says, but she doesn't seem to really care at all. She's searching the ground for the tart berries that grow here along the brush. We boil them down into a syrup that's tangy and sweet.

"You know," she pops a berry in her mouth, "I saw the way he watched you the other day while we were swimming. I think he's got his eye on *you, Birdy.*"

I grit my teeth, because something about her stealing his nickname for me *again*, something about her claim...that Moses was looking at *me* when—of course—he was really looking at *her*…

"*Shut up!*" I scream, staring her square in the face, my cheeks feeling like they're on fire.

Shocked, we both stop. Neither of us has ever spoken a harsh word to the other. She looks slapped. Color surges her skin.

"*Birdy,* I—"

"Don't call me that!" I scream even louder. "*Don't you ever call me that again!*"

I move on as fast as I can when one of Papa's cousins who still wears a lip plate comes around the bend. Relieved for the distraction, I call out to her about Mama's baby. She responds with a nod toward Great Mountain and the typical Kilokie greeting—

"The gods have been kind."

She speaks with the slur that always comes with her chosen look. Most of the younger girls don't pierce and stretch their lips like hers anymore, but this cousin is about Mama's age and wears her round lip plate with pride. A baby peeks from behind her back where he's tied tight. I swipe his soft foot with my thumb, trying to let his giggle pull me from the shock of myself, from this jealousy for Desta that has grown so big— so big, it's no longer a secret.

Shut up, shut up, shut up, the words explode through my mind in spite of the baby's laugh. And at once, I'm both crushed and relieved. Part of me wants to fall into Desta's arms and beg forgiveness. But the other part of me wants to scream again and again into her shocked face.

So I say goodbye to the cousin and speed up, leaping over a rocky patch—still without losing a drop of water. *Shut up, shut up, shut up!!!* I think of Mama, of how direct she can be.

So I try to imagine her yelling at Desta, but I can't. Because she would never…

※　※　※

Still, Mama doesn't hold back. One time, a traveling doctor said it was because of this mineral-rich water balanced on my head that we villagers have such hard, white teeth. He even tried to look inside Peter's mouth with a tiny light, but Mama "breathed fire on him," Papa said afterward with a laugh. She waved her fist. She yelled in English, "We need a well drilled here—not a medical exam!"

He was such a funny-looking man, with skinny legs and a fat, round body. He wore a safari vest and his arms were full of papers. His mouth hung wide when Mama yelled in his own language. She backed him out of our village, his papers scooching up and out of his arms, swooping high in the sky and fluttering down all around us like enormous white leaves. He scrambled, slapping at the air then crawling in the dust, his white skin coating itself red. And then, looking like an enormous fire ant, he snatched a paper from a little boy who'd wandered into his path.

Papa came to help. I saw them speaking quietly as they gathered up the papers. I could tell Papa was saying something like, "Don't mind my wife's temper." That was his way.

※　※　※

I turn around to see my cousin with the lip plate talking to a distraught Desta.

"I'm fine—I promise," I hear Desta say. Her face is covered with sweat. She won't look up, yet she denies herself the chance to find comfort in our shared friend. She could confess the reason for her tears, but of course she doesn't. Desta would never betray me.

CHAPTER 23

Talitha
the panther

I SLOW DOWN UNTIL DESTA is right behind me. She has the same crushed look Nala gets when she remembers her mama. My heart winces, and once again, my legs grow wobbly just thinking about Shani. But if I can't walk, how can I fetch our water? So I try not to think of her, even though I always do, with questions rolling forever through my mind: *Was she snatched before Weeping Rock or after it? Will Nala remember her when she's grown? Will she remember me if I'm taken too?*

Like Adia, Shani was hard to know. She had deep dark skin like Nala's and pretty eyes like Nala's, and a quiet way about her. Often, I find myself wishing we'd both been less shy, wishing we'd visited a little more. I'd like to tell Nala about her one day …especially if she never comes back.

☀ ☀ ☀

I was thinking about this very thing the other morning when—out of nowhere—Nala called for her. It's strange. She'll be fine for days and then something will send her searching, searching, searching, as if we're playing "hide."

With a mischievous smile, she peeked in the giant cloth basket, then ran behind the hut. She looked everywhere, up tree trunks and into tiny tin cans, only to fall into my arms, howling until she finally slept. I dozed off and woke in a mess of sweat. The sweet potatoes she'd eaten midday were smeared all over my chest, but I didn't move for hours. Later, when Nala woke with a spark, ready to let Moses crawl on all fours playing "cheetah," I was so relieved.

※ ※ ※

While I pass beneath the acacia tree that grows at such a slant you can walk up the side of its trunk, a smile cuts my face as I think of Moses and Nala together, playing in the hut. But also, the last time we were here, they picked these same droopy branches clean of blossoms, with her riding up high on his shoulders. My fingers rustle the prickly leaves as…the faintest rumble drifts through the sky.

I freeze. Goose bumps prick my skin. I turn around only to spot Desta. I'd assumed I'd also see the black jeep. But there's no jeep, no truck at all, nothing moving anywhere except wind through the trees.

Desta's eyes are a storm, searching for mine. Her mouth opens slightly, as if to say *"I'm sorry,"* when another engine growls—this one louder and closer. Her face changes in an instant from sad to scared.

"What's that—?"

A cloud of dust explodes from behind a patch of trees and heads straight for us. A black panther comes to mind, even though I know it's the jeep full of miners.

"*Run!*" she cries, stumbling forward. A wave sloshes from her *mtungi*, laying down a dark swath in the clay. While all my senses agree with her, I stubbornly hold back, walking as fast as I can, like there's a lion on my trail and to run would make it give chase.

"They'll only take a girl if she's alone!"

I hear my words, but don't believe them. Holding onto my *mtungi* with both hands, I glance back, a little faster this time. The jeep is closing in on us, but I stare it down, willing it with all my might to turn—to head north or south—anywhere but in our direction. Because *Mama needs this water!* To drop my *mtungi* now would be the same thing as putting a knife to her throat. So I hold on as if it's gold.

"Just some miners," I try to sound calm, "trying to scare us."

Cold sweat snakes down my back. Something in the air feels wrong—*very wrong*. There's an electricity all around, like the fat fullness before a storm. A rotten carcass appears suddenly on my right. A gazelle. Its broken neck is twisted back. Its beady black eyes stare lifelessly up at the sky, catching the reflection of drifting clouds.

How did I miss that before?

The question is quickly scared off by the jeep that's now *way too close!* And without another thought, *we run too!* Mama and Nala disappear from my thoughts along with the *mtungi* from my head. The instinct to survive kicks in as we kick up the clay. I'm prey—I open my mouth and scream with all my might.

Desta falls behind, crying in a high-pitched voice, begging me not to leave her. I glance back just in time to see two

men—not much taller than us, but wide, with black masks on—
hop out of the jeep. I've never seen such masks before and my
shock must slow me down. But before I can scream again, one
grabs her. Then, very quickly, the other one grabs me. The rest
I see in flashes—

A ripped shirt.

My teeth bite a hairy forearm.

A man's scream.

My hair yanked out.

A silver knife.

My head cracks on a rock.

Dark silence.

CHAPTER 24

Flora
the lines around those eyes

SHE SHUFFLES ON QUICKLY, knowing the pains are about to return. She knows they'll grow to the point of being unbearable, swelling in waves so strong Flora's afraid she'll die without Jaia and Eshe. As she stumbles along, leaning onto tree trunks and stray boulders, breathing heavily through the contractions, her last glimpse of Deaf Man stays with her. He was agitated today, slapping her ankles as if he wanted attention. She talks to her baby.

"I wonder if he could tell you were coming…"

The thought of meeting this child who's been kicking and stretching within her womb makes her hum. She rubs the sides of her hard belly as she reflects on Deaf Man, remembering how her husband was always so fond of him.

Deaf Man had shot Flora a harsh look as she walked away from Weeping Rock, and the smile lines around his eyes—

the ones that crack out from the edges like crevices in the sun-parched clay—remind Flora of *someone*.

She shakes her head and squints her own eyes as she *searches, searches, searches* the parched trail before her, but also the endless picture catalogs of her mind for this *someone*. It's a *someone* she can't place at first, but as the baby jabs her ribcage, she gasps…*"Father."*

※ ※ ※

She hasn't thought of him in years, but now he's begging her not to leave. It was the night she last saw him. He wore tan slacks, a blue dress shirt, and wire-rimmed glasses. Salim, Flora's handsome young suitor, stood behind him on the grass off their back porch. Salim was dressed, as always, in the burgundy hunting robe of the Kilokie.

The night was balmy. The only light was from a lone porch lamp that zapped bugs, its noises startling Salim again and again. Flora tried to explain that the light killed insects, but he couldn't understand her. They'd made great strides in learning to communicate over many months of letter writing, but still, this buzzing light confounded him. His jumping shoulders gave way to her laughter, which she fought to contain through cinched lips. Her father's mood was explosive.

"I am listening to you, Papa," Flora said, her hands on her cheeks to hide the dimples that deepened when something made her laugh.

Earlier that day, Salim had arrived unexpectedly with five bolts of cloth and displayed them with great pride on the front steps of Flora's home. A few were coarse, for dragging home a kill or stringing a tent. But the last one was purple silk—for a wedding dress. The five bolts, two chickens, and a good milking goat were the traditional Kilokie barter presented for a bride. Salim had walked barefoot over Great Mountain, dragging the goat on a rope and pushing the rest of the goods in a cart for three days and two nights to make his claim on Flora.

"Papa—I promise, I am taking you seriously," Flora spoke through muffled hands, her laughter impossible to contain. The bug zaps were making Salim's whole body leap, which stirred up the goat. The goat started to bray, making the chickens go crazy. Salim stumbled over a flapping hen and Flora yelped.

Her father's anger heightened to something she'd never seen before. His eyes narrowed into slits and his brow beaded with sweat as he tried to push his daughter back into the kitchen. He'd already told Salim not to take one more step toward the house. Salim stayed on the grass, the bolts of cloth strewn and scattered at his feet, lying there from when Flora's father had launched them into the sky.

"I pay for school uniforms and cello lessons, and now…now you want to throw it all away to live out in the bush?!" Her father seethed, "No, Flora, no! The answer is no! You will not go! You will never go! You will never marry this heathen while I live and breathe!"

"But he's not a heathen, Papa." Flora gasped, struggling to stay calm. "Salim's been baptized. We want to be married in the Church. Ask Ibrahim. He'll tell you. Salim's had a conversion of heart—a powerful and real conversion."

"Fine. Good," Flora's father replied, his words neat and clipped. "The boy's found religion. Good. I'm happy for him. Still, you will stay here in the city. The young man will get a job, perhaps an education. And in time…possibly…you'll marry…"

"No, Papa! Salim wants to take our faith to his people, and I'm going with him!"

Flora's father was about to interject when she raised her eye-brows and her voice in a way that made people listen—a manner-ism she learned from him.

"His people need us more out there than anyone needs us here!"

Flora motioned with her hands toward Great Mountain. "Some of them have never even heard the Gospel before! They still practice rites that involve mutilation or—"

"Ach! Stop!" *her father covered his ears.* "Listen, I'll send Bibles and rice and whatever else you want!"

"No, Papa, that's not enough!"

"What do you mean? That's not enough?!"

Flora could hear her mother and sister Jane crying in the kitchen. Flora hated to upset her family. She knew they thought the letter-writing was cute and romantic, but they, like Flora at first, didn't think it would lead to anything. Flora was the prac-tical one. The one with perfect grades and a scholarship to study medicine at the university. Jane was the silly, sweet one who had a long string of boyfriends. She was the one who was supposed to run off young and get married. Flora, on the other hand, was to earn a degree and take over their father's pharmacy. Of course, Flora would marry eventually. But she *was the one who was supposed to make them proud.*

Ibrahim, Flora's older brother, had already upset the family a few years back by "taking religion too far," in their father's words. It all started when he went to the university and got involved in a group that met in the evenings to pray and on the weekends to work at a soup kitchen. Ibrahim would come home for visits and want to talk to his parents and sisters about his faith.

"Why does this make you uncomfortable, Papa?" *Ibrahim asked at the kitchen table one morning, his Bible open. The bustle of*

127

breakfast in their sunny kitchen suddenly turned tense. Their father dealt with the discomfort by tucking his face behind his newspaper.

"It doesn't make me uncomfortable, Ibrahim. I go to church every Sunday and probably know that book better than you. I just don't think you have to be so happy-clappy *about it all the time."*

※　※　※

Happy-clappy, happy-clappy, the phrase taunts Flora now as she curls in a ball under the blistering sun. The next contraction is starting and she's terrified of the pain…

Happy-clappy, happy-clappy, the phrase cuts through her now the same way it did years later when she got the devastating word of her brother's violent death.

CHAPTER 25

◪

Talitha
lightning flashes

A s I lie on the trail, Papa comes to me in a dream…
He's in the middle of the river, casting a net. He sees me and opens his mouth to speak, but a shiny green fish jumps from his lips, then another, then a whole streaming school of them. They pour from his mouth, filling the river, flopping around his waist. Happily, he grabs one, slices it open, and throws its skeleton high to the darkening sky. Lightning flashes. Thunder claps. And the rain, the hard, driving rain—it pounds down. I look from the purple sky back to Papa. He covers his face with his hands. The rain meets the river so fiercely it looks as if it's boiling over, steaming up, becoming one with the dark, stormy night.

"Papa!" *I try calling to him, but no sound leaves my lips.* "Papa!" *I try again, but my mouth only whispers. All of a sudden, he reaches for me, but his face has changed. He's become Moses.*

I go to him. I look into his palms. Nala's mug shines up from his hands like a pale pink shell. Picking it up, I rub my thumb along its crack, finding the line like Nala always does, tracing it like a favorite scar…

☀ ☀ ☀

The wind licks the gazelle on its way to me. As I lie on the trail dreaming of Papa, dreaming of Moses, I smell death.

CHAPTER 26

Flora
a red-winged bird

SHE GROPES FOR SOMETHING to grab on to as memories of her brother distract her from the pain. Groaning, she falls forward on a skinny tree trunk and bites a branch. Wood fibers splinter between her teeth, filling her face with a tang that, surprisingly, brings Ibrahim even closer—his whittling knife against soft wood, carving toys for her children.

※ ※ ※

"Flora-girl, whatcha' know?"

He'd always say this with a wink, teasing and complimenting her at the same time. He'd then wait expectantly for her answer, since he genuinely did want to know what obscure fact his little sister had accidentally memorized that morning. Something like the periodic table or all the regions in a country. So many brothers would be threatened by a sister with such a gifted mind, but Ibrahim was fascinated by Flora's abilities.

"Nothing much," she'd respond with a smile. But they both knew it wasn't true. Sometimes, if they were all alone, she'd be honest and tell him what remarkable thing had caught her attention—

"The chemical composition of soil in the Falkland Islands," she'd say, and they'd giggle like children.

So even though the two of them were close, Flora wasn't worried when Ibrahim decided to travel deep into the bush with a priest he'd met through his group. They'd wanted to visit the Udi, a friendly tribe whose chief was rumored to have fallen under the spell of a traveling mshirikina—a traditional healer known also to use witchcraft. Years later, it became clear that many of the Udi elders had disagreed with their chief's decision to welcome this deceiver into their fold, but by the time they voiced their reservations it was too late.

Apparently, the chief was so taken by this charismatic man's charm and healing arts that the Udi were tricked into trading their hand-pounded spear tips, which they used as prized barter with neighboring tribes, for his curative potions. Even worse, this man convinced the chief that he could "ward off evil" with strange forms of human disfigurement, specifically the painful piercing of body parts with sharpened branches. Such non-traditional mutilations were performed by the mshirikina himself as a means of atonement for illnesses and wrongdoings—both real and imagined.

For example, if a child fell ill, the mshirikina would carve lines across her belly "to let out the darkness." Or, if a man was suspected of stealing from another man's field, this new leader would drill a hole in his cheek with a thorn to mark him as a thief.

The strange scars and thorn-like "jewelry" worn by these people was to their shame. And according to Ibrahim's letters, just about every one of them was heavily adorned. For this reason, Abba Yosef, Ibrahim's priest friend, prepared a message he hoped the chief would allow him to deliver before the evening meal in exchange for his typical gifted sack of grain. This visit was not out of the ordinary, as the priest had been welcomed warmly by the Udi many times in the past, always into the chief's hut where they'd sit together talking and drinking tiny cups of salted coffee.

So Ibrahim and Abba Yosef braved the long journey to the remote Udi by boat and by foot. They sang hymns and prayed aloud the entire way—to worship God, but also to scare away the snakes. Each night as they camped, Abba Yosef would labor over his notebook, preparing his message. The good priest also brought with him a visual lesson in his satchel—the instruments of Christ's torture, including three metal spikes and a crown of thorns.

❋ ❋ ❋

Pounding the clay with her fist, Flora imagines a baby elephant collapsing on the side of her abdomen again and again. But when she opens her eyes, she sees only sun-bleached grass batting in the breeze. Drenched in sweat, she scours the landscape, searching for a shady spot to deliver this baby. Sweat blurs her vision. And without meaning to, her mind flies far away again to escape the pain only to land on her brother's letter, the one she wept over countless times. It lies, stained and crumpled, in her memory:

Dear Flora,

4, May

Abba Yosef stood before the Udi.
He held spikes in one hand and a woven
crown of thorns in the other: "By His
wounds, we are healed!" Abba yelled.

All the villagers were silent. They turned
to look at the mskirikina, who paced back and
forth behind them, his eyes wide with fury. Then
the villagers began to whisper among themselves. They
all seemed confused—all except their gray-haired
chief, who asked if he could touch the crucifix
Abba Yosef wore around his neck.

When the chief kissed the cross, all the people
gasped aloud. And I couldn't help but notice that
this chief wore the strangest scars and piercings
of them all.

Abba Yosef then went over to the chief and
knelt before him. And as the priest washed
the chief's feet, the chief slowly removed the many
piercings from his own nose, ears, and cheeks.
You see, the Udi had heard the message of
Christ many times, but the chief never received
it until that moment.

The contraction passes. Flora musters her last drop of strength, pushing herself up and stumbling on. Dying for relief from the heat, she loosens her wrap, letting her sweat meet with the breeze. Her mouth yearns for water, for a taste of the frigid spring. And with that, worry leaps for Talitha, a flame in her heart. But she talks herself down.

"The girls are *together*," she says aloud as she almost loses her footing over a patch of rocks, not being able to see beneath her belly.

With her peak in sight, a gush of water courses down between her legs.

Knowing the next contraction may bring the baby, she's tempted to despair when, all of a sudden, a turaco bird—her brother's favorite—catches her eye. It hops from branch to branch above her head. Then the red-tipped creature flies off to a nearby warka tree on the backside of the slope, in a direction Flora never travels. She follows the bird to find the tree's branches that kick out shade in a dusky circle. She barely makes it beneath the umbrella-like covering when the flow between her legs begins gushing.

Her trembling hand is covered in so much blood, she should be alarmed. But instead, the sight takes her back to Ibrahim's slit neck five years ago, to the moment his body was laid out before her, cold as stone.

❈ ❈ ❈

She didn't cry that day. She didn't beat her heart with her fist. She just stared, her mind refusing to accept the body before her as real, as once having belonged to her dear brother.

Nothing made sense. The rest of Ibrahim's letter spoke of a mass Baptism where Abba Yosef took the chief and almost the entire tribe into the lake, where the tribe's elders celebrated after hearing his sermon and chasing the mshirikina *from their midst. That's why when Abba Yosef's and Ibrahim's lifeless bodies were discovered the next morning, the entire village was horrified. The heartbroken chief even tried to hunt down the* mshirikina *with the other men, a task he'd typically leave to those with youth on their side.*

To this day, the Udi revere Ibrahim and Abba Yosef with a memorial at the top of their lake, a wooden cross where they were all baptized.

᚛ ᚛ ᚛

The red-tipped turaco looks down on her from a lofty spot as Flora labors below. The bird preens its silky feathers and returns her cries with loud, cackling caws.

᚛ ᚛ ᚛

Usually, especially here, lying so close to "her peak," Flora's only thoughts are of her husband Salim. When he was alive, she'd pause to take in the view, and if she was having a particularly tiresome day, she'd look out in dismay at "her valley." She'd shamefully wonder if her father had been right when he yelled, "Love won't be enough! Go ahead, marry the boy, but you'll be back!"

She'd wished so many times to go back. To take Salim and their children back to her family's home. To run a hot bath and give them all a good scrub. She'd sit at the kitchen table sipping tea while her mama roasted a chicken. Utensils would rattle against pans, filling the air like music.

Flora also yearned to sit by her father in the evening. He'd look up from his book or his newspaper to say something about politics or his work at the pharmacy. He'd always listen thoughtfully to Flora's ideas. Then he'd lean back and look at the ceiling with a little smile as if her opinions were pleasing to him, as if they tickled his mind in a delightful way. He rarely disagreed with her. Rather, he often seemed impressed by how similarly their practical minds seemed to work.

Most of all, though, over the years, Flora missed her sister.

When she first came to the valley, she'd hear Jane's voice in the quiet corners of her day. She'd turn around quickly, only to find an auntie or Salim or any random barefooted member of her new tribe staring at her, speaking words she didn't yet understand. One afternoon, a woman brushed by Flora in the market. The woman's neck was erect and her voice trailed the sky like a string of glittering sand…

"Jane!" she gasped. "Sister, it's you!"

Flora chased the woman, forging through the crowd, bumping into carts full of fruit and knocking against tables piled high with fresh meat. She whipped under swaths of heavy burlap to finally grab the woman's shoulder from behind. A barrel spilled. Barley grains poured out in a brown wave around their ankles as a mouth too small to be Jane's cursed in a strange language. The barley vendor had a fit, and Flora's children, Talitha and Peter, were so young and nowhere to be seen in a world where Flora simply did not belong.

CHAPTER 27

Flora
like a machete

I T FEELS LIKE HOURS HAVE DRAGGED by since she first started feeling this pain. Now, she's down on her hands and knees, dripping with sweat, delirious beneath the warka tree. Her body demands her mind return to the present with searing blows she thinks are impossible to endure. She's labored before and knows the baby is almost here. Even so, the pain is so shockingly crushing. It's as if her mind keeps departing from her body to fly away with the red-winged bird—the turaco that departs every now and then to coast out over the valley, only to return each time to the branches above her.

Flora presses her cheek against a fallen log, narrowing her eyes on a row of juicy black ants marching back and forth through clods of tan sand. One carries the clear severed wing of a cicada. Flora sucks in a deep breath and bears down, trying with all her might to push the baby out. But he won't budge.

She throws her head back and hollers a long, strangled moan. Again, she yearns for water.

※　※　※

Jane's face appears out of nowhere. She must be about six because she's wearing that stretchy top, the one with the purple and white stripes. An older boy knocked off the fire hydrant's cap, so she's jumping and running and splashing in the foamy white spray.

The whole street went wild that day. It had been so devilishly hot for weeks, even the mothers came out. They let the spray hit their arms and chests where they'd unbuttoned their blouses a bit. Jane saw Flora walking home in her green school uniform.

"Come on, sista'!" She cupped her hands and scooped water through the muggy air toward Flora. A few drops kissed her brow. The wetness on her skin, her neighbors dancing in the streets— the moment was a bottle of pure happiness captured, shook up, and exploding into the sky all around them. But Flora backed away. She didn't want to mess up her freshly starched collar. Also, she had to get home to study even though she was only in her first year at the academy.

"Come on, Flora!" Jane called as her big sister passed her by. "It feels so nice. Play with us!"

Jane had found a spot where the water pooled on the blacktop. Lying on her back, she propped herself up on her elbows, her chin tilted to the sun.

A neighbor blasted a giant stereo. Another grilled kebabs. Music and the smell of smoky meat filled the air. Life surrounded them, full and rich like sweet sliced mangoes after a heavy meal.

But Flora walked on, down the street and into her dark room.
The ceiling fan pushed around stale air. She itched under her collar.
The guava nectar she poured from the fridge was warm before she even
took a sip. But still, she studied the periodic table to impress her father.

᠁ ᠁ ᠁

"Hydrogen, helium, lithium, beryllium!" Flora screams the
elements in order as what must be the final and most painful
stages of labor slam through her. After all this time, she's surprised she still knows them. But that's how Flora's mind works,
capturing words as permanent pictures.

"Boron, carbon, nitrogen, ohhh!" Flora senses someone
approaching before she sees him. Even through the thick veil
of pain, she hears the shuffle of feet and twigs snapping.

Like Deaf Man and her father, this man too has creases at
the corners of his eyes and a deeply concerned brow, though
he's about her age. His flushed face is now just centimeters from
hers. He speaks, but she can't hear him over her own screaming.
She's seen this man before, but can't remember when.

His skin color is striking—almost white, like coffee thick
with cream. His light brown hair, even the golden flecks that
wheel out from his dark irises speak of a *mzungu* papa. And
then the man's identity cuts her like a machete—one splitting
her mind as well as her entire torso in two.

The mine owner . . .

Lucian!

She's only seen him a few times, but those times he was
screaming mad and turning over their bed mats, yelling that
the villagers were hiding his emeralds.

Fury erupts in Flora's heart as she realizes that this is the very same man who mocked Salim's stutter in front of the entire village, the one who refused to properly support the mine's shafts with enough steel rafters.

It's you! she thinks as she looks at the cruel mine owner through blurry tears. *You're the reason my husband is dead!*

Venom rises from deep within her. It's a churning sulfuric storm in the back of her throat, creeping to the tip of her tongue. And as she opens her mouth to unleash its vitriol, Lucian tips a canteen of icy water to her parted lips. It pours down her throat and tastes blue as the sky. She gulps the clean flow down greedily. A cold stream trickles from the corner of her mouth into her ear.

"There now," he says gently, turning his terrified eyes to meet hers.

And there's something in his eyes. Perhaps it's the golden flecks deceiving her. Or perhaps it's the fact that they look like they're about to cry too. Whatever it is, these eyes know pain, and they're looking straight into hers in a way—she can tell— he's deeply worried for her. And all she knows is that, in this moment, it feels so good to have someone—*anyone*—worried for her.

This must be why Flora doesn't fight him when he scoops up her entire pregnant frame and carries her as if she were a doll made of wheat. He slides down the steep slope on the backs of his heels and runs swiftly into the valley, her body secure, buoyed up high in his muscular arms. And even in the throes of labor, and in spite of who he is, Flora is immediately overcome by the strength and smell of him—the scruff on his neck that tickles her cheek, a spicy cologne, his sturdy chest.

"*Salim,*" she cries as he sprints to his pickup truck.

"It's gonna' be all right," Lucian says confidently between heavy breaths, his lips accidentally brushing her forehead. "I won't let anything happen to you—*I promise.*"

NOON

CHAPTER 28

Talitha
pawing through quicksand

OPEN MY EYES TO THE world on its side.

I see a gray rock. A patch of dry grass.

Why isn't it dark? I wonder. *Where's my mat? Where's Nala?*

But then, like a whirlwind, it all comes back.

"Desta!" I try to scream, but her name comes out in a whisper.

Frantically, my eyes dart around—*searching, searching, searching*—behind boulders and skinny trees. But she's *gone.* Our *mitungi* are spilled. Blooming stains the color of wine spread wide in the clay. I push myself up. Pain explodes through my shoulder like a knife. And I remember the shiny one pressed against Desta's neck...

"Help..." I say, "*...help,*" this time a little louder. My hands move as if I'm pawing through quicksand, as if I'm in a dream where I'm trying to run, trying to scream, but my mouth won't make a sound.

The sun blinds my eyes. My head is thick with fog. I touch my temple to find a welt swelling there like a hungry leech, making everything I see blurry. Bushes and trees are shadowy creatures, crouching and growling, ready to jump and…

"Aaaahhh," I scream, sitting up and hugging my knees, startling at the slightest breeze, the faintest rustle of the branches.

When what's happened rushes in.

A blow to my head.

Men with black masks.

There's blood all over the rock where I fell—my head must have hit its corner.

Try to breathe, I tell myself, *try to breathe.*

"What's that smell?" I wonder aloud as I look over to see the gazelle carcass buzzing with flies.

One lands on my swollen eyebrow. Its iron jaws clamp down on my already torn flesh. I imagine its evil green stare and how it's bringing a bit of the rotted gazelle to me, how the dead creature's blood now intermingles with mine—and hot bile fills my throat, emptying my stomach on the trail in loud, choking hacks.

My vision blurs. But still, no tears. I struggle to stand, feeling through the air like a sleepwalker.

Squinting, I look back to the spring in the distance to find it empty—surrounded by trampled grass, but empty. Women won't gather there again for another few hours.

Then I turn home, toward Nala and her tiny pink mug that's most certainly empty right now.

And Mama! My mind races—*Mama and her baby! But… I have to find Desta!*

"Desta!!" I yell, my voice scratchy but finally here, "*Destaaaa!*"

As more of what's happened returns, the memories hit me like falling rocks…

The masked men! They've got her! Just like Adia and Shani… Chase them! Find them! Get her back!

My mind commands me to run, to follow the footprints right here in front of me. But even if I had the strength to obey, Mama calls to me as well; she could be giving birth at this very moment…

I don't know what to do. I'm too dizzy to even keep standing, so I fall to my knees and crawl around, searching the cracks in the clay for an answer, peeking behind a wide stump, but finding nothing, when…

Shut up! My words hit me like a slap in the face. My stomach heaves again, but it's already empty.

Shut up! Shut up! Shut up! The memory echoes, haunting me, taunting me, bringing with it Desta's shocked expression… I turn to my left, searching the high grasses for her. I turn to my right, straining to see behind the furthest row of trees. *But she's gone.* And everything all around is suddenly so strangely quiet, it's screamingly loud. Yanking my hair from my eyes, I shriek with all my might—

"*DESTAAA! DESTAAA!!!*"

My fists pound up a wall of fresh dust as my voice carries through the valley.

"*DESTAAA!!!*" I scratch slashes in the clay for seconds or minutes or hours—I can't tell. I only know that my sister-cousin, whose song is strong and high to mine, soft and low—*is gone.* My Desta, who weaves the brightest feathers in my hair first and takes whatever's left over for her own, was stolen right in front of me.

And the last thing I said to her was…

The last thing I said to my cousin who let me cry for hours when Papa died—back when I still knew how to cry; to the friend who never once told me *"stop now,"* or *"be strong,"* as Auntie Eshe and Mama always did, but rather would finish my crying with her own. The last thing I said—or *screamed* at her was…*"Shut up!"*

How could I?

CHAPTER 29

Talitha
everything all together all the time

DON'T KNOW WHAT TO DO—*who to tell?* But I know I'm
thirsty. And I know Mama and Nala are thirsty too. Also...
maybe Desta escaped! Maybe she got away and ran home!

I grab my *mtungi* and struggle back toward the spring.
Because I *can't* go home without water, no matter what's happened. Even though it will slow me down, and then slow the
uncles down...*they'll form a search party! They'll grab their spears.
Some have machetes—they'll take those too!*

But then I remember the panther, that black blur with wheels.
Its tire tracks...*they're right here on the ground in front of me!*

I place my bare foot into one and then another. Before I
realize what I'm doing, I'm running away from the village, away
from the spring, the tread marks taking me to Desta!

I'll find her! My heart soars. *I'll rescue her, and I'll never be
mean again!*

But each thudding footfall is a brick against my head. I make it as far as the tall grass but can't go any farther. The pain behind my swollen eye would surely make a river of tears if only my heart wasn't so cruel and dark.

Shut up, shut up, shut up!

I fall on my knees and think about how awful I've been to Desta lately. Every time she skips up our path and the men stare and the women wave and the little ones reach for her like she's made of sap.

※　※　※

That's how it was when she visited a few days ago. I was mixing up sugar with spices to coat the deep-fried pastry balls—Peter's favorite food and a special treat we only have a few times a year. She pointed to a can of dirty oil. "Oooh," she smiled, "is the syrup ready?" I knew it wasn't syrup. I knew it was gross, but gave a nod anyway. She gulped it down, covered her mouth, and ran outside. When she returned, I couldn't look at her. She didn't say a thing. But then, later, I wanted to cry when I found the perfect white feather she left for my hair.

※　※　※

Snot burns my tongue. My vision is so foggy, I think for a second I'm crying. And for a breath, I'm thrilled—which sounds impossible, to be thrilled that my eyes may have finally remembered how to cry. It's just that I've yearned for it so often lately. To go off to a secret spot and feel that release. To be washed clean from the pain of losing Papa and all my mixed-up thoughts about so many things—about Moses and Desta, about life and how it can be so full of sadness and thirsty people and tiny birds fluttering in my stomach and Mama's anger and Mama's baby and everything all together all the time…

Am I crying? Am I really crying?

I touch my cheeks, but they're dry.

"Damn it," I swear aloud, sounding just like Mama.

I can't believe it! Desta was stolen and still, I can't cry! *But I don't want to think about me. It's so stupid to think about me.* I could just hate myself for thinking about *me* at a time like this!

Reluctantly, not knowing what else to do, I shuffle back to the spring and fall into a fluffy mound of sweetgrass. Shoving my hands into the icy water, I drink until I have my fill, then lift a cold palm to my eye.

My reflection stares back at me. My slug of an eyebrow doesn't shock me as much as the sun's position—*it's Nala's naptime already!* At least Peter is there with her today, stuck in the *Others'* hut with his injured leg. But even though Nala likes to play with Peter, she's horrible about lying down with anyone except me, and she probably needs more to drink by now. And of course—so does Mama! All they have are the drops left over from yesterday's *mtungi*, not nearly enough for a new baby.

And so, without any other choice, I press my *mtungi* down beneath the water's surface. While it fills, I lift my head, straining my eyes, searching, hoping with all my might for one tiny glimpse of Desta, for a stray rattle of her ankle beads or a snippet of her laugh sailing in on the breeze. But all is quiet and strangely bright. There's a crisp blueness to the sky, as if it's blind to what's happened down here.

Surely it should darken, I think, with rain clouds and thunder…

I heave up the heavy *mtungi*. Water streams down loudly from its sides. And with Mama's and Nala's faces ever before me, I head home.

CHAPTER 30

Talitha
the chiming song

I CARRY THE *MTUNGI* IN MY ARMS like an overgrown baby.
Because there's no way—I'm too dizzy—to lift it onto my
head. But it's so heavy, I end up thumping it ahead of me on
the ground and then walking two steps, then thumping it ahead
again, and walking two steps more.

Thump-step-step, thump-step-step—slowly, I make my way,
remembering how I'd hatched my plans for this *mtungi* just this
morning. *First give Mama a drink, then Nala;* it all seems so silly
now, so childish.

As if I'm in control of anything...

Precious water sloshes out with every thump, making the
parched clay where it spills dark as the inside of a cherry. And
even though I'm trying to be careful, a huge wave lunges out
across my foot. Cussing like Mama would, I stop to watch the
water carve a clean line across my toes. Staring at my bare feet—

one filthy and the other swiped clean—*they're just like my lives,* I think. And I must have been living another one when I hatched those plans this morning.

I didn't realize it back then—just minutes ago, really. I didn't realize what a simple life I had, a sweet life. One where Desta was my cousin-friend and our only real problem was getting back in time for the new baby. I can't believe that old life shared this very same day. Nothing hurt back then—not my shoulder or my eye. And now, I think as I force my legs to move along, that old life feels so far away, as if a hundred years have passed in a minute.

Suddenly, the trail wobbles...

A parched tree hunches over like a baboon and walks with a limp. A lopsided boulder spills into a long gray puddle. Stars explode behind my eyes. Tingles rush my skin and my legs fold beneath me, collapsing my heavy bones into the clay like a bag of bricks. But I don't spill a drop this time. No, I set my *mtungi* off to the side, just as my own breathing rushes as loudly as the wind whipping up sand all around—batting my curls, filling my nose and mouth with dust.

⁂　⁂　⁂

If it weren't for these winds, the ones that blow up hot and dry during harvest, I'd have waited on the trail, collecting my thoughts until the dizziness passed. But it was the wild winds, lifting long-abandoned strings tied up with tiny sun-bleached bones and shards of broken glass, ripped-up shirts and bells and seashells— a Spirit Tree Desta and I made ourselves by tying things that were important to us to each of the branches. Something I'd forgotten

about almost entirely, until this moment. But it was these winds
and this tree, and they called to me.

᠅ ᠅ ᠅

Following the chiming song, thinking for a second it's
Desta in the flesh, I crawl away from my *mtungi*—I can't carry
it anyway—and find the nearby slope. It's a steep one, hidden
behind an enormous prickle bush. Carefully, I push back the
thorny branches with a stick and slide down the straight drop
on my bottom into a dark, shady spot. Clay clods and pebbles
roll beneath me. A broken root nips my thigh, ripping open my
skin. But I don't feel a thing except the throbbing in my head.

Water shocks me with a *splat,* deep in a puddle. I'm too dizzy
to hop up, so I just sit as marsh seeps in all around, soaking my
kitenge, slithering up my back.

All is still, but not quiet because above me towers our tree.
Decorated, hidden like a secret. When I look up at it again for
the first time in years, with its flying strings tied with bits of our
life, I feel so small. Alone and lost. But at the same time…found.
And even though I can't see her, Desta is here too in this damp
place that's dotted with flies, smelling of ferns.

The mud that's landed on my shoulder feels so good I
scoop up some more and press it to my forehead too. I haven't
forgotten Mama, but I've got to catch my breath or I'm no
good to walk at all. So, reluctantly, I lean back and watch the
countless flying strings—the long brown and white ones that
were all Desta's idea. And suddenly, I'm in awe of her. Just like
everyone else…

Shut up, shut up, shut up!

"Cousin!" My voice cracks. I grab my head. I rub my stinging eyes with filthy hands, but they're dry as dust.

"Why...why can't I cry?"

Paralyzed by all that's happened, I lie still, watching strings flutter all around, flying high to the blue sky beyond the black branches.

"Mama took *two days* to have Peter," I tell myself. "And there's no one better than Jaia to help deliver a baby..."

I resolve to get back to my *mtungi* just as soon as I can see straight, and my eyes land on the strings tied with scraps of a ripped-apart *netela* Mama once loved so much—too much. She wore the purple sheath every day until it turned into a mess of threads.

My eyes dance branch to branch some more, amazed, remembering *that orange feather from Desta's hair* and *those bent spoons we used to dig up roots.* My hands knead the mud at my sides, raking up sloppy leaves and broken branches. Another fast wind whistles around the nook where I'm hidden, and memories rush in on the smell of soaked bark.

Everything's just as we left it, I think as my eyes land on a chunk of our hair tied tightly around the trunk. It's frayed, but still braided.

❋ ❋ ❋

"I just need a couple curls," Desta laughed. We were bustling around the hut, packing up to move her home, when she hatched the idea of this Spirit Tree. How my heart ached. She was sad too. I could hear it in her voice, but she missed Auntie Neema and wanted to help her.

So I went along with Desta's plan even though it's not the kind of thing Mama and Papa would have liked—a Spirit Tree. It's an old practice and not of the faith, but Desta's mind was set. She said our souls would fly here at night, to meet with each other when they were lonely. I don't know if that's true, and I don't think the tree holds any special powers. But I do believe in our prayers for each other. The Shepherd God sees the Spirit Tree and knows what's in our hearts.

"My hair," I gasped as she grabbed a handful and held it straight above my head. It was morning time in our hut. Sunlight streamed in from the open thatch as Desta tipped her head back, laughing. I tried to stop her but before I knew it, her knife made a sawing sound as it chewed through my curls. She tied the lock with twine, dropped it on the pile, and began biting apart the seams of Papa's only dress shirt.

"Don't," I started as the fabric's rip sliced the air long and loud.

"He never wears it," she said with a wink. "He even wore his hunter's robe when he stole Mama away from the city."

And now, as I lie here watching that shirt's collar flutter like a starling, I smile. This was so typical of Desta's charm, calling my parents "Mama" and "Papa" even though she's really Papa's cousin. This was—is—her way with everyone, familiar and funny. I remember how she charmed Uncle Ibrahim on his last visit before he died. How he even included her in the secret reading lesson he'd insisted on giving us that night. She squeezed in between Peter and me as we watched Uncle Ibrahim draw words on his notebook by the light of a kerosene lamp.

"What do you mean you've stopped teaching the children?" he had questioned Mama earlier that evening. Smoke swirled up from the fire, outlining his face with a long gray curl. We were all happy

157

and full of meat, having shared a few pheasants Papa trapped for the occasion.

"Oh, Ibrahim," Mama sighed, "If you only knew how difficult it is for us. The Kilokie want us to keep following the old ways. They don't like how we won't take part in all the traditions. The elders tolerated our faith at first, but lately they've been losing patience with us more and more when we try to practice it out in the open. I fear what could happen to the children..."

"If you're afraid of suffering, Flora," he spoke softly, then paused as if he were carefully choosing his words. His damp eyes twinkled in the firelight before he continued, "If you're afraid of suffering, you've chosen the wrong path."

❊ ❊ ❊

Afraid of suffering, Uncle Ibrahim's words from that night echo in the rattle of the strings, making me glad he never saw us later, after he was killed. Because that's when—after Uncle Ibrahim's neck was slit through with a spear—we all became something so much more than simply afraid.

Resting here in this cool, shadowy place that's dark in so many ways, so many years and so many wounds later, I'm hit now by Uncle Ibrahim's words in a way that's so peculiar I actually laugh out loud. And as I listen to the sick sound of my own voice, I realize just how brave Mama and Papa were back then—that last night we were all together around the fire, sharing stories and passing greasy pheasant between us, nibbling meat until there was only bone.

❊ ❊ ❊

That cool, starry night was his last visit. A few weeks later, his body was carried into our village. His stretcher was made of skinny trees, and there were smooth white circles in the spots where the branches had been snapped off. My fingers tingled with the need to rub the scar of each one. And as I did, as I knelt beside my dead uncle, disbelief filled my heart.

Sit up, I commanded silently. Tell me a joke.

But he was cold as stone. My fingertips found his bulging eyelids as well, brushing over them fast before anyone could see. The skin there was thin, rippled with purple veins. Peter made a choking sound beside me, his hand finding mine and squeezing it so tight it hurt.

"He sleeps, ch-children, he m-merely sleeps," Papa said as he gathered us, like a mother hen, into our hut. But Mama stayed beside Ibrahim's body, her limbs pulled tightly into a ball. I think she wept, I assume she did, but she didn't make a sound.

CHAPTER 31

Talitha
a churning volcano

"*IF YOU'RE AFRAID OF SUFFERING, FLORA…*"
Do my uncle's words haunt Mama like they haunt me now?

I spot his dried-out pen strung up on a low branch and wonder. I wonder all these things, and wish Uncle Ibrahim could have seen just how afraid Mama and Papa became *after* he died. If he could have, he would have cheered them for their courage that last night we were all together. Because *after* he died, Mama and Papa turned into worried little mice, hiding their Bibles under their mats, praying in secret or not praying at all. They'd heard the report from the Udi—that the traveling *mshirikina* was to blame for what happened to Uncle Ibrahim and *Abba* Yosef. The light in their eyes grew dark. The excitement in their voices hushed to a whisper. Who knew if something similar could happen among our people?

And this is simply what we grew used to, which makes these dangling memories all the stranger. Mama's icon of the Virgin Mary dressed in blue catches my eye—sunlight glints off the image's gold paint. An old string of Papa's prayer beads— a *mequeteria*—rattles back and forth where it's tangled in a low branch. He had a couple sets of these beads, and he'd say the same prayer again and again when he sat on the stump in the evening and when we lay sleeping at night. The beads made the softest clack between his fingers. His voice was even softer— "*Lord have mercy, Lord have mercy, Lord have mercy…*"

A *mequeteria* in his hand was his most constant companion. That, and his Bible…. Whatever *did* become of his Bible, with its crinkly pages and Mama's old letters tucked all throughout it?

☀ ☀ ☀

It's so strange to remember a time when Papa actually brought this Bible out to the fire every night. He'd lay it open on his lap and talk and fight with the uncles about its stories. There was one about a flood and a boat where Papa's Shepherd God saved two of each animal. There was one about a tree and a snake and a delicious fruit that God told the people not to eat, but they did anyway and were suddenly naked. That story gave me nightmares. It still does.

Back then, back before Mama and Papa actually were afraid, they had the same sparkle and glow about their faith that Desta had about everyday life. They'd look forward to Abba *Yosef's monthly visits with such excitement that Papa would stay awake the entire night before, gently rattling his* mequeteria *that now dangles before me in the breeze, catching my eye again and again.*

When Abba would arrive, we'd sneak out into the woods for Divine Liturgy. Ibrahim would translate for the one or two villagers who were curious enough to tag along. Then Abba Yosef would feed only some of us Communion on a tiny golden spoon.

But then Ibrahim and Abba Yosef were killed and everything changed. A new priest took Abba Yosef's place. And even though we had always gone to the woods to pray, now there was something extra scary about it all. Papa never brought anyone new anymore. Also, we'd sneak off after dark without telling a soul what we were doing.

"Where's Abba Yosef?" Peter asked the first time the new priest came, not realizing he had died with Ibrahim.

Mama wouldn't answer him. She clenched her jaw the way she does when she's in a hurry, pushing through the waist-high brush as if it were on fire. The long strands snapped back and stung me and Peter as we tried to keep up—our arms and legs itched with welts for days. Papa's hands shook like his voice on those nights. He'd follow behind us, looking over his shoulder again and again until we reached the spot deeply hidden behind the trees. The new priest would be waiting there, chanting prayers and burning incense.

☀ ☀ ☀

"Talitha! Talitha!" A voice cuts the sky and my thoughts.

Desta? My heart is hopeful, even though I can tell right away it's not her.

I knock the mud off my forehead and pull myself up, gripping knuckles of rock to climb the slope. My soaking *kitenge* slops behind me, so I have to stop to wring it out. As I do, I realize I can see so much clearer because of my short rest. Peeking around the pricker bush, I see a woman in the distance.

"*Taaa-liii-thaaaa!*" she calls again, then turns to see me coming. And I realize it's Jaia, our wet-nurse and medicine woman, even though I don't think I've ever seen her anywhere but inside our hut or leaning on the stoop beside it—always with a baby on each breast or grinding up herbs for her remedies. My heart jumps in my throat. Why is she here? She should be with Mama, helping her with the baby.

Her face scrunches up when she sees me.

"What *happened*…?" She reaches for my eye.

The story of the morning spills from my mouth. Hardly pausing to breathe, I tell her everything, about Desta and the men who stole her, about Mama having her baby, about the black jeep and how we have to follow its tracks…

She starts crying, but I can't stand to look at her. Her thick frame shields the blazing sun from my eyes, and I'm thankful because its glaring light is as blinding as my guilt, my grief, and the fact that I told the entire story without shedding even one single tear, as I should have, *as I'm trying to*—but can't. She grabs me, hugging me with the strength of a lioness. When she finally pulls back and looks into my eyes, her own are extra spooked.

"Talitha," she whimpers. "*Your mama must have been stolen too…I would have passed her on my way…*"

I step back. The weight of her words is crushing—as if I were being run over by that black steel panther.

"You never saw her? She's not with Peter and Auntie Eshe?"

Jaia shakes her head frantically side to side.

"But that's not all," she cries. "Nala's really sick. That's why I came. Eshe, Brave, and a bunch of *Others* started retchin' right after you left this morning and they can't stop. The usual draught I mix isn't working; they can't keep it down."

My mind spins—faster now than ever before. I step away from her, cussing, "Damn river," sounding just like Mama. "Damn filthy river.... But what do you mean, *Mama didn't make it back?!*"

Jaia sinks to the ground, covering her face with her hands. I watch her, but I feel like I'm watching myself and something about the weakness I see fills me with a fury, with a feeling I've never felt before, like a churning volcano just before it erupts. I drop to my knees and grab her limp shoulders. "No!" I yell, seeing Adia and then Shani in my mind's eye. "They can't do this to us again! We can't let them! No, no, *no!*"

I push my full *mtungi* of water into her arms as a flash from this morning—from my old life—visits me. It's the black jeep coming out of Dekadente's gates, driving in circles, kicking up dust.

And at once, I simply *know* where Mama and Desta have been taken. And at once, I know—I must go there too.

CHAPTER 32

Flora
the sound of heaven

SHE'S PROPPED UP ON A WHITE, fluffy bed with cushions behind her back. Blood gushes from between her legs in a way she knows isn't right. An older woman with tan skin and dark freckles attends her. This woman, Clara, has a gentle voice and cold, nervous hands. She wears a white apron smeared with Flora's blood and is yelling to someone on the other side of the door.

"I told you," her Spanish accent is thick with anger. "We *need* a *doctor!* This baby's stuck on his side!"

The door has a brass handle, and Flora focuses in on it as she writhes among twisted bed sheets. In the hall outside the door, Lucian reaches for the handle's other side. He's about to turn it when he changes his mind and continues pacing. His brother laughs.

"You'd think the child was yours, Rot. I know—you like your women as dark as your teeth…don't you?"

Lucian jumps at Nelson. "*Stop*," he says, unable to muster anything more. He'd been driving toward the mine that morning with the windows down when he heard Flora's agonized screams and pulled over to investigate. What he found shook him to his core—an indigenous woman writhing in labor. He watched her suffer from afar for a few seconds and the experience was unbearable. It was as if he heard all the stolen girls' voices in her desperate screams.

Now, his face is flushed and his teeth are streaked with the mine soot that hides under his nails. He's been so nervous since he brought Flora into the house that he's chewed his cuticles raw.

Lucian looks down at his hands. Embarrassed, he shoves them into his pockets. A glance at a passing mirror reveals his darkened teeth. They're always shadowed from the mine soot, from the habit of chewing his nails. He looks away quickly, feeling weak, feeling like he'd do anything in the world for a hit of junat.

Nelson flops back on the leather couch. He props his feet on a gold-rimmed coffee table. A smile cuts his face as Flora's screams cut the air.

"I hear Badru's boys got that girl today," he says. "We could always sell this woman and her baby off too—a package deal."

Lucian flies at his brother as Nelson shakes with laughter. His shin bumps an end table, and a stack of books falls to the floor. Lucian grabs his brother by the shirt so hard his collar rips. Nelson startles.

"*Have you no shame?*" Lucian seethes, his beet-red face a centimeter from Nelson's. Capillaries surface, casting a pink veil around his amber eyes.

Stunned, Nelson pushes droopy curls off his angular face with a familiar swipe of the hand. He sinks back into the overstuffed sofa and, like a spoiled kitten, studies his brother with a look of amusement. Lucian is already back to chewing his fingernails and pacing the floor. A slick retort takes shape on the tip of Nelson's tongue but is interrupted by the wide oak door swinging open. Clara walks out, her smile serene.

"Boys," she says, drying her hands on a towel. "He's here."

✹ ✳ ✹

Flora accepted Lucian's help because her labor was so strange. Many years ago, Jaia had helped her deliver Talitha and Peter— two healthy babies—but since then she's miscarried countless times. Flora knows childbirth is a threshold of pain unlike any other. But what she felt this time under the warka tree was different and wrong. When she attempted to push, the baby wouldn't budge. Only blood gushed, so much that Flora felt her eyes closing and the urge to sleep overwhelming her, even in the middle of labor.

Once inside Dekadente, Flora trusted Clara immediately. The way the older woman fed her ice chips and breathed silent, sighing prayers. Just when Flora was about to give up—succumbing to the urge to sleep—Clara looked up and yelled something loud in another language. Then, she reached inside Flora and felt around. When her pinky hooked under what she knew was a tiny armpit, she gently pulled the baby around and down, and delivered him. The sight of her son's limp body revived Flora quickly. She grabbed him, smacked his little bottom, and blew into his face until his screams united the two women—strangers until that moment— in laughter that is certainly the sound of heaven.

Clara cut the cord, swaddled the baby, and gave him back to Flora. "What will you call him?" she asked gently.

Flora couldn't answer right away. For months, she'd planned to name her son after his papa, but something happened during labor that made her change her mind. Just before Lucian found her, her brother's memorized letter led to another letter captured perfectly in her mind's eye—her husband Salim's shaky handwriting back when they were dating, something she hadn't recalled in years.

25, September

Dearest Flora,
    I made this print with the red clay of my people.
    Love, will you place your hand in mine?

Father Damien of Molokai

friend of lepers

    I cannot believe I have found a soul who also cherishes Fr. Damien and how he said "I make myself a leper with the lepers to gain all to Jesus Christ."

by Philip Kosloski

    Flora, if you marry me, I will give you a life of hardship. But I will give you all my love Seven Mountains Publishing that burns body, mind and soul — only for you.
Answer me please,

                   Salim

Nuzzling her nose into her baby's fluff of black hair, she returns to the letter again, complete in her memory, every word sprawled on a page torn from Father Damien of Molokai's biography—the saint to whom both she and Salim shared a special devotion.

Flora, reveling in Salim's marriage proposal and relieved to be through with labor, puts the baby to her breast. He latches on. Clara sighs, but Flora's mind is somewhere else.

Whatever became of that letter? The one written on a page from the Father Damien book. It was a story Flora and Salim cherished about a missionary priest to Hawaii who caught leprosy ministering to the people he loved.

"*Are you calling the Kilokie people* lepers?" Flora had challenged Salim when he first shared this inspiration for wanting to take her back to his people.

"*No, no—my K-Kilokie are so b-beautiful, I am unworthy of them. For this reason, I go b-back—to become wo-wo-worthy of them.*"

Perhaps Jane found the letter and saved it. Or, more likely, her father fed it to the incinerator. The thought of her estranged family who promised to hold a funeral for her if she "*married that heathen*" brings tears to her eyes. She hasn't seen or talked to them in sixteen long years, since Salim walked with her, hand in hand, across Great Mountain.

᙭ ᙭ ᙭

Back then, when Flora first came to the Kilokie, she had her husband and the belief in their mission of ministering to his people not by simply dropping off Bibles and rice, but by being *Kilokie. She loved learning the traditions of Salim's tribe, the dances and songs of his people—his people who were now hers. She also had her brother Ibrahim, as he would bring news and visit when his work as an interpreter allowed. Flora had—maybe too idealistically—hoped that eventually her parents would catch the vision she and Salim shared, that there would be something concrete she could show her parents—like an entire tribe being baptized, or the chief allowing their priest to set up a Bible school for children, or—something, anything to prove her choice wasn't in vain.*

But then her brother was killed, and she began to doubt. So many hardships, big and small, followed. From the day-to-day work of surviving without electricity and running water, to having more babies miscarry than survive, to watching her husband struggle to carve out a living in dangerous and unjust conditions. The years passed. She doubted more. And her anger…it grew.

☀ ☀ ☀

Clara keeps pushing her take to sips of broth.

"Rebuilds the blood," she says with each lift of the spoon to Flora's cracked lips.

Clara says a doctor is coming, but he won't be here until evening. Flora protests the help and would grab her baby and walk out the door if she could. However, even lifting her head off the pillow is impossible. So she rests with her son in her arms. And really—the soft bed, the smell of clean sheets, and Clara's nurturing touch are such a relief, such an enormous relief.

CHAPTER 33

Talitha
this roaring fire

"**G**O BACK TO NALA," I SAY, forcing Jaia to keep my *mtungi*. "Make her drink and—"

"But Talitha!" Jaia begs. "Even Peter can't calm her down; she cries only for you. No one else can console her!"

My heart clenches, but I've got to find Mama and Desta, and I just know they're in that white mansion surrounded by coconut trees. I can't explain it, but something about how mad Mama got when she stared at Dekadente this morning is leading me there.

"Also," Jaia whimpers, "the sickness is my fault." Her eyes are wide. "Yesterday, I took the little ones to the river to cool off; I couldn't stop them from taking tiny sips—we were all so thirsty! I even drank some, and now my milk must be tainted."

Jaia's weeping, but my sole focus is Dekadente.

"Oh, Talitha," she continues, "what are we going to do? None of my medicines are working…. And look at your eye!"

She reaches for my face with a shaky hand, and something about her fear—no, her *weakness*—commands what little strength I have to show itself all the more. I grab her broad shoulders.

"*Stop it,*" I say, staring her straight in the eye. I squeeze her tight for a few seconds, trying to make a plan, trying to think above the sound of her whimpering. "Here's what we'll do—you take this water to the village. Tell the uncles and anyone you can find—tell Moses, *be sure to tell Moses*—that Mama and Desta have been stolen just like Adia and Shani. Tell them I've gone to Dekadente to search—"

"*Dekadente?*" Jaia gasps. "You'll be shot!"

"I have to." I try to sound calm. "If they don't have Desta and Mama, they're the only ones who can help me."

"They won't help you!" she begs. "Badru's probably got them. If you go to Dekadente, they'll sic a dog on you before you even get a chance to ask for help. *Don't do it, Talitha— the uncles will look for—*"

"*No,*" I whisper, my face close to hers.

She loosens her grip and backs away, looking so confused, I think for a second that she doesn't understand me. And to be honest, I don't think I understand this roaring fire in my chest either—except that in the seconds Jaia was begging me not to go, it was as if she had disappeared and all I saw before me was Dekadente. Even now, as I look off in its direction, my hands and feet itch to climb its iron fence.

"*No!*" she pleads again. "*Don't go!*"

I refuse to look at her, so she speaks even louder. "Why are you so certain they're there?"

"I just know," I answer quietly, staring at my muddy feet, my words dissolving into air.

I look up at Jaia, and suddenly, even though she's the sturdiest woman in the village, she appears so small to me, standing in the center of our worn-down trail. In her terrified eyes, I see myself. I see all of us, refusing to fight back, accepting even more of our women—*even Mama, even Desta*—being *stolen*. And a fire I've never felt before fills my veins...

Jaia's crying, wringing her hands, when a lonely orchid catches my eye, sprouting in a rocky patch behind her. It's curly and white with a violet-pink mouth—a thing of beauty among rubble. So much like Mama, so much like Desta and Adia and Shani.

This twisting orchid, the cool, dry breeze—the everyday normalcy of everything is maddening. The ordinariness of it all, of the squirrels racing up tree trunks and butterflies floating flower to flower—it all seems to mock me, to mock Desta and Mama. Shouldn't the squirrels know? Shouldn't they hide away in their nests?

I grab Jaia's shoulders one last time.

"I don't know *how* I know, but Mama and Desta are at Dekadente, and I've got to get them back. Now *please*—go take care of Nala for me. *Please!*"

With that, I run toward the peak. Jaia calls for me, but I don't look back.

CHAPTER 34

Moses
a tick on the scalp of a bald man

H E HAULS BUCKET AFTER BUCKET of water to the three special coconut trees that grow in the corner of the plot Talitha's papa used to farm. Uncle Tebaho showed him how a few months ago.

"It's a shame about the accident in the mines. That Bible man was very good," Uncle shook his head the first time he took Moses to this special place where foreign trees shoot up to the sky, tall and proud like three strong women. Trees that are at once strange to behold, but also beautiful with green, flapping fronds. Trees that drop hard, round fruits, furry on the outside and sweet with white milk in the middle.

Tears stream down Moses' cheeks as he dips the bucket he keeps hidden just for this job. Running back and forth between the river and the trees at least twenty times, huffing and puffing as he goes, Moses works until he's about to collapse. But he's relieved for the task that feels like the tiniest drop of atonement.

When he pours the final bucket, he stares down at the wet dirt, breathing in the earthy tang of stomped river weeds, wishing for some goat manure to fertilize the soil. He's been babying these trees ever since he learned they belonged to Talitha's papa. Moses never told her he'd been tending them, and he doesn't really know why he's kept it a secret. Except that whenever Talitha's papa is mentioned, she walks extra fast. Also, her voice drops off, talking so softly Moses has to read her lips. The fast walking, he thinks, means she's off to search for him, for her dead papa. The soft talking frightens Moses, makes him worry that all the sadness is weakening her, making her fade away. He always finds an excuse to touch her in these moments— a helping hand over the cliff, a tweak of a curl. It's his way of bringing her back, because he can't stand the thought of the world without her. Also, maybe Talitha will look for her dead papa here one day. So he'd like to keep the place alive.

He re-hides the bucket and takes one last look up at the trees, their fronds flapping against the bright blue sky like crazy, curly hair. And suddenly, these trees are the women he's come to know: the shortest one in the center is Flora, Talitha's mama, straight-backed and proud. The thicker one to the left is Desta, curvy with extra fronds shaking, full of ripe brown fruits. And Talitha is the most delicate tree, farther away from the other two, almost on her own. The sun shines golden on the lean swerve of her trunk. *A trio,* he reflects, *scattered, all because of me...*

He swipes at his tears, but just rubs dirt in his eyes. Finally, he turns away to move on, to cut through a field, trudging around corn stalks until he falls out onto an empty dirt road. It's the long way back to his uncle's shack. Moses looks both ways to find the road empty, then moves forward, loping along the rocky path because, quite simply, he doesn't know what else to do, where else to go. And maybe, just maybe, they let Uncle Tebaho go and he made it back home. Maybe he's waiting there now, anxious to see if Moses is safe. He stumbles along.

"*Talitha…*" he sighs, looking back over his shoulder at her tree, until it finally falls out of sight behind the slope, behind the green wall of rustling corn. He kicks dirt clods as he walks, choking on ghost-sized clouds of red dust. Moses groans, punching tree after tree, ripping the skin clean off his knuckles. And even though he passes a tiny trickling creek, he denies his throbbing hand a thrust in the dark water. Because the pain screaming up his arm and tingling his elbow feels right, like well-deserved punishment. He shakes his head as fresh tears flow freely.

☀ ☀ ☀

Crying has always come easily to Moses—almost too easily. When he was a little boy, his eyes would fill up at the slightest fright or tumble. The fact that he's always been overgrown and accident-prone (only exacerbated by puberty) never helped. His mama worried about his sensitive nature, especially because at the age of three, he was the size of a six-year-old; at the age of six, he was the size of a ten-year-old; and so on.

"Why is that boy crying like a baby?" a hired hand once complained when Moses was about four.

"Because he is a baby!" His mama defended him, scooping Moses up even though he was more than half her size.

※ ☀ ※

For years, Moses has struggled to keep his leaky eyes under control. But today, all alone on a remote road, he lets loose.

"*Talitha*," he groans, throwing his head back to the cloud-less sky. His fingers rake his hair. His blurry eyes are almost completely blinded by the glaring noonday sun. "Oh, Talitha…"

Imagining the worst—the masked men grabbing both girls; Talitha screaming for him, "*Moses, Moses!*" She's reaching out her arms for him to save her. And then Uncle—the hunter's knife held high over his tightly tied hands in the mine's dark cavern. Blood spilling everywhere. These images flash through Moses' mind more clearly than the rut-filled road right in front of him, when a curious thought flutters by, stopping him cold in his tracks.

I ran away. I wonder if the masked men are mad at me…

The idea arrives at the very same moment the black jeep whips around the bend in front of him. His jaw drops open. His eyes search frantically on either side of the road for a place to hide. But he's arrived at a clearing, surrounded all around by freshly cut fields.

Moses is a tick on the scalp of a bald man. The realization straightens his back and wicks his weepy eyes bone dry.

CHAPTER 35

Flora
my cup overflows

FLORA LIES IN THE WIDE, soft bed, studying her child. He looks much like her other babies, with a smooshed-in nose and mounds of silky black hair.

The sense of relief she feels is so overwhelming that when the baby scrunches up his face, as all babies do, she laughs until tears of joy sneak from the corners of her eyes. Clara notices the baby's serious expression too.

"What a frown!" the older woman laughs. "Oh my! What a serious little man!" She talks sweetly to the baby.

Flora giggles softly as she strokes his velvety cheek with her thumb. Clara leans over the two of them. "Well, hello there," she grabs his tiny hand. "Pleased to meet you."

Flora sighs and relaxes back into the fluffy pillows. Clara scoops up the child. Suddenly, Flora's emotions swing sharply, as emotions often do after labor. For Flora, the shift is especially profound, as she's been holding back so much for months, trying to be strong for Talitha and Peter. But now, with her older children away and her baby safely delivered, she can no longer contain herself. She covers her face with the blanket, trying to hide the fact that she's not laughing anymore. But Clara isn't fooled. The older woman strokes the tired mother's head. "There now," she whispers. "I understand."

And like a movie reel, the wounds of the past sixteen years appear in Flora's mind, as hot tears pour down her temples and into her ears:

Her father's back to her the morning she returned to the Kilokie with Salim.

Ibrahim's dead body carried into the village at dusk.

The dry bottom of the *mtungi* as her children begged for another drink.

Another bowl of tasteless yellow cornmeal in the months when food was scarce before the new harvest.

Eshe and the villagers turning away from Salim anytime he pulled out his Bible.

And finally, the merciless moon the night of Salim's death— so bright, so blindingly white. How often she'd lain on her mat since that night too scared to close her eyes, terrified she'd find the moon there in her memory, taunting her, screaming her father's words in its rays, *"Go on, go... love won't be enough... you'll be back..."*

So, for many endless nights, Flora never closed her eyes. Instead, she stayed awake with the crickets, curled on her side, listening to her children breathe. Better to lose sleep than to greet the morning sightless, with eyes burned from a picture, a memory so real she was certain it would leave her blind.

The memories continue to play as Clara hums to the baby and a fan clicks overhead. Memories captured like pictures in Flora's mind. Pictures—restless wanderers lined up straight, summing up her story, driving home the conviction she's been piecing together for years…

It was all in vain.

She and Salim should have heeded her father's advice and stayed in the city. They should have raised a family there.

A knock on the door snaps her to the present. She dries her eyes with a sheet.

Lucian speaks without peeking his head around the door. "May I…come in?" he asks.

"Just a minute," Clara replies, fluttering around Flora, straightening her blankets. "All right."

Flora would have protested if she'd caught Clara's eye, but now it's too late.

A tray appears first. It's loaded with fresh pineapple and melon, a steak, and a huge baked potato. There's also a tall glass of chocolate milk, sweating with condensation.

Flora's taste buds quicken at the smells, salty and sweet. She hasn't had anything but goat's milk, let alone chocolate milk, in ages. And salt! A whole shaker full of white salt sits next to the steak, which looks like something straight from the fanciest restaurant in her city—a place called *La Trec*. She ate there just once, on her sixteenth birthday. She'd made perfect marks that quarter at the academy, and her father surprised her with a blue velvet box when the waiter brought a dish of flaming cherries for dessert. The dress she'd worn matched the box perfectly, and when she snapped open the seal, a sapphire pendant glowed from the center of what looked like a hun-

dred tiny diamonds. Jane squealed. The sound, the memory—
one bathed in candlelight and laughter—slips in like a peck on
the cheek as Lucian sets down the tray.

Flora's never seen so much butter. There's a golden chunk
the size of her new baby's fist just wallowing there, slipping and
sliding through the ivory fluff of a foil-lined potato. Saliva rushes
to her mouth when she hears what can only be described as a
soft, still voice.

*"You-you s-s-set a t-t-table before me in the p-p-presence of
m-my enemies…"*

Her husband's favorite psalm. It's Salim. He's here. His
presence fills the room, and Flora jumps.

"Oh my," Clara gasps, reaching to steady the glass. Lucian
looks confused. Flora searches the room with a stunned expression, expecting to see her husband. Lucian backs away.

"Rest now," he says. "The doctor will be here soon."

Just as quickly as Lucian appeared, and just as quickly as
Salim's presence appeared, they're both gone.

Clara sighs over the baby, her face leaning into his, her
smile serene.

"Tell me, what will you name him?" Her voice is a song.

But the exhausted mother can't answer. Her head rests
limply on its side. The sight of the fruit makes her sour taste
buds twist like tribal dancers. Her mind begins to explain the
voice away when Salim returns to her once more.

"My c-c-cup overflows."

Flora gasps again sharply and almost jumps out of the bed
this time. But Clara, oblivious to anyone or anything but the
baby, coos over the bundle in her arms.

How many times had they sung that psalm that had captured

Salim's imagination, reminding him of his own boyhood days as a shepherd? How many times had he carved it with a stick into the mud of their hut's floor? How many times had he gently guided their children's small hands over its letters?

Now Salim comes to Flora on the wings of this prayer, and she catches him. She clasps him tightly in her bunched-up quilt and presses all the pain of his death into her own iron-clad heart as it—finally—breaks. Only this time her emotions swing sideways again, and a smile lights her face at the sight of her baby.

With misty eyes, she reaches out to dip her finger into the melted butter. She dabs it on the center of her tongue. It spreads like ripples on a pond.

And as Flora lies there, anticipating her meal and straining once again to hear her husband's voice, Clara sings to the baby.

"You are a sunrise," she sings. The melody is familiar, but Flora's never heard it with these words. "You are a new day…"

Clara sings the chorus again and again. Her voice is louder than Salim's and rings truer than all Flora's doubts. Flora can't help but fall in love with the song and even weakly hum along.

"You are a gift," Clara continues, "our hope for tomorrow…"

Clara finishes singing, and the two are quiet together for a while, with only the sound of a fan clicking overhead. Finally, Flora speaks—

"He will be called Damien."

In a heartbeat, Flora's changed her mind about naming the baby after his father. Instead, she names him for the saint who first inspired their mission to the Kilokie—a mission that only made sense for the first time a few seconds ago, when Clara laid the baby on the bed to baptize him, pouring water over his head three times. She then made the sign of the cross over the entire length and width of his tiny body.

She thinks I'm not watching, Flora smiled, realizing that Clara—with kind intentions—was quickly baptizing a village baby before the mother could protest.

But in that moment, Flora realized something quite clearly—their mission to the Kilokie had *not* been in vain. For she saw not only her baby's body under the shadow of that cross, but her husband's, her brother's, her own…

Sure, this cross was a symbol of death, but death didn't have the last word—resurrection did. And this new baby, this new life, was the proof Flora needed that there's still hope.

"I will call him Damien," she repeats again with a little more strength in her voice, "Damien Salim."

"Oh," Clara says excitedly, "I love it!" She opens the door and hollers down the hall, "Boys, come back! She's named him—Damien Salim is here!"

CHAPTER 36

Lucian
sparrows

Lucian and Nelson hear Clara's voice faintly from their father's old study. Nelson lights a pipe, takes a puff, and passes it to Lucian.

He reluctantly accepts. The vibrant room full of mahogany furniture and stuffed game, all bearing sharp claws and fake marble eyes, fogs quickly. Lucian's mental tension, however, is barely touched. It perches behind his shoulder with ravenous eyes, much like the endangered lynx his father shot so many years ago on a trip overseas—poised and ready to pounce.

"Badru's boys said that punk chickened out," Nelson says. "They said he found a girl, rode them to where she was, and ran away at the last minute."

Lucian can hardly believe they're having this conversation. He leans forward on the desk with his head in his hands. He went over the books last night, and unless he can pay off at least half the interest on his long-overdue loan by the end of the week, the bank is going to start collecting their assets— beginning with Dekadente. Part of him wants them to just take it, take it all—the marble floors, the bronze pillars, the hidden safes that were once full of diamonds, emeralds, and stacks of cash. Safes that now sit empty, drained by his mismanagement and his many addictions.

Lucian could probably even handle extracting his invalid mother from this palace he so despises. A palace his father sold his soul to build, once beating a worker close to death in front of him when Lucian was only a freckle-faced child.

☀ ☀ ☀

He'll never forget that day. He was seven and couldn't find his belt, so he was tugging up his pants with one hand while carrying a bird book in the other. His binoculars hung on a cord around his neck, as he'd been on his way to watch for the barn swallows that migrate south that time of year. The birds are a deep blue but have throats and bellies as red as the blood that covered the worker lying limp on the ground. The man's skin was black as night, but his teeth and his yellow shirt were drenched crimson. Unconscious, he was taking his screaming master's kicks to the stomach as if he were a sack of straw. Lucian tiptoed away, unnoticed and terrified.

For years, he couldn't bear the sight of barn swallows. When they skimmed by his lookout in the treehouse, he'd see the swish of red on blue and remember the blood on the whites of the man's eyes—eyes that stared up numbly, as if they too were searching the sky for birds. Lucian would grip the branches when the barn swallows passed and drop his binoculars. He'd squeeze his eyes shut tight, hear the woodiness of their flapping wings, and pretend they were sparrows.

✸　✸　✸

"Well, did they catch her?" Lucian mumbles as he mindlessly bends and unbends paper clips, one after another. He yearns for more junat, but he won't let himself reach for the pipe.

"Oh yeah. I'll go along when they take her to Badru's guy in the city tonight, make sure we get the money they promised. We'll only see a third of what we got for the last girl, but—"

"A *third*?" Panic ripples through Lucian. "I thought it was going to be enough to cover what we owe!"

"No, the price has gone down, and of course Badru still needs his cut. Now listen—"

Clara's voice interrupts them. Nelson knocks the ashes from the pipe into an oversized ashtray, and they reluctantly head down the hall. Both men heed the voice of the small woman just as they did when they were young, back when she taught them to tie their shoelaces. And now, even though they're grown, they'll still sit for meals and even say grace if she makes the request. Their father, when he was alive, marveled at the power the *Señorita* had over his boys.

"You don't even beat them," he'd say, incredulous at the sons who showed no interest in hunting or learning his trade.

"I don't have to," Clara would reply. And in her heart, she'd finish sadly, *Because, unlike you, I* love *them.*

Lucian's and Nelson's work boots clomp down a spiral staircase. Nelson's voice quiets as they near Flora's room.

186

"Badru's planning something for that Moses, something he won't forget."

"But didn't he do what he was supposed to? Didn't he get us…" Lucian can't bring himself to finish the sentence.

Nelson's eyes glint with glee, "Yeah, Rot, but he ran away. He didn't follow through. And it allows for us…a bit of fun."

Defeated, Lucian raps the guest room's door. The native woman had behaved so oddly when Lucian delivered the tray Clara ordered from the cook. He'd prefer not to return so soon, but he knows better than to ignore Clara.

CHAPTER 37

Flora
in the presence of her enemies

THERE'S A KNOCK ON THE DOOR.

"Come in," Clara calls over Damien's soft mews.

Flora's propped up in bed. The tray is on her lap.

The brothers look as awkward as the silence filling the room. Lucian chews his nails. Nelson smooths his black hair back again and again.

Clara tilts Damien in their direction. His eyes are closed and his lips are pursed pink.

"Um, uh," Nelson mutters. "You can stay here 'til the doctor checks you out…but then you gotta' go."

Clara shoots him a look. The brothers shrink back in the small woman's presence. They quietly look to Clara, then to the baby, and then back to Flora. Flora thinks their eyes remind her of an animal's at night—frozen in the light of a kerosene lamp.

"Thank you," she addresses them softly.

And as the words leave her mouth, she realizes she's look-ing into the faces of the men who abuse and overwork her people, who rest in luxury while their workers go without food, medicines, and even clean drinking water. Regardless, she's so overwhelmed with gratitude for her baby, for Clara's help, for simply having survived. That gratitude must go somewhere. She sits up straighter and clears her throat.

"Thank you," she says again, only louder, as her hand ges-tures over the room and the tray, "for everything you've done for us. I thank you."

And as the mine owners whom Flora's imagined herself screaming at and beating on with balled fists look on, Flora does what is only fitting. Finding herself at *a table set before her in the presence of her enemies*—she picks up her fork and eats.

CHAPTER 38

Talitha
flood of light so blinding

As MY HEELS KICK UP CLAY, the mansion fills my senses and my feet tingle cold at the thought of all that marble. Oddly, I feel as if I've been there before, even though I haven't.

The task before me is so clear, my feet are suddenly light and my mind is alert. Even my swollen eye has stopped throbbing.

As I run, flashes of color flood my vision—the green of the farmers' fields pop into sight as I curve around the bend. Dense trees line my path. Their branches clap together in the breeze, cheering me on. Tiny leaves spin with excitement. And for a moment, it feels so right to be running toward Dekadente to find Mama and Desta, like I'm doing exactly what I'm meant to do.

Pausing to catch my breath, I arrive at Weeping Rock to find Deaf Man sound asleep. His head's tilted back, his mouth is wide open, and he's snoring so loud that any other day it would be funny. The pile of yeheb nuts beside him reminds me of how little I've eaten today. Normally, I'd be starving by now. The sun's straight overhead, but I feel fine—even better than fine. My feet speed on, barely touching down on the trail.

And the thought that quickens my heart—*I'm going to save them. I'm going to get them back!*

I've never felt so alive.

Mama's peak comes into view as three long-necked gerenuks spot me from their grassy patch below. The deerlike creatures take off at a trot on the other side of the river, and so we race. Thoughts of Jaia returning to Nala trouble me with each high stride. But while I long to be with my little one, I've seen Jaia with the babies when they're sick—something that happens all the time.

She'll be fine, I tell myself again and again. *Peter is there to help them. Just get to Mama and Desta…*

The gerenuks stop to drink, but I speed up. And as I do, I consider the other instructions I gave Jaia.

Find Moses. Find Moses. Find Moses.

I imagine his face, and I can't help but smile. Even with all that's going on, I just can't help it.

Dekadente's closer now. The white glare of its walls is blinding, even from so far away. I stop in my tracks, my own breath deafening to my ears.

Find Moses.

The gerenuks turn toward the mansion as if they're leading the way. Their golden haunches shed sweat, their heels pounding up skinny clouds of dust that mix with the heat waves. The animals gallop like three miniature horses, leaving me alone on Mama's peak with nothing but Dekadente and my last two requests to Jaia looming loudly, much like the gerenuks' hooves thundering across the valley's floor.

Take care of Nala, find Moses, take care of Nala, find Moses… And as I stand here, confronted by the white mansion with its armed guards, an *understanding* fills my mind. But it's a flood of light so blinding, it hurts.

Moses—I suddenly know just who he is to me. Because in this moment, all the baby birds make sense. If it has a name, it would be something like *mine*. And if it were any other day, if Mama and Desta were safe in the hut and Nala sat happily on my lap, this *understanding* would lift my chin to the sky, like a flower opening to the sun. But right now, with Nala retchin' and Desta and Mama stolen, I simply need his help. I need him to call out their names with me, to search every abandoned emerald mine and every dark corner of this valley until we find them.

This *understanding,* though—the part that's blinding is his face the last time I saw him, dusty with mine soot, lined with tear tracks. And then his strange question—

"Will Desta be at the spring today?"

And then…the panther jeep…the black masks…Desta's scream…

A sharp pain, like a swift kick to my stomach, shoots through me.

"Will Desta be at the spring today?"

And as the reality of his question—what it means now, in light of what's happened—hits me, I grab my heart because I'm falling, collapsing to the ground. My fists rip up dry brush like an animal at the bottom of a trap.

"No!" someone screams. *"No, no, no!"* It takes me a second to realize that *someone* is me.

Moses couldn't *have been one of the masked men*, I tell myself. He's so much bigger than them, and so gentle…"He would *never*…" I cry without tears.

But still—something's not right.

"I have to find him," I mutter aloud. I have to ask…what… he…knows.

What he knows?

The horror of him knowing anything about Desta with a knife to her throat is more than I can bear. And even though all this knowledge comes with endless questions, talking to Moses will have to wait.

Quickly, I make my way down the face of the cliff, through the same steep dip where fog hung thick just a few hours—and yet a lifetime—ago. But now, everything is so warm and bright. I lift my *kitenge* to cross the river. When I reach the dirt road on the other side, a corn plot catches my eye. Its endless ripe kernels peek through silky husks, like so many yellow smiles.

All this beauty, I think, *it belongs to Mama, but it's a part of me too…*

I snap off a fresh ear of corn and keep walking. My teeth sink into its flesh, and something about the sweetness makes me *know* I'll find them! I'll take Mama and Desta home! We'll live in our own hut forever!

Dashing ahead, I follow the gerenuks' hoofprints, pushing this new understanding about Moses—so bright on the one hand, yet so blindingly painful on the other—from my mind.

The distance to Dekadente shortens with each running leap. I stare down its glaring white walls as if I can see right through them to Mama and Desta inside, hugging each other, terrified… encircled by lions.

CHAPTER 39

Moses
SHE KNOWS

H E LIES ON HIS SIDE in the back of the black jeep as it lurches and swerves along the dusty dirt road. Moses' wrists are tied so tight his fingertips are white and his hands are numb. Blood spills from a gash on his lip. His cheek sticks to the hot plastic seat. He lifts his head, and from the corner of his eye, Moses sees a red splotch in the shape of his face imprinted on the plastic.

When Badru's thugs attacked him a few minutes ago, they hadn't listened as he held up his hands, trying to explain why he'd run away earlier. The shorter one shrieked something in French and pointed a gun at Moses' head. The bigger guy smiled snidely as he jumped around like a boxer, swinging punches at Moses' face, like this whole thing was some sort of game. Moses could only understand a little of what they said, between their foreign language and their raucous laughter.

The jeep rattles as it zigzags through dust and over ruts and bumps back to the dormant mine. Hot, chalky air pours in through the open windows. The men speed up at the top of a hill and catch a jump, then slam down loudly. It sounds like the whole squeaky vehicle will certainly bust apart. The men howl with laughter and suddenly there's something small and hard in Moses' mouth.

Is that a rock? he wonders, rolling it around with his tongue. Confused, he spits out a bloody tooth on the floor. But the pain in his jaw and the throbbing welts all over his arms and ribs where he's been beaten black and blue hurt nothing compared to the mental anguish that's left him reeling. Because as he's lain here in the back of this speeding panther of a jeep, two words have appeared clearly in his mind, knocking him down harder than the punches the thugs kept throwing at his face—
SHE KNOWS.

SHE KNOWS, SHE KNOWS, SHE KNOWS—the words scream louder than the branches scratching the jeep's metal sides.

When he squeezes his eyes shut tight, Talitha's there. Her dark, almond eyes stare him down. As always, she sees right through him. And she's furious, because this quick-witted girl who can look at the grass rustling and sense that a hedgehog is about to sneak from its nest, this girl who can glance at the sun and mark the exact time of day down to the minute…Moses *knows* that she must know of his guilt.

Talitha can read him the way she reads everything—with a glimpse. That's all it takes for her to fully grasp the object or idea, person or passage of Scripture, hideout or wild animal—even memorize it—forever. Apparently, Talitha's mama has the same gift, and he's certain the two of them have already figured out what he's done, that they've pieced together his question *"Will Desta be at the spring today?"* with their dear cousin being stolen.

They hate me! he mourns, thinking of Talitha and her tiny mama with the tornado of a temper. The older woman already terrifies him, even though he could surely pick her up with one hand. *They* should *hate me…*

Moses' body is in a state of shock. He's never been beaten like this before; he's never been beaten at all before. Now, with a tooth knocked out and bruises covering his body, he throbs all over. But no injury to his ribs or face hurts nearly as much as the realization tormenting his soul, screaming louder than the French rap music blasting from the speakers, wracking his mind as the jeep speeds toward some ominous destination. None of this tortures Moses as much as the fact that *SHE KNOWS.*

CHAPTER 40

Lucian
a ton of dark, sooty rocks

"BADRU CAUGHT THAT KID MOSES, the one who ran away this morning," Nelson comments, smiling darkly as he opens the fridge. Lucian ignores him.

"So Rot, are you gonna' join us out at the mine?" Nelson flips through the cabinets. "You know…help us teach this kid a lesson?"

As if in a trance, Lucian stares out the window just as three long-necked gerenuks trot by. Usually, their shiny coats would send him outside for a closer look. But today, the unusual creatures run on without Lucian giving them the smallest second glance.

He can't face his brother. Frayed nerves have soured his stomach. The sandwich Clara made him lies untouched, pushed off to the side of the counter. He tried to eat it, but the conversation he's just had with Flora set his mind spinning.

᪥ ᪥ ᪥

Lucian returned to her room a few minutes ago without Nelson. Drawn by a compulsion he didn't quite understand, he brought her a stack of blankets, which was silly as the room was already warm.

"Should I go to your people?" he asked her as he set the blankets on a chair near her bed. "Should I find your husband, tell him you are well?"

And Flora, although exhausted physically, was emboldened in spirit. For some reason, she told Lucian everything—about how she's from a faraway city and how she'd come to the Great Red Valley. She told him of her adopted tribe, the Kilokie, and of Salim's death. While the story would have been sad to any listener, there was something exceptionally disturbing about it all that left Lucian deeply troubled.

Yet in spite of his piqued mind, he couldn't help noticing baby Damien, who seemed to cast a glow of his own. To his surprise, the child struck him as remarkable, even otherworldly. Lucian had never actually seen a baby that small before—his tiny fists, the striking thatch of black hair.

᪥ ᪥ ᪥

"Nelson," Lucian says as he leans against the kitchen counter, "what was the name of that miner? The one who wrote the letter to the bank?"

"Oh, the one we knocked off?"

"Shh!"

The shaky handwriting on crumpled paper, the memory of his casual nod of assent when Nelson suggested *"Let's bury it,"*

assails Lucian like an avalanche of dark, sooty rocks as the letter
flashes in his mind's eye:

Dear Sirs,

    I write to the Credit
Union today to inform you of
unfit and unjust working
conditions of your "holding"—
Kerr Emerald Mines, Great Red
                  Valley.
    I speak as one of
the miners for all the miners—

The letter went on to describe extremely long shifts—fifteen
to sixteen hours at a time. It talked about children being forced
to work and about a community of laborers whose families
lacked the most basic necessities while their employers lived
in luxury.

Lucian had read that letter aloud to Nelson about six months
ago, wanting to get his advice. The bank had sent a copy of it to
Dekadente, stating it was the third one they'd received from the
same person—a man who was brave enough to sign his name at
the bottom of the letter. And at the same moment, both Lucian
and Nelson say the name aloud:

Salim Befenge

At the sound of this name, Lucian catches the powdery smell of Damien on his hands. Lucian hadn't wanted to hold the baby, but Clara had insisted.

What have I done? Lucian thinks as the baby's soft cry wafts down the hall.

Let's bury it. Nelson's suggestion now haunts Lucian, because the *it* wasn't an *it* at all, but a man who simply wanted to make a living for his family. The *it* was a husband and a father—the father of the baby who is now crying in the guest room.

Lucian knocks over a chair as he dashes around the kitchen's corner and out the sliding glass doors.

"Hey, Rot," Nelson calls after him. "Are you going to eat that—"

Lucian's heart beats so hard he thinks it will explode from his chest. He doesn't know what to do, where to go, but he needs to escape—from Nelson and Dekadente. If he could, he'd escape from himself, leaving behind his own body and mind to forget what he's done.

Lucian's legs think for him. He tears past the bright blue pool and through the wrought iron gate, leaving it swinging wide open behind him. Then he runs as if being pursued, crossing the stretch of flatland at a sprint.

When Lucian hits the row of jackalberry trees, he slows to a walk, going to a special spot and pushing up the brambles with a stick. It's been so long, but he drops down on his belly and scooches under the prickly vines as if he'd done the same thing only yesterday.

And here it is, hidden out of sight behind a swath of dark leaves. The boards are still nailed to the trunk as a makeshift ladder. Lucian hasn't been here in twenty years; he stopped coming as a teenager. Yet the sight of this treehouse with its trapdoor hanging open fills him with the feeling of coming home.

CHAPTER 41

Lucian
a small sapling

LUCIAN POPS HIS HEAD UP through the open hatch, the old wood creaking under his weight. The place is so much smaller than he remembers. Red dust lies like a blanket over a stack of comic books and a row of empty soda cans.

An important moment finds him, one he's totally forgotten until this second. It's a memory of Clara. She'd caught him stealing those same sodas for this treehouse from the mini-fridge in her bedroom. She sat him down on her blue flowered rug with his back against the wall, her arm resting lightly across his shoulders.

"It's good that you feel badly, Lucian," she'd said gently, her Spanish accent curling at the edges. *"Whether you take something big or something small, stealing is wrong."*

Lucian pushes himself all the way up into the shrunken fort and sits cross-legged amid so much debris that was once a treasure to him. As he surveys his dusty binoculars and field guides and crinkled candy bar wrappers, the weight of what he's done to that man in the mine—the one who wrote the letter, the one whose baby sleeps in his home—crushes him.

The guilt feels infinitely more painful than the weight of those stolen soda cans so many years ago. Stealing a few sodas is nothing compared to ending a life—or *lives*, as many died in the mine explosion. The hollowness in his gut that he felt as a child…it's grown into something more monstrous, a gaping pit threatening to swallow him whole. Stealing sodas was wrong, but stealing girls? Murder? There is no word for it other than *evil.* His guilt is so real, so heavy, he struggles to breathe.

"Your conscience is the little bit of God in you." Clara's wisdom planted decades ago suddenly sprouts a small sapling in the center of his soul.

"My God," he cries into his hands. He knows no one can hear him. Still, he whispers, "I'm sorry. I'm just so sorry."

He weeps, and time seems to disappear. As he cries, so many faces fill his thoughts: Nelson, laughing at him on a night long ago when he fell from that trapdoor and broke his leg; their father with bright red cheeks—the shade they turned when he was screaming; Flora in the white, fluffy bed and Clara beside her, smiling down at the baby. And although he never met Salim, he imagines a dark-skinned man climbing down into his mine, never to return.

Seconds spill into minutes, and the minutes evaporate in the intense afternoon heat. When he finally dries his eyes, he senses a release deep within himself, followed by a calmness falling over him like a misty rain. He inhales deeply. He can't tell if he's been sitting in the treehouse surrounded by dusty comic books for five minutes or five days, but there is one thing he knows for sure. He wants to be—*needs to be*—a better person from now on. He wants to be good, like Clara, starting the very second he leaves this old hideout.

Lucian pulls his hands back from his face, flips them over, and examines his short, scabby nails, all the places where soot has carved its way deep into the ridges of his knuckles. And, just for a moment, he glimpses—he envisions—his hands *healed*. His fingertips clean, the moons of his nails peeking out white. He gasps aloud, a sound almost like laughter.

He dries his face with his sleeve. There's a wholeness in his chest, a peace he hasn't felt in years. Clara's profile comes to mind, her frizzy hair, her aquiline nose. She's leaning over his childhood bed to whisper their nighttime prayers.

His heart leaps at the thought of telling her about this decision.

"Teach me again," he'll say, *"about what's good and true. I don't even know what I've forgotten."*

Her wrinkled face will explode with joy.

But before he can go to Clara—before he can tell her of her answered prayers—there's something he must do first.

CHAPTER 42

Talitha
into the lair

I REACH THE OTHER SIDE of the cornfield and am surprised by a buggy marsh.

I didn't know this was here…

The realization isn't surprising. Straying this close to Dekadente is like drinking river water—forbidden, but also unappealing.

"Too wide to walk *around*," I mutter under my breath, so I trudge forward until the warm, almost hot water is at my knees, then up to my hips, then weighing down my *kitenge* as I trudge up the other side.

That was easy, I think, just as I spot the leeches—black as ink, thick as fingers, wriggling across my thighs, fighting for a taste of my blood. One latches on as a farmer startles me, popping out from behind the brush.

"Whatcha' doin' here, girl?" His shoulders are slumped beneath a thick branch. On each end of the branch hangs a bucket, swinging back and forth, sloshing with water for his crops.

I'm dying to rip off my wraps—both top and bottom— to smack myself clean of the leeches, squirming now, cold and slippery around my waist. But the farmer stares me down with his full-moon eyes because I really shouldn't be here, this close to the mansion. So I slip a hand inside my tunic and pull out a dozen leeches, slick with the pink sheen of my blood.

"Just hunting for mushrooms," I say, "but I found these instead."

I flash the kind of smile I've stolen from Desta, because everyone knows the dangers of coming this close to Dekadente, where the guards use villagers for target practice.

He doesn't return my smile. Instead, he nods downriver. "Some down there," he says, "big ones; now, go on."

"Thanks," I say, reaching behind my shoulder and smacking some more leeches into the water before they can bite me. "Just after I get rid of these."

The creatures squirm back toward my foot, but I hop away. They disappear into the silt as the farmer moves on. The brush closes behind him, and I glimpse a peek at his wheat field. I can tell by the fullness of its crackly heads that his stalks are ready for shearing.

If that were our field, we'd harvest it in a day…

My heart swells at the thought of Papa swinging his sickle wide with a stalk of wheat tucked in his cheek, working our field whenever he wasn't in the mine. Mama and Peter and I helped too, especially at harvest, gathering up the sheaves. But I'd always be grumbling back then, not knowing what I had at times like those, thinking only of my own thirst or the scrap of *lahoh* in my hip sack and how I didn't want to share it.

The last bloodsucker I find is a long one, latched on tightly to the bottom tip of my shoulder blade. I give it a tug, but it won't let go. So I slide my fingernail underneath it real careful, the way Papa taught me to, and dislodge its teeth from my skin. As soon as it lets go, I toss it high, watching it twist in the sky and return to the marsh with a *plunk*.

Quietly, I wait to see if the farmer's coming back. And after it seems he's truly gone, I *do not* turn to search for the mushrooms he mentioned. Instead, I push on ahead, straight through the dense trees, heading closer to Dekadente than I've ever been in my whole life.

Spotting a waterberry tree on its side, I dart to the enormous round shield of its exposed roots and crouch down. Twisting tendrils drip dirt into my hair, but I feel so safe in this cool, dark spot I wish I could stay here forever. Because as I peek around, I realize all that's left between me and the white mansion now is open land and the tall iron gate.

"Help me, Lord," Mama's prayer slips from my lips. I look over my shoulder, thinking for a second she's here, that she's the one praying.

Knowing I'd better move quick before I lose my nerve, I catch sight of the guard. He's extra wide and definitely from one of the tribes, but he wears Western clothes and sunglasses and carries a big black gun. He walks toward a potted plant in my direction, then back toward the mansion, his shoes clicking loudly on the concrete.

Next time he turns around, I tell myself—my heart hammering so loud in my ears, I swear he can hear it—*Next time he turns around...*

RUN!!!

I fly across the open patch, dive into the small bit of cover at the bottom of the wall, and *freeze.* Every muscle in my body is so tense it could snap, and my ears strain with all their might to hear...*gunfire? footsteps?*

But there's nothing; no guard with a gun. No one at all. And finally, I exhale.

What kind of man would shoot his own people?

Mama's rage fills my heart. The thought of her. How she'd wave her fist at the very idea of a villager guarding Dekadente. And now, to think of her weak and trapped somewhere deep inside that white palace—so bright with the sun ricocheting off its sides, but so dark, so deeply dark.

Even as I lie here in the dust, there's a presence I can't describe. I think of the men in the black masks, the knife at Desta's throat, and a wave of fear threatens to crush me.

"Though I w-walk through the valley of the shh-shadow of death..."

Now Papa's voice sneaks in on the breeze. The way he'd sing this psalm in our wheat field. I know he's not actually here, but still...I feel like he could walk out of the trees, his sickle slung over his shoulder, his voice loud and clear:

"...Thou art w-with me ..."

Papa's song. It arrives more like a question than a comfort.

Really? Is the Shepherd God really *with* me? I think of Papa dead, crushed by enormous black rocks. I think of us left behind, thirsty, sad, and now some of us stolen. And Mama's anger—bottled up and shaken—churns in my chest.

Frustrated, I flip on my back to take a break from inhaling the dust. The sky above is hazy, like it might rain. But I know it won't. Such teasing clouds pass over us all the time. Still, I imagine our cisterns filling, spilling over into Nala's happy mouth.

Oh, Nala! I check the sun and send up a prayer that she's being good for Peter and napping, that she's not retchin' her guts out.

Turning back over on my belly, I snake a little closer to the spot where the iron gate sprouts from the concrete that's hiding me. And I stop. To my shock, the gate is unlatched. I peek up at the guard. He's close, just a few feet away, but his back is to me. He sits on a blue and white striped chair. His legs are kicked up on a small table and his head is tilted back, like he's staring up at Great Mountain—or hopefully, like Nala, he's sound asleep.

My heart races even faster. Yet, without another thought, but with the feeling that something—or Someone, bigger than me, brighter than me—is guiding me on...I rise from the dust.

CHAPTER 43

Talitha
a myth that is real

SILENTLY, I SLIP INSIDE THE GATE. It doesn't squeak or creak, and so I exhale softly. Placing one foot in front of the other, I pass between the napping guard and the bright blue pool. Its smell burns my nose, making me think of black pepper or an enormous pile of chopped onions. For a second, I pretend the mansion is mine and I'm simply arriving home from a trip to the spring. Excitement brews in my heart like mash water in a forgotten pot.

Arriving at a clear door, I don't know what to do. I touch it. My fingertips leave tiny brown smudges. My eyes widen as I realize it's glass—I've never seen a pane this huge before. No one's on the other side, so I lay my hands flat. It's smooth, the same temperature as the air. I'd like to lean forward to lick it—the thought comes and goes quickly, but a cool taste like mint lingers in my mouth.

I push the glass forward, and like a miracle—it opens.

A quick look back at the guard; he hasn't moved a bit, so I walk in.

And all at once, the air around me is overwhelmingly icy and charged with my nerves. There's a humming sound, loud and steady, but I don't know what's making it. And the marble floor beneath my feet is even colder than I imagined. Its silver-speckled pattern makes me think of Weeping Rock and Deaf Man and…*Who's going to feed him if I get shot?*

The thought arrives, a full-bodied shiver.

᯽　᯽　᯽

Dekadente is a legend in our valley—something like a myth that is real.

"I hear old man Kerr counts his gold pieces in teetering stacks, filling room after room." *It's a common thing to hear around the fire at night. Or,* "My brother got pulled in to work at the mansion. He saw trays of food lined up, spilling over with chickens and lambs, passion fruit and papayas."

We villagers seem to equally despise and desire this place, and no one is immune. Even Mama and Papa with their talk about being content and finding joy in their faith—even they would say little things. Typically, Mama refuses to even look at Dekadente each morning at her peak. Yet one day, when the sun was beating down something fierce, she turned to the mansion with longing in her eyes.

"Oh, to fall into a pool of blue water," she said slowly, as if her tongue were lagging behind.

Another time, Papa and I were out checking traps and I sliced open my foot on a jagged rock. He carried me back to the village, but when we passed the peak, he stopped and stared off at Dekadente. He didn't say anything, but I imagined he wanted to take me there and care for my foot with actual bandages—not whatever ripped-apart cloth Mama could spare.

"Oh, Papa, I'll be fine," I remember saying. "Just get me to Auntie Eshe."

❀ ❀ ❀

Now, here I am, freezing cold and standing inside this place of scorn and envy. Frantically, I look around. To my right, there's a long, rectangular opening in the middle of a white wall. On a shelf at its bottom sits a plant, and on the other side of the opening there's a table spread with food. A warm smell assails me and my hunger pangs rush back. So I tiptoe around the corner, grab what looks like a fluffy piece of flat bread, and stuff it into my mouth whole. My cheeks bulge as I try to chew. Also, there's a sort of pink meat; it had been hiding under the bread. I snatch it up and it tastes amazing—like a roasted pig that's been soaked in brine.

Eyes wide, nerves taut, I turn my head left and right, scanning the rooms for guards or a sign of Desta and Mama. A long, shiny knife catches my eye. It sits over by the sink spicket that must be like the one Mama grew up with—all tall and pretty with a neck like a crane. I stand in front of the spicket, watching the water come out drip…by…drip. Bending over, I catch a few precious drops in my mouth, as the salty meat has parched my tongue.

These things aren't so great, I think as I touch the spot where the droplets creep out ever so slowly. *At least our water at the spring gushes.*

Someone must have sliced a tomato, because the knife lies beside a scrap of green vine and a pile of soupy red seeds. I grab the knife, grip its hilt tightly, and try to calm myself down. The knife shakes as I step out of the room and, "Ahh!" I scream as someone appears—a girl with springy black hair tied in braids. She screams too, but I don't hear anything.

Then I reach out, and to my relief—she's me. I've never seen a mirror so big or so clear before. It's up on a wall and lined with gold, just like everything else in this room, the vases and tables and chairs.

Stopping at the mirror, I touch my reflection with the tip of the knife—I look so much like Mama, with her eyes that slant on the sides like I'm squinting at the sun. I'm filthy, with dried mud all over and leaves in my hair. Still, I've never seen myself in such a clear mirror. I'd like to stop and look some more, but, *"Mama? Desta?"* their names cross my lips in whispers, because *what if they're hidden in this very room with me right now*—tied up in *that* wooden chest or behind *that* glossy door…

The humming sound is louder now, coming from the end of this skinny passageway before me, and for some reason the sound draws me in. Also, there's a rustling down there, like someone's lashing a roof with reeds. *Quick, quick, quick*, I follow the sound, peeking back over my shoulder, and *oh, I've left a trail of brown footprints!*

A baby cries. I gasp aloud—"Mama?"

And someone really strong—someone from behind—grabs me. I scream and my feet run in circles through the air as he squeezes so tightly I suddenly can't breathe. I can't see his face either, except out of the corner of my eye. And he seems to be smiling. Also, his black, curly hair—oddly—looks just like mine. He grips my wrist and holds the knife out and away from both of us.

I go wild, thrashing and scratching and biting, but he holds me firm and lets out an amused sigh. Before I know it, he's carried me through an open door, and the first thing I see up on the ceiling is the source of the hum—an enormous fan with spokes in the shape of wide palm fronds. And below it, on a bed as high as my hip, sits Mama. Her face is confused. I'm sure mine is too. There's a baby in her arms, and they both look so perfectly black surrounded by bright, white blankets.

"Talitha?" Mama asks incredulously.

The man loosens his grip. I fall to the floor in a heap, but hop up quickly.

"Mama?!" I can't believe my eyes.

She smiles through exhaustion and lifts the bundle, tipping his tiny face in my direction.

"Come," she says. "Meet your brother."

CHAPTER 44

Desta
the happiest song

BLINDFOLDED AND BOUND, SHE SITS in the cold, dark cave, waiting for something to happen.

"*Birds watch us as we work,*" she sings, whimpering through the happiest song she knows. It's the song she sings with Talitha. The one she hides behind, running off to the woods alone when her mama's headaches are so bad that she'll beat Desta if she gets in her way.

"*Oh, to be a woman with legs.*" Desta weeps "the Song of the Birds" even though it puts the man assigned to guard her in a rage, punching her down with iron fists, echoing Talitha's "*Shut up! Shut up! Shut up!*" from this morning.

With her eyes swollen shut, Desta wouldn't be able to see where they've brought her anyway. Even if they hadn't covered her head with a foul-smelling bag. So Desta does what she always does when she finds herself drowning in darkness—she sings about the jealous birds. These creatures who want to trade their wings for legs, who see what girls like her do even if nobody else does: *"That one walks for days,"* her throat is scratchy, but she still hits the high notes perfectly; *"her* mtungi *is painted bright; oh, to be a woman at the spring!"*

Tears sting her cracked lips. She hasn't had a drop to drink all day.

"I said *shut up*!" her kidnapper yells as he thwacks her head with his gun's handle.

And as she passes into a state of terrified, semiconscious sleep, as she listens to the man curse her and taunt her and tell her all the horrible things they're going to do to her, all she sees is Talitha's scowling face.

CHAPTER 45

Talitha
broken stalks of wheat

THE GUARD LEADS ME OUT of Dekadente the same way I came in, past the pool and out the high metal gate. It's a different guard than earlier. He makes a *tisking* sound under his breath—the kind a mama makes when a child is naughty.

I ignore him even though I'd like to *tisk* right back. Instead, I turn away and dash across the open patch and into the woods, feeling much better now that I've eaten and had some rest, but also feeling…lost. What should I do now? I was so *positive* Desta was at Dekadente, that the people there must have had *something* to do with stealing her, because everyone knows the mine owners are good friends with that awful man Badru. But after what Mama told me—that Mr. Lucian had *saved* her— I just don't know what to think anymore…

The air has cooled and shadows stretch long behind the trees. My head, my mind floats like the hippo-shaped cloud in the sky up above me. I think I must be drunk from holding my new baby brother, from the otherworldliness of this endless day. The sun's position tells me it's almost time for the evening meal, and I don't care if Nala's napped, I don't even care if she's still retchin', I just hope she's not crying for me, missing me the way she misses her real mama.

And so I swing my arms. I'm too tired to run, but still, I move as quick as I can, passing soybean and sweet potato crops, rustling my hand over the weedy tops of ripe carrots. A farmer passes, then a miner.

"Have you seen my friend?" I ask, describing Desta, the men in black masks, the jeep.

Their reactions are the same—shock, but then a drop of the head and they're gone. Even if there was something they could do, they're both too hungry and tired to think of it. With ribs showing in long skeletal rows, each man's skin is thickly coated with dirt from the day—the farmer's in shades of red, the miner's black as night. He's small and had bright eyes before I told him about Desta. But as the story left my mouth, it was like the light there was snuffed out.

My feet snap into the dried wheat of Papa's plot. I don't recognize it at first, but the three stolen coconut trees in the corner give it away. Amazed, I stare up as their brown-edged fronds smack about on the wind, and I remember how Papa would run back and forth from the river with heavy buckets.

※ ※ ※

Watering these trees was always the last task of the day, and he covered the distance between the skinny trunks and the river in a few swift leaps, every leg muscle straining, every neck and arm tendon perfectly taut.

"We're starving," Peter and I would moan. "Can't we just go?"

Papa never wanted us to help with this task.

"It's na-na-nothing," he'd say with a laugh, "it's no work at all."

He claimed he loved the sweet milk from the center of the coconuts. But we all knew these trees meant something more. Legend was they started as saplings stolen from Dekadente ages ago. While the mine owners took years to learn how to grow these tropical trees here in the clay, we Kilokie figured it out fast. Extra water, of course, but also rotten goat manure, eggshells, onion skins, and anything else that stinks like death in the sun.

※　※　※

The fronds slap at each other like enormous green birds, so high in the darkening sky and…the sight of these trees, the memory of Papa tending the ground that holds their roots, makes me keenly aware of the soil beneath my feet. All I can say is it feels something like *holy*. Catching my breath, I kneel. Broken wheat stalks cut my scarred knees, but I don't care. My heart swells as I think of Papa. It swells even more as I think of my new baby brother he'll never meet. The intense pain of it all squeezes my eyes shut tight, leaving me alone with nothing but the sound of the swishing trees and my time with Mama running through my mind…

※　※　※

"Nala will be fine," she kept saying, her head nestled deep in the white pillow, assuring me again and again that Jaia would care for her. "Peter's there too. Everyone gets retchy now and then. Stop worrying," she smiled such a relaxed smile. "You worry too much."

That's when I exploded into a fit about Desta and how "I just know she's here too!" I ran from room to room, searching for her until Miss Clara took me into her arms, assuring me that Mr. Nelson—the man who grabbed me—promised Mama was the only guest here today.

Miss Clara then pulled me into a bright room and forced me into the hottest bath. It felt sooo good, but rather than enjoy it, I scrubbed up quick, wrapped myself in a fluffy white robe, and went back to try to convince Mama to search the mansion with me.

"Come on," I whispered, "I'll carry the baby."

That's when she told me about the mine owner, Mr. Lucian, and how he rescued her just in time, when she was terrified she'd bleed to death.

"All right, all right," I said, feeling totally defeated. I guess the mine owners really didn't have anything to do with stealing Desta. And even though I could tell Mama was worried about her too, she wasn't her usual fiery self. She seemed exhausted, totally worn out from the birth. So I just sat there in that soft chair with baby Damien asleep in my arms while Clara washed my kitenge. I ate the rest of Mama's food, and even though I was heartbroken at not finding my best cousin-friend, the food and the goodness of finding Mama with Damien was so wonderful. As if the sight of them shone brighter than any darkness, so much you'd think the darkness had simply disappeared.

"Try this," she said, placing a large piece of buttery bread in my mouth—using gursha, the custom of feeding her guest a bite. It's a custom she hasn't practiced in years, but today she insisted. And oh, the bread—it was both crunchy and soft at the same time, nothing like the lahoh we use to scoop up wat. I took a sip of her water, but it was so cold it hurt my teeth because there were actual chunks of ice in it. I popped a crystal in my mouth and cracked it with my molars, and the crunchy cold feeling made me smile. Mama laughed. I hadn't heard her laugh like that in ages.

For a while, I stayed by Mama's side, curled up next to her on the bed. I was so tired I fell asleep, but just for a few minutes. See—the baby, the food, even the ice—it was like a dream, like the happiest dream! There were just so many distractions, so many amazing things that kept me from finding Desta like I should have. Also, I think that deep down, I was wishing my cousin had met the same amazing fate Mama had—that she'd jumped from the back of that jeep, that she was waiting for me in our hut with Nala in her arms.

"Do you know why I named him Damien?" Mama asked. The fan hummed overhead. Her blankets rustled as she reached for the baby.

※　※　※

Of course I did. And as I kneel here in Papa's fallow field, as broken wheat stalks pierce my knees, a story is caught up in those flapping green fronds—a tale about Father Damien at sea. It arrives on the golden rays of the setting sun, like a gift.

CHAPTER 46

Talitha
something that feels like courage

"**F**ATHER DAMIEN WOULD FILL HIS BOAT with these." *Papa tossed a shaggy coconut to Peter as we sheared last year's harvest. Machetes swung from dawn 'til dusk. Wheat was piled high and laid out in stacks. We carried it home in great bundles on our backs. Mama and Auntie Eshe ground the dried kernels down between two flat stones—an all-day, floating-dust-mote kind of job. Auntie Eshe would hold the bottom stone steady while Mama turned the round one on top. Our plot raised enough wheat in one season for our family's lahoh for almost a year, and lahoh for the Others, as well. For this, Papa was proud, especially as the farming was something we did as a family in the rare hours he wasn't in the mine.*

Papa held himself up high in the coconut tree by gripping its skinny trunk with his thighs. He tossed the hard fruits down at the ground near us as we jumped and laughed and he told his story.

"When they'd bring the lepers to the island of Molokai, there was no harbor. The sailors didn't want to catch the disease themselves, so sometimes they'd just toss these dying men in the ocean and make them swim for shore. But they were so sick, they'd drown or lose body parts along the way."

Papa talking about Father Damien and his lepers—even lepers losing fingers and toes—was a normal part of any afternoon with him. Papa had only learned to read right before he met Mama, when Uncle Ibrahim taught him how. One of the books he learned on was Ibrahim's biography of Father Damien, the missionary priest to the lepers in Hawaii.

"I like to imagine Father Damien riding out in his raft with a boatload of these." Papa shook a coconut by his ear. "He'd be smoking his pipe—the tobacco helped mask the smell of leprosy, so he smoked it a lot. When the sailors would throw the lepers overboard, I can just see him bombing their boats with coconuts."

"Why would he do that?" Peter asked.

"To shake up the sailors," Papa laughed as he hopped down from the tree and slapped his hands together.

"Why?"

"So they'd stop throwing the lepers into the ocean; so they'd take them to shore."

Papa cracked open a coconut on a pointed rock and drank the milk. He passed the other half to me. I broke off a piece and chewed the sweet flesh.

"That's what it means to be a Christian, children. It's not just about believing in our Shepherd God. Yes, you must believe, but you must also 'tend His sheep,' as the Bible says. You must fight for the oppressed one—for the fatherless, for the widow."

☀ ☀ ☀

Fatherless. I see Damien's scrunched-up face in my mind's eye. *Widow.* I see Mama, her weary head asleep on the enormous white pillow.

And even though I know my baby brother and Mama are resting safely now, I sense something new inside myself. I sense a bit of Papa.

"I'll fight for them," I whisper as I burrow my thumbs into the neglected soil, "I'll fight for them, and I'll find Desta too; I'll fight for them all."

Then like a thwack on the head from a falling coconut, I remember my weakness—the quivering, the fearfulness in my soul, the one that's so much like Papa's stuttering voice.

Can I really make this promise?

And suddenly, I think of Dekadente and the guard by the pool—the idea of sneaking past him and into the mansion just a few hours ago. Of grabbing the knife, the long, shiny knife— seeing my own eyes in its silvery reflection.

Was that really me?

Fireflies flicker on and circle beside me. Trapping one, I peek at it between laced fingers. And as the tiny creature casts a soft glow, another light fills my mind, one from that same harvest day last year…

Papa didn't stutter when he talked about Father Damien.

Coconuts bombing the sailors off of Molokai, coconuts bombing Peter and me in this field—it's like a flame spreading on the parched grass of my heart when—

"Someone's been watering these," I gasp at the circles of damp soil and trampled eggshells at the base of each tree. Looking over my

shoulder, wracking my mind, I wonder who would do such a thing,
when something even more wonderful catches my eye.

There at the bottom of the tallest tree, as if it's waiting just
for me, sits a perfectly ripe coconut on a mound of sweetgrass.

Fruit from a tree I thought was dead. The idea is the brightest
one yet.

I snatch it up and shake it beside my ear. The way this coconut makes me feel—it's just what I needed. Milk sloshes loudly
against its insides, and I can already taste its sweet flesh between
my teeth.

I have to get back, have to take care of the little ones, have to
get help for Desta and tell everyone what's happened to Mama.
Clutching the fruit over my heart with both hands, I run along
quickly; climbing up the last steep slope to our path, I set off
a mini-avalanche of clay clods and speed up until, finally, the
thatched roofs of our huts are in sight.

My feet know the rest of the way, so I glance often at the
coconut in my hands. I found it at the same moment I found
something new inside myself—something that feels like courage.
And so I hold it tightly.

CHAPTER 47

Moses
blue ice

THEY LEAD HIM INTO THE DARK dormant mine through an underground passageway. He's sore all over from the thugs' beating, but fortunately he can walk fine. He touches his shoulder and forearms. They're bruised, but nothing seems to be broken.

The men nudge him on. At his back, there's a crumbling wall. Below his feet, a thin ledge. And out before him, nothing—a vast, misty drop down a narrow shaft. Moses is chilled to the bone and relieved that at least he can't see the bottom of the pit below.

"Listen to this." One of Badru's men on his right pulls out a handful of coins and tosses them high over the edge. They clink down the shaft's walls, setting off a cacophony of echoes before splashing into water somewhere below.

"Gotcha'! Gotcha'! Gotcha'!" the thug on the left prods Moses' ribs with the butt of his rifle. Spooked, Moses tilts forward, screams, then throws his weight back against the wall to regain his balance.

"Quit it!" Badru's other guy yells. "You'll kill us all!"

The man cackles, and the three of them shuffle to the end of the ledge. There's a rod jetting out of an enormous damp rock. They take turns grabbing it and pulling themselves onto a wider, underground stone plain. Moses looks behind his shoulder, back over the foggy hole. It seems the rod used to be part of a handrail that stretched the length of the ledge, something miners must have grabbed on to years ago when this deep underground shaft was still worked, before it was concluded to be "dormant"—stripped clean of emeralds.

Now the gun is pressed into Moses' shoulder.

"Go on." The weapon nudges him toward a dim light a few meters away. He bows his head, stoops his broad shoulders, and walks through the dark tunnel. Icy pellets of water drip, their *plunks* sounding near and far. Some echo as they drop into puddles buried deep in hollowed-out passageways. Others plop straight onto the crown of Moses' head and send chills down his spine that don't stop until they burrow their iron coldness deep into the very core of him. He can't stop shivering. He tries to control it, as it makes him feel weak, but he just can't stop.

Moses hears his uncle before he sees him. There's a muffled *whoomp* and a soft gasp. He runs ahead to find the small man folded over, his mouth taped shut, his trembling hands covering his head.

"Leave him alone!" Moses runs to Tebaho's side. He covers his uncle's lithe body with his own. The ever-feared Badru is there too, along with another man. Moses has never seen him before, but he guesses by his icy blue eyes and a head full of curly black hair that it must be one of the mine owners. They're both tittering with amusement. There are several bottles of liquor and a few tall pipes of junat on the card table below the swinging lamp. The syrupy junat cloud is thick and sweet, and at once it makes Moses both dizzy and nauseous. The men must have been drinking and smoking for a good while. Their eyes are fiery, and the mood in the dim room is a mixture of happy and mean.

"Anyone feel like fishing?" Badru speaks with a gust, exhaling the smoke that had puffed out his rib cage.

"Oh yeah, it's been a while," the mine owner laughs. "Get their feet, boys!"

Badru's men tear Moses off Tebaho and bind the small man's hands with a rough rope. Moses struggles, but he's no match for the four of them. Also, one has a rifle fixed straight at his forehead. Badru leaves and quickly returns, clanking in two long, rusty chains. His gold tooth glints as he flashes a wicked smile. He laughs gruffly and drops the chains on the ground. As Badru leisurely lights a pipe, one of his men winds a chain around Tebaho's skinny ankles.

"*What are you doing?*" Moses panics.

"Don't worry," Badru smirks. "You'll go down with him."

Moses kicks furiously, but the men chain his feet as well. The iron is heavy and even colder than the air in the cave. The chain's rough edges cut against Moses' Achilles tendons where they've been wound too tight.

Then one of the men lifts Tebaho onto his shoulder like a feather. The other three drag Moses as he thrashes and screams all the way back down the walkway. With each step, the rocky floor slices into his back. They drop him hard a few times only to hoist him up again. Laughing loudly, they carry Moses back to the shaft they'd passed earlier, where, finally, they leave him beside his shivering uncle—the two of them teetering on the edge of the misty hole.

"On the count of three," Badru calls. His men count aloud as they swing Tebaho out over the drop, "One…two…three!" The small man's bloodshot eyes flash at Moses right before they let him go, before he yelps and flies off into the fog. He sails easily, bound like a small bundle of firewood. The rusty chain unravels, clanking loudly as he descends all the way down.

To where?! Moses panics as he stares, unblinking, unbelieving, at the empty spot where he saw his uncle hover for just a second before he dropped.

"*Uncle!*" Moses screams. "Oh, God, no!"

"Come on, boys; this one will take some muscle." Badru rubs his hands together as he walks toward Moses.

"*Nooooo!*" Moses yells. He tries to break free, but his tied hands and chained feet won't budge. "Please don't! No!"

The men surround him as Moses throws his body side to side, yelling and fighting with all his might.

"No! Stop!" he begs, his voice scratchy and high. "Where's my uncle? *Tebaho!*" he calls as the men push him forward, "*Tebaho, I'm coming for you!*"

Moses looks at Badru's men, hoping to appeal to any scrap of goodness left in them. But the glare in their eyes is inhuman, reminding him of the rabid dog he once killed with a mallet, beating in its skull when it cornered him—growling with white foam dripping in strings from its snarling mouth.

"Don't forget to come up for air!" Badru laughs as calloused hands tip Moses off the ledge into the darkest night he's ever known. Immediately, his head hits a jutting rock. But then he falls.

And falls.

And falls.

Blood rushes to his brain, rings in his ears and tingles his toes. He's weightless. His stomach, an empty drum, lurches to his neck. And for just a breath, the feeling is a freedom like he's never known.

A flying.

A falling.

Talitha's face flashes to mind. Her knowing eyes, her delicate hand sweeping a white-tipped wave in his direction.

Until *snap*—the chain loses its slack. And with a jolt, the shock of stopping threatens to unhinge all his limbs from their sockets.

The feeling of blue ice surrounds him, cutting through his face and hands until instinct kicks in and he lifts his head, lurching, searching for air. When he finds it by tightening his stomach muscles and pulling himself up and out of the water—so he's bent in half at the waist—his first greedy breath echoes loudly against the pit's tubular walls.

"Uncle!" he cries, spotting Tebaho's chain and body hanging limp. There's enough light to see he's submerged to the waist. Only, unlike Moses, his beloved uncle doesn't struggle.

"*Tebaho!* No! Oh, God, help me! *No!*"

Moses bounces his upside-down, dangling body against the sides of the narrow shaft. His chain crashes and rattles over the sound of splashing water. The men up above are laughing. One of them yells something as a few bottles fall from the sky. One just misses Moses' head while another smashes against rock, pelting the pit with a crescendo of broken glass. A few shards lodge into Moses' neck and arm, but he ignores their bite. His sole focus is his uncle.

If I could just get to him, he thinks, I'll grip his shirt with my teeth; I'll pull him up...

With his stomach flexed tight as a clenched fist, Moses keeps his own head out of the water. And slowly, bit by bit, he swings closer to his uncle, who hasn't moved at all, but whose half-submerged body hangs slack from the ankles, limp and lifeless.

CHAPTER 48

Talitha
red splotches

I SHAKE THE COCONUT BY MY EAR, but my happy daydream of sharing it with Nala comes to an end as soon as I reach the twisty gray marula tree. I can tell right away something's terribly wrong. Up ahead, the village looks empty. There's no fire lit, no cast-iron pot bubbling up a meal, no aunties pounding out cassava or babies babbling at their feet.

There are, however, the first of the uncles coming home from the mines. A tall, skinny one, called Mosi, stands by the center stump. His hands and face are coated in soot. He's rubbing his scruffy chin. When he sees me, he calls out, "Your brother and Nala are in there." He motions to the hut, "But be careful; whatever they have, it's as bad as the typhoid."

Typhoid! The word makes me see red splotches, running the length of Peter's legs when the disease almost killed him the last time it was here.

"I thought they were just retchin'!"

A breeze blows up from behind the hut and out through the flimsy green curtain, lifting it, ruffling it toward me. I cover my mouth and run inside.

CHAPTER 49

Lucian
the misty pit

HE RUNS THROUGH THE WOODS toward the dormant mine. Two guards follow closely on his heels. They ditched the truck in front of a marsh and crossed to this point on foot. Lucian knows the path well. He began following it back when he was a teenager, when Nelson finally invited him to run with *"Badru and the guys."* For years, just stepping into this shaded path that leads to the abandoned mine would fill Lucian with the welcome sense of belonging. But today, fury and a mission he doesn't fully understand drive him onward.

"Lift your feet high," he calls over his shoulder to the guards, both deeply black-skinned Korins who long ago left their tribes in favor of Western wear and a wage at Dekadente. "The roots will trip you," Lucian warns, pointing down at their feet.

Between heavy huffs and long, leaping strides, the guards

shoot each other knowing looks—*The mixed-breed thinks he knows our valley…*

Their feet fly high above roots that arc out from the rich soil. The path they tread twists and turns on what was once a dirt road, but is now overgrown with waves of rustling weeds. If they had been moving more slowly—inquisitively, the way Lucian had when he was young, when a single spider's web could hold his attention for hours—endless striking sounds and sights would mark their wooded journey. But the men sprint on, oblivious to their surroundings. None of them notice the finch's nest smashed on a rock. None pause over the sharp contrast of colors, the yellow yolk against its bright blue shell.

Because they're *running, running, running.* The roaring current of each man's own breathing deafens his ears. Lucian doesn't stop as he would have when he was a boy to kneel beside the nest, pondering pithy wing feathers in the hollow of his hand, studying them with fascination and sharing in the mama bird's sorrow.

No, Lucian doesn't see the finch's nest. He sprints right by it, snapping vines and crushing ivy as this and so many other wonders pass him by. A spotted cheetah sleeps beneath a canopy of ferns. They don't hear her growl when their feet thunder the earth beneath her belly. They don't see her slink away, tired and annoyed.

Only Lucian's sense of mission and the guards' sense of gain—Lucian promised them extra pay—mark their way through the woods.

"There it is!"

A guard points to the dark triangle at the base of the mountain. This—the mine's opening—is nothing more than two flat sandstones leaning against each other, pitched at a point.

And even though this entrance leads to a whole underground world, it could easily be missed if one didn't have a guide.

Lucian slows his pace, tiptoeing toward the opening so as not to rustle the brush. He lifts his pistol to his lips, shushing the guards. Then he crouches down and crawls in. Immediately the tight space is so crushing he's tempted to panic. But he presses on. Having crawled through this short tunnel many times in the past, Lucian is experienced in the art of forcing his claustrophobia behind him. Still, the ancient rock hurts his knees as his elbows are scraped clean of skin.

When at last he makes it through, he finds himself in a dark cavern. Immediately, a voice echoes nearby—

"Bring me up some emeralds, boy!"

Right away, he recognizes the raspy voice as Badru's. He must be just around the corner. Again, Lucian turns to his guards to shush them.

Lucian can tell by the jeering sounds that Badru has someone down in the pit. This is one of the mercenary's favorite "games." People have a way of finding the money they owe him— often borrowing it from another extortionist—after they've hung, chained by their feet, for a while.

Lucian and his guards make their way along the first narrow ledge that overlooks the misty shaft. With their backs to the wall, one of the guards yells when the spot holding his foot crumbles away. He catches himself by grabbing on to a pointed rock.

"Who's there?" Badru calls out.

Lucian reaches for the metal rod and pulls himself up onto the landing. He levels his pistol at Badru.

"Bring up the boy!" Lucian demands with a passion rare to his nature. "I know you have him. Now bring him up!"

Lucian's guards also quickly point their rifles at Badru and Nelson. Nelson's hired men raise their hands, but Nelson laughs, his voice echoing loudly in the dark mine.

"It's just Rot," he slurs, finishing the last of the liquor and tossing the bottle into the pit. "Come on—dig me up some jewels!" Nelson yells over the side of the cliff where the two sets of chains hang attached to pulleys.

"I said *bring him up!*" Lucian screams this time, his face burning red with anger. He runs over to the man by the pulleys and jabs a pistol into his chest. There's a rage in his voice no one's ever heard before. Still, Nelson's dismissive of his typically mild brother.

"Oh, Rot…"

Badru steps forward with a smirk, taking his cue from Nelson. Lucian aims his pistol straight in Badru's face this time. "Stay where you are," he orders, squaring his shoulders as he enunciates each word, *"Bring. Him. Up!"*

"You don't want to do this," Badru puffs out his chest, his voice dangerous, "I promise. You *don't* want to mess with me and my business."

Lucian knows exactly what he means. He also knows the only reason he hasn't been punished for failing to pay Badru back his money in the past is because Badru and Nelson are childhood friends. Lucian's heard the many stories of severed ears and thumbs and worse. He's known of powerful people who fell out of Badru's good graces, only to be found floating in the river, bloated and blue and feasted on by fish. Everyone's heard the stories of his unpredictability and his temper. Regardless, ever since his time in the treehouse this afternoon, Lucian is determined to undo the evil he's been a part of, at least as much as he can. And the first step of his plan is to rescue this boy who now hangs below him in the dark pit. It's as if Lucian's too focused on his mission to be afraid, even though he knows he's finally pushing Badru too far.

"Turn that crank *now!*" Lucian fires a shot that barely misses Badru's cheek. The mercenary drops to the ground, taking cover, and his men throw their weight into turning the first pulley's crank.

CHAPTER 50

Moses
the strength to carry on

DANGLING IN THE DARK, Moses hears the fighting and the gunshot above. He tries to call out for help, but his voice hardly carries. With his hands bound tightly, it takes all his strength to hold Tebaho in the curl of his chest. Moments ago, he was able to pull his uncle's head out of the water by grabbing Tebaho's hair with his teeth.

Now, as uncle and nephew hang upside down, Tebaho utters jumbled prayers, but mostly he's barely conscious. Moses is just glad his uncle is still alive.

Every second they hang suspended, Moses' body threatens to give out under the weight. Succumbing to gravity would thrust his own head back into the icy waters for only a second, but it would mean certain death for his uncle. So he holds on, squeezing every muscle in his body, forcing himself into a curled nest for Tebaho. Gritting his teeth, he shakes violently all over.

And just when he thinks he's about to collapse, he feels the chain tighten around his ankles—he's being pulled up.

"Please," Moses yells with what little strength he has left. "Pull the other one up first. Please!"

His own chain loosens while Tebaho's links clank tight. Moses watches with enormous relief as his uncle's slack figure rises away slowly, back up through the misty cloud.

Relieved beyond measure, Moses sucks in a deep breath and falls back, relaxing his stomach muscles and thrusting his head into water. His eyes flash open to the blue, and for just a second, he glimpses those knowing brown eyes he's pondered underwater so many times—tormenting him, but also calling to him, giving him the strength to carry on.

CHAPTER 51

Talitha
a plank to the face

"**N**ALA, PETER, I'M HERE," I call, bowing my head into the hot darkness.

And the smell, the stifling air, the moaning—it smacks me hard, like a plank to the face. My foot slides through a puddle, and I fall back with a bang on my rump. My newfound coconut flies from my hand and rolls into more of the foul, brown mess. I look around the dim hut, searching and squinting until finally I spot them—there, against the far wall, Auntie Eshe and Nala lie side by side.

Peter is next to them, trying to clean up the mess as much as he can with his leg in a splint. He's pale and coated in a sheet of beaded sweat like everyone else. But he brightens when he sees me, his voice sounding relieved. "Talitha, thank goodness you're here. The aunties and uncles are still coming back from the fields and the mines, but I wasn't sure what to do. Everyone's so sick and the babies can't keep down the medicine Jaia mixed…"

A strangled cry cuts him off. It's the little boy Brave—Nala's friend and the child who was always Papa's favorite. He's on the ground, grabbing his stomach and scrunching up his tiny face. Peter goes to him, picking him up and rocking him back and forth. "*Oh*," I gasp, covering my mouth with a corner of my *kitenge*. "I'm sorry, Peter, I didn't know it was this bad! I should have come sooner!" I start toward Nala when I realize I'm all covered in human waste. Horrified, I look around. The mess is *everywhere*—on my hands and my freshly washed *kitenge,* but also in puddles all over the hut. Places where aunties and babies have gotten sick but were too weak to clean it up. Also, the flies have gotten in. Their buzzing and swarming in the trapped heat is maddening, making me feel as if they're feasting on my filthy skin.

I smack the air to keep them away as I search for *anything* the least bit clean—an untouched *netela*, a tiny scrap of cloth— when Nala sits up. Seeing me, she smiles sleepily, rubs her eyes, and is toddling in my direction when the illness seizes her. She bends over, gagging and heaving.

"Oh, Nala," I whisper, "It's gonna' be okay. I'm here now."

Every muscle in her tiny body strains, but nothing except a spitty green trickle escapes her mouth. She coughs and wipes her face with a pudgy hand, smearing bile into her messy hair.

"Litha." She reaches for me, but I don't know what to do. I'm too filthy to pick her up. So she crawls across the floor, her hands touching a spot where someone's gotten sick.

"No! Nala, stop!" I beg, but she ignores me, making her way into my arms. And even though we're both covered in waste, holding her is such a relief I want to cry—if only I remembered how—but I don't want to think about that right now. So I just hug her close.

"It's all right. Litha's here. I'll clean you up. I'll make it better." I look at Peter, instructing him, "Mosi and some of the miners are coming back now. Go ask them for rags so we can clean this place up. Oh, and tell them we'll need more water—lots more water. I'm going to the river, but I'll be right back."

Peter nods tiredly, and I duck out of the hut with Nala in my arms, careful not to slip again. I go around back and find a few slivers of white soap and two cloths wide enough to serve as wraps after we bathe.

Heading down to the river with Nala's hot breath in my ear, my thoughts rage.

First Desta, then Mama, now Nala and Peter…

I search the darkening sky for an answer.

Why? Why so much pain?

I look to the top of Great Mountain, that place so sacred to the Kilokie, hoping for the Shepherd God or his Son to appear from behind a cloud—that Child, the sweet one who slept in the hay with the cows and the lambs.

Why, Baby Jesus? Why so much suffering down here?

It's the same question I've been asking for months. But there's nothing in nature, not in the birdsong or the purple-streaked sky, to explain all these terrible things that keep happening to us. There is, however, one full *mtungi* of water by Auntie Eshe's kettle. It's a green one with no cap—definitely not ours.

How did Auntie Eshe miss it? I wonder, but it doesn't matter now. I'm back. I'll clean us up and then care for the *Others*. I've fought the retches before; I'll fight them again.

The sight of the gifted *mtungi*—now I remember—it's the one my cousin with the lip plate was carrying. She must have made two trips when she heard about Mama's baby. The sight of this full *mtungi* is priceless, like Nala's kiss on my neck, her gentle pat on my back. The small amount of water will never be enough to cure everyone, but the fact that this cousin cared, that she went out of her way to help—it means so much.

If we'd had any medicines left from the missionaries, Jaia would have tried them already. And if her herbal remedies aren't working, all we can do is drink and drink and drink, hoping to wash away the sickness from the inside out. So even though the sun's setting and my whole body aches for sleep and I still need to tell everyone about Desta and Mama, I'll be running back to the spring again tonight—maybe even a few times.

The spring…

Fear shoots straight through me like a lightning bolt: Desta with the knife at her throat, the men in black masks, my own throbbing head cracked against that sharp rock.

But then Nala cries as a choking heave rips through her.

"It's okay," I whisper, holding her out so she can spit up off the side of the trail. Immediately, my fear is replaced—at least for now—with the need to cure Nala, with making her well. And if that means walking back and forth to the spring all night long for the next three days, I'll do it.

I smooth her fluffy hair and think about how odd it is that her filth doesn't bother me at all. Any other child's vomit on my neck would make me gag. But with Nala, I'm just relieved the retchin' makes her feel better. She lays her head on my shoulder and rubs my ear.

"Good girl," I whisper, "we're almost there."

The pebbles on the shore hurt my feet. It must be Nala's extra weight in my arms, since I usually don't feel them at all. And as I wade into the slow current, as the water rises to my knees, the thought of bathing Nala in the same river that made her sick to begin with feels like swallowing a bitter pill. But I have no choice.

"Shut your mouth tight," I say to her, stressing each word and then sealing my own lips in a straight line. It's a command Kilokie babies learn young. Nala sucks in a deep breath and squeezes her lips into a pucker. And despite all my worries, I giggle. Because that's the magic of Nala—she's the laughter in the center of my anguish, a blossom sprouting from ash.

"Good girl," I coax her to stand still as I lather her up with the smallest sliver of soap, washing her hands, her hair—even the tiny spaces between her toes have to be scrubbed free of the disease.

I hum our psalm as I dip her back, and my voice—I sound just like Mama.

Rinsing Nala's scalp makes giant rainbow-streaked bubbles float out, like rays of sun across the dark water. She brightens as she squints up at the sky. I finish and toss her back up on my hip. Her pointed toe pops bubble after bubble on the water's skin.

Soaked through and smelling of soap, I tie on our new wraps. Once mine is tight over my shoulder, I drop my old *kitenge* down to my feet and step out of it. Then I search the pebbles for the last few slivers of soap. As my eyes rove over the gray speckled stones, I remember when these slivers were pungent white bars, dropped in the village with bags of rice by a missionary who'd stopped to baptize someone traveling in his group.

᛭ ᛭ ᛭

The river-bound boy was about my age, only white. But what was most remarkable about him were the silver jewels on his teeth. Also, he wore a blinding green shirt marked with that skinny fish that means Christian.

Afterward, Papa sat with the milk-faced mzungu *who did the baptizing. He had a loud way of talking and nostrils that flared when he spoke, looking like tiny, dark caves.*

"Would you like to receive this gift?" The missionary motioned at the river with his Bible, his scalp hot pink from the sun. The cloth he used to wipe his forehead couldn't keep up with the sweat pouring down his face. He wore heavy glasses that kept sliding down his nose.

"Oh, I've been b-baptized, sir." Papa bowed his head, pausing quietly as he did when he spoke of his faith. He then looked up at the man and without a stutter said, "But, I thank you for your kindness."

The missionary studied Papa's burgundy robe and his bare feet. Then he frowned and walked away. When I asked if the man was angry, Papa told me, "Sometimes, the mzungu *expects us to take his ways along with his religion." He sighed. "But in faith, that man is my b-b-brother. Even if I am not his, he is mine."*

☀ ☀ ☀

The smell of our fire fills the air as I wring out our clothes. Nala runs from me to a row of bushes. She covers her eyes with her hands as she "hides" beside one in plain sight, crouching down beside its branches.

"I can still see you!" I call, relieved she must be feeling at least a little better. She moves on to a chasing game, charging up the slope as the setting sun paints the clouds with pastel brushstrokes. But at the farthest corners of the sky, a bruising blackness creeps in quickly, like river water after a hard rain.

CHAPTER 52

Talitha
it's all my fault

NALA HOPS WITH EACH STEP. Her fresh white wrap catches on the breeze.

Maybe these retches aren't so bad after all! The happy thought appears just as Nala freezes a few meters ahead of me. She lets out a gasp as a yellow-brown slick runs down her legs and pools at her feet. But before I can stop her, she squats down, smacks the puddle with both hands, and touches her hair.

"No!" I scream. She turns to me. Her eyes fill with tears. She looks side to side quickly, the way she does when she remembers her mama. I want to snatch her up, but I can't let myself get covered in the sickness again. So I pick her up carefully from behind, my hands under her armpits. She kicks out her feet as if, once again, we're playing a game.

"Simmy?" She floats on her belly in the shallow water this time, splashing her hands and feet, practicing her swim strokes.

I click approvingly with my tongue, as keeping one's head afloat is a skill we Kilokie learn young too.

I wash her again and wrap her bottom in what's my very last scrap of clean cloth. Then I carry her all the way back to the village and prop her by the fire to dry. She smiles weakly as the aunties gather around, having just returned from the fields. I take a deep breath, summoning my loudest voice to catch everyone's attention. Most of the time Auntie Eshe would be the one telling the latecomers what's going on with the *Others*, but because she's sick, I holler over the noise—

"Auntie Eshe and the grannies and the babies—all the *Others* have a nasty case of the retches."

As I share the awful news, two uncles arrive, looking for a meal. They're covered in mine soot and they probably haven't eaten since morning.

"They can't keep down Jaia's medicine. If we don't get them drinking," I motion to the hut, "they'll only get worse."

Then I explain the day.

"*Desta…a knife…men in masks…*"

The words fly from my mouth and draw a bigger crowd.

"*Mama…Dekadente…baby Damien…*"

Our chief has been away on a trip for a few days, negotiating a livestock trade with a neighboring tribe, but the elders are quick to assign tasks, splitting everyone into groups to take action. Before I know it, a few uncles have lit torches and are heading out to search for Desta. Their slapping footfalls against the clay hush softer and softer the farther out they go, until their running feet sound like a distant rain. A few others grab empty *mitungi* and dart off to the spring. Some of the married aunties, although weary and caked with dust and sweat from a day of working out in the fields, hover around me in shock. They offer hugs and words of kindness, but—even more—words of defeat.

"Oh no! Not the one you sang with! She was taken too?"

Someone fills my hands with a steaming bowl of sweetened *teff*. For even though Desta's tragedy overshadows everything, news of baby Damien is still reason to celebrate…quietly.

"Flora," they marvel at her strange fortune. "Another boy! Waiting for a doctor…in *Dekadente?!*"

I'm relieved for the darkness, that the aunties can't see into my soul. If they could, they'd see it's as filthy as the sickness now covering our village. They hug me and wet my cheeks with their tears. They give me more *teff*, and the warmth of the crackling fire feels so good on my back. But these aunties—they should scream at me. They should pound me with their fists because… It's all my fault.

Shut up, shut up, shut up! My last words to Desta ring in my ears, because all the jealousy, all the hate I've nurtured toward her—I just know it's the reason behind this evil that's come down on her, and on us all. My guilt is as foul as the cloud of sickness filling the air around us, but none of them know that I'm the one to blame. Part of me wishes they did. Part of me wishes to receive their wrath, but not one of them accuses me of anything. They are too taken, too amazed by Mama's fate— by how the cruel mine owner actually *saved* her and the baby.

"A boy!" The happy news keeps spreading further and further out into the night with clapping hands and gasps of joy:

"She calls him Damien!"

"The gods have been kind!"

But all this is quickly interrupted by Jaia's soft moaning.

"Please!" she calls. "Please help us!"

Jaia carries Brave from the hut. All the uncles turn away at the sight of her, as Jaia's *kitenge* is loose and both she and the child are covered with vomit.

"It started with him." She holds out the little boy—and oh, he's so pale. His skinny arms and legs hang loose, his mouth slack. "Look—he's the sickest of all."

Jaia pinches the flesh on Brave's arm and it stands up straight—a sign of dehydration.

"He can't even keep water down. Please help him!"

Jaia fumbles toward me and drops Brave into my arms. Then she runs behind our hut to retch. And again, I'm covered in filth. I'd like to not care, but this means I can't touch Nala or fill her tiny pink mug until I've cleaned myself again.

"Come, give him here." Auntie Eshe limps toward me. She's damp from the river and wears a fresh wrap.

"But you're sick too," I protest.

She receives Brave in a clean cloth and lays him by the fire.

"I don't get sick," she says, although her words don't match her expression. "Now, you go. Get us some water. We'll be needing every drop."

CHAPTER 53

Talitha
the petrified tree

AUNTIE ESHE ORDERS US AROUND as only she can, and it's
times like this that I can't forget she's one of the most
respected of our people's elders. Shadows dance across her face
as she leans on the stone ledge near the glowing fire pit, sending
this uncle for lye and that auntie for a stash of clean clothes, the
fastest runners going to the Korins to tell them what's happening
and see if they have any medicine left from the missionaries
they could spare us.

Soon all the sick *Others* are washed in the river. Their shivering bodies are laid by the hearth and draped with borrowed
cloths from nearby huts. Jaia's draught is helping some of them,
and I'm glad to see Peter looks a little better already. The ones
who can't keep anything down are the real problem, though.

Clean again and having eaten a large portion of tasteless
but warm food, I know I need to unwind Nala's arms from my

neck. But this task is proving hard as she's wide awake from having slept most of the day. Fortunately, she hasn't been sick again since we were at the river, and she's asked for her mug to be refilled twice.

"Pay cheetah!" she says, pulling at my braids. She wants me to *play cheetah*, and even though her happy eyes are hard to refuse, the sound of Jaia crying over Brave, a baby who isn't even her own, drives me back to my *mtungi*. We used up the first jug—the precious gift from my cousin with the lip plate—within a few minutes. Some aunties brought up river water to mix with lye to scrub the hut, but we'll need so much more clean water than usual for drinking if we're to have any hope of flushing this sickness out of the village.

"You'll stay with Peter and Uncle Azizi," I say as I pass Nala to my brother, who's sitting by the fire with his leg set out straight in the splint Jaia made from a walking stick and twisted rags. He bounces Nala on his healthy knee, but I see it in his eyes— he's heartbroken about Desta. Also, the restless way he watches the uncles run off into the night with torches; he's dying to help with the search. All the while, Azizi stands nearby, staring off into the distance.

"Azizi…Azizi…" I call the kindhearted uncle's name. But this gentle shepherd who was so close to Adia, our first lost girl, doesn't respond. Rather, he mumbles prayers toward Great Mountain as he rubs the carved face of his walking staff. Around us, torchlights dot the night like so many orange eyes. Azizi sounds just like he did in the days and weeks after Adia was taken. His brow furrows as deep as the crack in the wide oak tree, the one whose bark is so weathered they call it *petrified*. And in this moment, Azizi looks to me like that tree—his back hunched, his face twisted. I say his name again, but again he doesn't hear.

"You can't go to the spring now!" Peter looks up at me pleadingly. "Not after what's happened!" His almost-man voice cracks. His eyes catch the light of the fire. They're glossy, as if they've been singed with smoke. "What if they take you too? Please, Talitha, *don't go!*"

It feels like ages since he's been that honest with me, since he's let his fear show. But before I can answer, a figure steps between us, casting a dark shadow. Immediately, I recognize the shoes with the cut-out toes. My mind quickens; my lips part, forming his name: *Moses.* It takes me another moment to remember this morning, his strange way and his even stranger question—*"Will Desta be at the spring today?"*

By the time I look up at him, my smile is gone.

"I'll go with her," Moses says to Peter, refusing to look me in the eye.

He carries a torch. His hair is soaking wet, and he smells like iron and sweat—the odor of the mines. Also, his eye is bruised and his cheek is cut, like he's been in a fight, which is confusing as there's no fight in him. Aunties lean in to hear our conversation, but there's nothing for either of us to say because there's *too much* for both of us to say. A log explodes in the fire. The *Others* moan.

"You," I hiss, angry but also perplexed by his swollen face. *"What did you do?"*

"Please," Moses says, "let me take your *mtungi*. You stay here."

I search for his eyes, but he won't look at me. The tiny birds that once nested in my stomach and flew throughout my body at even the thought of him must have died.

"What happened? Tell me what happened!" I demand once again.

Silent anguish slumps his shoulders as he reaches for my arm. He touches my elbow and—*oh, shame*—those baby birds are alive! The tingling doesn't stop even though I shake free quickly, even though I scowl, trying hard to disdain him.

The birds scatter, but I'm left dizzy as Moses lopes ahead down the trail. He has the torch in one hand and both my *mtungi* and another empty jug in the other. Any Kilokie who can gather water is on the trail. Their bright, burning torches light up the night, bobbing back and forth, sending up smoke and the hope that comes when so many work together.

Auntie Eshe's voice pulls me back to the task at hand.

"If this baby doesn't keep something down, he's not going to make it," she whispers to one of the uncles as he kneels beside Brave. I can tell she doesn't want Jaia to hear her. Auntie Eshe is spooning little sips into the baby's mouth, but they just trickle down the side of his cheek. The cloths she's used to swaddle his bottom already overflow the soiled basket. She changes him every few minutes, but his retches won't stop.

A sharp pain seizes Jaia. She bangs the clay with her fist and lets out a strangled moan that seems to sum up this endless day. In her cry, I hear Mama in labor—her screams echoing against the valley's walls. In Jaia's cry, I see Moses, the way he looked this morning with tears carving lines down his face. And as Jaia's moaning turns into wailing, I see the hopeful look in Desta's eyes when she spoke to me last: *"Sing with me, Birdy! Sing with me please…"*

NIGHT

CHAPTER 54

Talitha
too much of everything

I WALK AS QUICK AS I CAN beside Moses, but we don't speak. Rather, the sounds of busy feet scampering off to the spring fill the silent space between us.

The trials of this day and now this night seem to make being alone together all right. Also, we aren't really alone. So many Kilokie are with us, walking and running—*quickly, quickly, quickly*, swooshing by each other, bustling bodies with lined foreheads and worried eyes. The temperature has dropped sharply as it always does at night, but hardly anyone stops to swathe their arms and necks in winding wraps.

Men who typically hunt—the ones who aren't out searching for Desta—drape enormous sticks across their strong shoulders. Buckets typically saved to water the fields are attached at both ends. Only tonight, these buckets will water us Kilokie, hopefully washing away the sickness before it kills off our weakest ones, our grannies and our babies. Not that the strong ones are beyond its reach. We know that diseases like this can kill even the young mothers with sinewy arms hardened from tilling their fields.

I remember one wicked bout of typhoid when I was little. It took our mighty Kondo. He was a nephew of Auntie Eshe's and stood a full head over Papa. His chest was as thick as a baobab tree's trunk and his skin as dark as its branches, but his eyes and voice were full of the sweetest light and laughter. Typhoid killed him first that year. It took a few babies too, but it stole the flame from our strongest one first.

Men and women from Desta's tribe, the Korins, have joined us on the trail too. Their women look especially distraught at what happened to Desta, and I'm sure many of their uncles have already gone to join the search for her.

The Korins recognize me. They search for my eyes, but I can't look at them. I can't look at anyone. So I keep my head down as we run through the dark of night, hoisting *mitungi* but also barrels and buckets, any sort of drum or jug, on our backs and shoulders and heads. Sad faces, frantic faces flash by, running in rows along little seams in the earth, like ants.

Since I refuse to acknowledge Moses, who's huffing along beside me, my eyes search the dark valley to my right. Deka-dente's lights flicker on in the distance. I think of Mama there. I think of Damien. He cried before I left and sounded pitiful, like a kitten fighting for a teat. The thought of him—of his face with his tiny nose and his soft skin—pushes me on, even though my legs ache almost as much as my mind.

Moses coughs. Faking a Desta-like resilience, I skip ahead, like my eyes have seen a prize. And so we travel to the spring at a pace close to a run, breathing the cool night air deep into our lungs. I try not to notice, but a smell besides the mines lingers on his skin. It's woodsy, making me think he's been waist-high in river grass, clearing trails, catching fish. I want to turn to him. I want to lean into his neck and breathe this smell in more deeply, studying it, knowing it—knowing *him*. Of course, I don't. But if it weren't for the very real stench of *untruth* between us, this moment—with its whispers on the wind and all the smoky, swirling torchlight—this moment would be magical.

Without warning, he speeds ahead, then turns to stop in front of me. His desperate eyes dart from my chin to my ear, to the sky.

"I can explain!" he pleads.

But without giving him a chance, I demand the truth.

"*Why* did you ask if she'd be at the spring?"

His head falls forward.

"Talitha…I'm sorry." He sighs, stepping to the side of the path and putting out his torch by rolling it in the sand. Its smoke twists up, a skinny curlicue between our faces.

I lean in to whisper—no, to growl—"Then you *did* have something to do with it!"

My hands form fists, and the spark of Mama inside me explodes.

"How *could* you?" I beat his chest. If I could cry, there would be tears. Instead, spit flies from my mouth on my words. Usually, I care about how I look to him, how I sound. But right now, I don't care if I'm ugly as a snarling fox. The person standing here is no longer the Moses I thought I knew. He isn't the clumsy hippo-cheetah I thought he was.

He's a snake. And as much as I want to crush him, as much as I want to destroy him, my fists bounce off his chest like pebbles off rock. His meaty hands reach out to grab my wrists gently.

"*Please,* Talitha." He leans into my ear. His voice shakes, "Badru was torturing my uncle…and," he chokes on his words, "I couldn't let them take…I couldn't let them take…"

His eyes finally meet mine. He stops stammering mid-sentence and stares straight into my heart. His long lashes are damp as if with tears. They flutter like moths by a flame. I want to reach out and touch them with the pad of my thumb. I want to feel them on my cheek. But also…*I wanna' kick him in the stomach!*

Warmth falls from his mouth onto my chin as he whispers the one word that—once it sinks in—will change everything:

"*You.*"

"I couldn't let them take *you,* Talitha."

His hands slide from a tight grip at the tops of my arms down to tenderly cup the backs of my hands. Our eyes lock tight. He whispers in my ear.

"I couldn't *live* without you."

And suddenly, along with the realization that Moses had somehow been forced to betray Desta, there's a *knowing* between us. A *knowing* about the baby birds. A *knowing* that they fly through him too, at the sight, at the sound of *me.*

Silently, we stare at one another as the wind blows through my hair and endless sets of feet run by on the other side of the tree that's kept us hidden. We stay this way, without uttering a sound, until finally, shyly, we both…smile. Instinctively, our hands flip. His fingertips trace circles on my palms. Time melts away, but only for a few seconds. Because regardless of his reasons—

She's gone! Desta is gone! Floods of fury rush in stronger than whatever warm feelings dance between me and this boy, because *it's his fault!* And I can't forgive him for that—not now, maybe not ever! The fact that he was cajoled, even forced, to cooperate with those men opens a small door of understanding, even though I don't realize it yet.

I look into his eyes. He looks away. I look out into the night, to the bobbing orange torchlights at the bottom of the slope. I stammer and gasp, but I can't find any words because nothing seems real. Mama's in Dekadente. Papa's dead in the mine. Nala and the *Others* are sick. Desta is stolen. Once again, I can't tell what's real or what's a dream.

The only thing I'm certain of are these invisible baby birds, attacking me so fiercely now, making my heart and my mind race. Their typical tiny pricks have become sharp slashes up and down and all along the entire length of me, pecking me raw.

So I grab my *mtungi* and dart away from Moses, away from the trail and toward the swamp. Looking around, I didn't think I'd ever come back here again—not all alone, not without Papa. But within seconds, I'm hidden by the swamp's kind branches. These skinny old-lady arms pull me in and hide me from the boy-man now hollering my name.

"Don't go down there!" He begs, "*Please,* come back!"

It's not that I'm scared of Moses, not at all. It's just that I'm too much of everything—too mad, too sad, too…*elated,* but also furious that I'm elated.

And I just need to run.

CHAPTER 55

Talitha
this bright moment

I SPRINT AWAY AS FAST AS I CAN. The swamp's cold night air closes in all around me and, immediately, my head clears. Like the lightning bugs swirling around my face, I too come alive. So many Kilokie hate it down here, but I leap along the first narrow log at the swamp's entrance. Even with my *mtungi* under one arm, my balance is perfect, and the feeling in my heart when I cross into these woods is like coming home.

It's probably because Papa and I have done so much hunting down here. Peter would complain about not being allowed to tag along, but Papa would just tell him, *"When you're older,"* giving me a wink. He knew it was a special place, just for the two of us. I could wander to one of our secret spots in my sleep. But there are crocodiles. And while the whip of their tails on the water's skin doesn't frighten me like it used to, it does make me focus hard on staying balanced, tightening up my belly and making sure I'm *sure* of each step.

"*Come back!*" Moses keeps calling. "*Talitha, come back!*"

He knows I know this swamp better than anyone. He also knows it's the fastest shortcut to the spring—one that would have been impossible to take earlier when I was with Mama. Moses won't dare follow me in the dark, though; he doesn't know the path. But a few other hunters have had the same idea. I can tell from the flattened brush they've beaten me to it. Probably Mosi and Daneer; they left right when they heard the awful news. So they've certainly made it to the spring and are heading home the long way by now, as carrying a full *mtungi* back this way through the swamp is impossible—too many long leaps, tight spots and trees to climb; you'd spill every drop.

I hop quickly from mossy rock to fallen tree, from one of Papa's tightly lashed floating pallets to an island made of rock and sludge. I'm so used to our high, landmarked trail that not even one of my toes swipes the leech-filled water. My chin is up. My head is high, but still…"If I only had a kerosene lamp!" I yell the thought out loudly, as Papa always did, to *scare off beasts.*

Because if I had a kerosene lamp, I'd hold it out to see their eyes—the big red ones reflecting back are crocs. They'll leave you alone unless you fall all the way into the water. Smaller red eyes mean a giant frog. I used to hunt for these tasty creatures with Papa. Only we'd hunt when the moon was fat and low. We'd never have taken to the swamp on a night as dark as this one, with the sky covered over in a blanket of clouds and only a mild middle moon lighting the way.

A roiling croak lets me know a frog is near. And *swish-tat-tat*, Papa's footing is in my ear. He'd fly across the fallen tree trunk and leap onto a mound of cold, mossy rocks. He'd slay the frogs through their centers and push them up onto his spear until we had a giant kabob of fresh meat.

The memory of Papa teaching me the swamp's landmarks—the ones set too high for crocodiles to climb—warms my soul in the very center of my chest. I look down, half expecting my heart to glow through my skin like a fiery coal. But nothing's there, no seething ember tucked inside my *kitenge*, no burning light.

Still, I press my hands over my heart, clinging to this bright moment, before darkness returns—the hollow feeling of loss, grief's steady ache.

☀ ☀ ☀

The moon that last night we were here was full—a perfect night to hunt frogs.

"Take my spear," he said. "I'll h-hold the lamp."

He would never have done this during the day, as teaching a girl to hunt is against Kilokie ways. But as soon as the spear was in my hands, the fattest frog I'd ever seen bobbed out from under the floating brush. Its belly was bloated white. Its legs splayed as it treaded water. Without hesitation, I popped it onto the end of the double blade. Red swirled out from its back.

"That's my girl!" he whooped. "You d-d-don't need my help at all, d-do you?"

Auntie Eshe fried that frog whole—it was big as a chicken and tasted like one too. She added a handful of hot peppers to her sizzling pan—and oh, how the fat screamed!

᷻᷼᷼   ᷻᷼᷼   ᷻᷼᷼

Tonight, as my fingertips and toes feel their way through the cold soil of this pitch-black swamp, the thought of all those frogs rolled in coarse salt makes my mouth water. Time and worry slip away as I relive that last night of hunting…until I trip. Snagging my toe, I fly forward into the leaf-studded mud. I've landed on a stick as thick as my arm. So I fight against the sludge and, finally, it pulls up with a sucking *pop.*

Smacking the stick loudly into my palm, I yell again, "This'll make a perfect club *if I need it!*"

Just as the thought leaves my lips, the brush beside me rustles. I jump and yell, swinging the stick again and again, but I don't hit anything except a few branches. Squinting into the darkness, I can barely see a thing. So I climb to the nearest high spot and press my back against the bark of a tree. And just as I kick myself again for forgetting a kerosene lamp, the clouds above me part. I catch my breath as a perfect stream of moonlight shines down through the dense trees. Outlines of fallen logs with their branches pointing up to the sky are suddenly easy to see. Mosquitoes swarm in circles above the water's green, dimpled skin, spots where fish are feeding.

I move on, using the stick to push back vines and scratchy branches. As I creep along the last few landmarks, I force Moses from my mind so I can think about Desta—how I'll find her tomorrow, once Nala is better. But Moses' eyes and what he just said, the touch of his hand on my arm…it all threatens me with the dizzy feeling only he brings, but I fight it back. With each swish of my stick, I fight it back. An owl screeches. Mosquitoes bite my ankles, and I hop across three wide stones, *slap, slap, slap,* sticking to these high spots as if my life depends on it—because it does. While I haven't seen any crocodiles yet, I sense them crowding in like the swinging vines all around me.

From here to the thick wall of trees that marks the swamp's end, there's only a perfectly round sinkhole full of black water left to cross. For this short crossing, Papa lashed a raft together from fallen logs and vines. We'd stand on it side by side and push it over the water with his spear. He always left this raft lying right here by the rocks, but it's gone. I search all around, lifting branches with my stick and cussing like Mama, but it's *gone*.

Scratching my head, I face the sinkhole. Everything I see— every floating speck of dust and every twisted branch—it's all bathed in just enough moonlight to tell I'm *definitely* in the right place.

My heart pounds faster. A gust of wind prickles goose flesh on my arms. I crouch down, gathering my courage, thinking I'll just leap out as far as I can and swim quickly to the other side. I say a quick prayer and count aloud, "One…two…" when something enormous and definitely reptilian splashes into the water ahead of me.

CHAPTER 56

Talitha
the branch speaks

MY BREATH EXPLODES IN TINY PUFFS of vapor as I scream and stare and scream and stare at the now lifeless sinkhole, smooth as silk.

There's no way I'm turning back now—not when the spring is just behind this short patch of water. So I turn my eyes up to the heavens, begging for help. Now that the clouds have passed, stars peek out, lighting my way to a solution in the treetops. My heart skips a beat, and quick as I can I climb up a skinny tree trunk to a limb that stretches across to the sinkhole's other side. I lie flat and scooch on my belly across the rough bark.

Halfway there, a howling wind blows, tipping my whole bendy tree almost completely over on its side.

"Papa!" I scream, *"Help me, please!"* My voice fills the night, but I'm not even sure myself if I'm calling for my papa or the Shepherd God who's supposed to be everyone's Father.

The wind dies, my tree rights itself, and I freeze, hugging on to the branch. But my relief lasts only a moment because I accidentally look down. And everything I see—from the shimmery water to the yellow stars behind my ears—spins fast and blurry, like it's all rushing at me at once. My belly flips. Two crocodiles do the same below, switching places, slapping tails. The spot where they swim boils.

I scream even louder and lose my grip, slipping over the side. But then I catch myself, holding on as tight as I can. My *mtungi* strap snags and starts to unfurl, but a flailing thumb hooks its latch just in time. I try to stay calm, but I'm shaking as hard as the leaves all around me.

Staring at the sinkhole, searching for another sign of the crocodiles, I see nothing—the water is perfectly still. The creatures seem to have disappeared...

"I see you!" I shriek, trying to scare them off by hurling a stick into the water. *"I know you're there! I see you!"*

Hugging the branch tightly, I inch forward along the narrowing limb. Up ahead, the tree I'll climb down on is getting close.

"Almost there," I say at the same moment the branch I'm on speaks.

And with a *crack*...

It snaps.

In half.

CHAPTER 57

Flora
a feeling of flight

"**TELL ME ABOUT YOUR HUSBAND.**" His words are hushed. Lucian sits on the chair beside Flora's bed. His cheeks are crimson. His powder-blue shirt is smeared with signs of the mine—soot, sweat, and the smell of iron-tinged water. When he returned to her room a few seconds ago and asked to see the baby again, Flora was stunned. Carefully, she had placed Damien in his arms and pulled her blanket high until it almost covered her neck. Searching for words to make small talk with this strange man, she's found none. A wrung-out cloth, Flora is weak from losing so much blood. But now the silence is unbearable. So she interrupts the clicking fan overhead with a simple offering—

"Salim was a good man."

Lucian lets out a sigh and sinks lower into the chair. His grimy forehead almost touches Damien's when Clara scoops up the baby.

"Now, now." Clara pats Lucian's shoulder as he chokes back what sounds like coughing or crying into his stained hands. Then he tries to hide his emotion by rubbing his glassy eyes and forcing a smile.

"Excuse me," he says, standing abruptly, "I'm so sorry to bother you. The doctor will be here soon."

With that, he strides toward the door. Halfway there, he pauses and looks back at them pleadingly. His lips part as if to speak, but no words come out. Awkwardly, he turns away once more and accidentally kicks over a golden urn containing a tall plant with knifelike tips. He jumps back to avoid its sharp points while the plant turns on its side, spilling a wave of soil across the floor.

"I'll get that," Clara says, but Lucian's already down on his hands and knees, scooping the dirt in his cupped palms and replacing it into the pot. With all his effort, he seems to only make the mess worse. But still he tries, swearing softly, his hands swirling white clouds in the blackened spot of marble.

"Lucian?" Clara's dumbfounded. In all their years together, she's never even seen him tidy up his room.

"I'm sorry," his voice cracks as he works quickly, his face to the floor. "I'm just so sorry..." He wipes his nose with the back of his hand and fakes a quick smile again in their direction. Then he motions to the dirt. "You two relax. I've got this."

Clara bounces the baby and moves over to stand beside Flora. Together, they observe the man before them with the wonder one would give to a paradox in nature—a dog suckling a kitten, a river reversing its flow, a falling star. The silence continues after he leaves. Their eyes favor the closed mahogany door he's clicked shut rather than one another. The quiet between them is heavy, as if neither wants to dishonor Lucian by questioning his odd behavior. Clara eventually speaks, but she tries to keep things light.

"You say your husband was a good man," she sing-songs, tilting the baby to Flora. "Does Damien look like his papa?"

Flora stares at her child, thinking of Salim...

❊ ❊ ❊

He was handsome—tall and broad-shouldered, with a depth to his stuttering voice (oh, this "ailment" she found incredibly ador-able and—secretly—wouldn't have minded if it was never cured). Once, Salim guided her out the front door of her childhood home for a walk. His hand barely grazed the small of her back, but a sen-sation so strong swept through her body she had to stop to catch her breath. It was a feeling of flight—of baby butterflies or birds. His touch released thousands of them, fluttering and flapping, tickling all her hidden spots—under her arms, the backs of her knees, all the places she kept covered from the sun.

Salim saw the blood rise to her face as it rushed to his own as well. Together, on the front porch, they were quiet, holding each other's gaze for a long, heated moment.

A few boys passed on skateboards and paused to look at them. One of the boys pointed up at Salim, who even on his walks into town attracted a lot of looks by wearing only his burgundy kitenge and, of course, no shoes. But Salim ignored them, his gaze fixed only on her.

"Flora," was all he said, staring boldly into her eyes. The sweet smoothness of the sound—said without a stutter—made them both grin.

That had only been his fifth day at her home, when he was visiting with Ibrahim to learn more about Christianity and to seek healing at the local shrine. But within a few weeks, there was an understanding between Flora and Salim. They hadn't discussed a future together, but Flora saw it clearly each time she looked into Salim's eyes. She saw children and a lavender kitenge—a flowing one made of silk that she'd wear on her wedding day.

The world Flora saw through Salim's eyes compelled her like nothing she'd ever known. When they were first getting to know each other, she would share with him her anger at the unfairness women faced in her country when trying to receive an education and employment. He trumped her troubles with stories of famine, disease, and oppression—all faced by his own people who lived just on the other side of Great Mountain. And yet, when she watched his face as he and her brother discussed the faith—the way Salim's eyes lit up, the way he marveled over simple truths she'd long taken for granted—Flora felt she had nothing to offer him. Still, when Salim would turn to her to ask a question about the sacraments or Church history, she'd give an answer so elaborate that even Ibrahim would be left speechless.

While Salim was impressed with her knowledge, Flora was humbled to the point of embarrassment when she heard Salim speak about his people: his love for them, his desire to bring them the Gospel along with food and clean water. Listening to him, she felt she was in the presence of one of the saints whose biographies she'd read when she was young. These saints were regular people who'd chosen important things to live and die for. Long ago, she had concluded that such folk were fine material for books, but that they didn't exist in real life anymore. Until now.

Salim's passion both inspired and ruined Flora. She wanted to catch hold of it. She wanted something to live and die for too. But above all, she wanted her hand in his.

᜴ ᜴ ᜴

Flora dreams peacefully with the baby in her arms. Clara is nervous at first to let the young mother sleep deeply after she's lost so much blood, scared she won't wake up again. But Clara pities Flora, noticing the dark rings beneath her eyes.

"When was the last time you slept?" she murmurs as she places a chair beside the bed. Holding a tiny mirror to Flora's lips, Clara guards her patient's every breath. In her other hand, she holds a rosary, praying fervently that the doctor will arrive soon as she watches the tiny mirror fog with steam.

CHAPTER 58

Lucian
the knowledge of his crime

LUCIAN STANDS IN THE HALL pressing his fists against his closed eyes. He'd been listening to Flora and Clara's muffled conversation until they suddenly got quiet. Glancing down at his hands, he realizes he's chewed his nails to the bone. A smudge of blood covers his thumbnail and, having just been in the mines, he hears Nelson's voice ringing in his ears…

"Nice teeth, Rot."

Disgusted with himself, Lucian shoves his fists in his pockets and tips back his head, beating it softly against the door. A crack in the ceiling catches his eye. The fissure appears endless, stretching the entire length of the hall. For a second, he imagines it splitting open and the walls crashing down all around him. And if he was the only one involved in this tragic mess—if Badru wasn't certain to seek revenge on that poor boy, Moses—Lucian wouldn't care if this very thing happened, if these white walls crumbled into rubble at his feet. Dekadente was Lucian's inheritance, but it's always been more of a curse.

Only a few minutes ago, Lucian hid the truck in the woods with Moses inside, cradling his semiconscious uncle in his arms. "Please, stay here," Lucian had implored, "I've got something inside that will make Badru leave us alone!" The boy nodded, wide-eyed and mystified as Lucian ran into the mansion.

Lucian plans to beg his mother for her wedding ring— a rare, enormous diamond with two equally impressive emeralds on either side. It's the very last speck of wealth Lucian knows to exist in this entire mansion. His plan is to simply tell his mother the truth: about the drugs, about his addictions and how he's failed to run the mines, and even…about the stolen girls. Then he'll beg for her wedding ring to save his and Moses' lives.

Lucian only quickly stops by his filing cabinet on the way to see if his suspicion about Flora's husband was correct—to not rely on memory, but to confirm with his own weary eyes that Flora's husband was the same man he had targeted in the bombing.

Salim's last letter to the credit union now shakes in Lucian's trembling hands. He was surprised to find it so easily, but it was right where he left it. A handwritten note on blue paper. No letterhead; the same one he read aloud to Nelson six months ago. They'd been smoking junat, sitting together in their father's old study.

"You want me to make sure this guy has an accident?" Nelson had asked as he inhaled a long hit.

Lucian only remembers giving a quick nod, then reaching over to grab the pipe. It was that quick nod, that dip of his chin that sent Salim Betenge, Flora's husband and Damien's father, to his rocky grave. With the baby's powdery smell still lingering, Lucian again chokes back tears.

"I'm sorry," he moans. "My God, I'm so sorry…"

This simple prayer Clara taught him long ago is the only thing getting him through the day, as thoughts of Salim being crushed by falling rocks have become his constant torment.

※ ※ ※

Badru had pulled off the task with a simple pipe bomb set on a timer. Dressed in a disguise, he joined the miners in their cart and set the bomb to go off after twenty minutes. He then returned just as Lucian arrived for the day.

"The one with the stutter was in good spirits," Badru said. "He even offered me a drink from his waterskin." A faint shadow crossed his eyes. "A shame he has to go."

Seconds later, the explosion shook the valley. It was bigger than Badru had planned and took out a team in the next shaft as well. Lucian was furious with the loss of manpower, but Badru just laughed.

"Look around," he responded. "This valley's full of roaches, all begging to work your mines. You'll be fine."

※ ※ ※

"My God!" Just the idea of that day is torture. "I'm sorry— *Jesus, I'm sorry!*" Lucian smooths the letter on his chest, then forces himself to look at it. The bottom section, a part he missed only minutes before, has him reeling…

And so, kind bankers, I ask you
to remember the words of the One
who is Master of us all: "Whatever
you did for one of the least of
these brothers, you did for me. For
I was hungry and you gave me no
food, I was thirsty and you gave
me no drink."

Will you continue to take food
from the mouths of hungry children
by helping to sustain the holdings
of the Kerr Mines?

I am your servant —

Salim Befenge

Lucian sinks to the floor, the knowledge of his crime more than he can bear.

Salim was like Clara! The realization is a knife, sharp and stabbing. *He was good—truly good—and I killed him.*

Lucian escapes to his room in a distant wing of the mansion, where he punches the wall again and again until his knuckles bleed and he finally has to stop. Trembling with nausea, he falls to his knees to pray, only to find he doesn't know how. So he turns his hands over to look at the damage, and he catches a glimpse, another vision of his hands…washed clean, without cuts or blood, *healed* in every way. But just for a moment.

The vision this time—he can't deny it. He's baffled. But what he just saw brings something else: a lightness, a feeling of hope, even though he doesn't understand any of it yet.

So, with bloody hands, a broken heart, and his mind made up, Lucian mounts the stairs to visit his mother. She's the only one who can help him now.

CHAPTER 59

Talitha
the monsoon

THE SHOCK OF THE FALL leaves me rigid, almost forgetting how to swim. Underwater, my eyes flash open to shadows, blackish and green. I fight for the water's surface, kicking wildly, and find my yellow *mtungi* within reach. Relieved, I tuck it beneath me and hold on as it lifts me up and out of the water. Cold air hits my skin as my eyes dart around the darkness for crocodiles. Papa's warning echoes loudly—

"D-don't thrash! Go st-st-stiff as a log and they'll swim around you."

I'd fallen into a shallow spot that day. The water was up to my waist. But rather than pull me out, Papa calmly stepped in beside me.

"Sss-see," he said as a midsize crocodile swam between us, "it thinks we're a c-couple of trees."

And so, fighting against instinct, I hold perfectly still. Floating in the middle of the sinkhole, listening to cicadas drum and the water lap up against the sides of my *mtungi*, I know that I should be dead, that the crocodiles should have attacked me as soon as I fell into the water. But somehow, I'm still here. Is it a miracle? Or was I only imagining crocodiles?

Slowly, I brush wet leaves from my cheek and—*even more slowly*—I push out my tongue to spit grainy sands from my mouth. Then, squeezing my *mtungi* so tightly my muscles start to hurt, I squint through the fog, straining to see the other side.

And there's our raft! Caught up in a snarl of roots! My hand loosens to paddle forward when…

You know that feeling you get when someone stares at you while you're asleep? As if their eyes are letting off heat? As if their stare is the softest touch? Well…

Trembling all over, squinting into the night, I try to make out the things around me, but the moon shines dimmer down here, cut by the shadows of swaying branches. And in spite of the darkness, in spite of the fog, a gauzy light still reflects off things shiny and red—*like the almond-shaped eye right in front of my face!*

I freeze. The creature does too. It blinks, and—somehow—*I hold in* what would be the loudest scream ever.

"*Sss-stiff as a log,*" Papa said, "*and they'll swim around you.*"

Digging my fingertips into the sides of my *mtungi*, I don't move a centimeter. And in a flash, I see the monsoon I survived with Peter long ago—the closest I've ever come to dying. We held on to a tree just as tightly as I'm holding on to this *mtungi* as howling winds bore down, threatening to devour us, to suck us away into the rushing river already full of dead bodies.

That storm's force was like nothing I'd ever known. And even though I hadn't realized it at the time, I must have stored up some of its power within me. Because as I battle my own instincts, staying perfectly still when everything inside of me begs to scream and thrash and kick for the other side—I become that monsoon. *Only contained.*

The giant eye disappears and scattered moonlight reveals a shadow long and lean beneath me. So I push that monsoon down even deeper, and as I do, the creature slowly swims away.

Still, I don't move. I float, listening to the lapping water and the dance of the wind in the trees. For a moment, life seems to exist somewhere else, somewhere outside of me, maybe even outside of time.

Clouds pass along. The water shimmers with darts that look like silver fish jumping. And oddly, in this quiet moment, everything suddenly feels all right. Looking around, I sense a Presence greater than the darkness around me. Greater than the swamp, greater than that monsoon so many years ago, greater even than all the horrors and wonders of this endless day, this painful life and the happy-sad-confused way I feel about everything all the time.

Again, Papa's here. This time, in song.

"Even though I w-w-walk through the valley of the shadow of d-death, I will fear no evil for Thou art w-with me…"

And so, with Papa's prayer on my lips, I float peacefully among crocodiles. These creatures with their sharp teeth and scaly backs—they're feared more than lions because they'll attack anything that moves. But tonight, I share their swimming hole untouched. A realization fills my heart—

"I am not alone…"

The whispered truth feels like the love I lost when Papa died. It's no wonder I had to come deep into our swamp to find it. So I speak the words a little louder—

"I am not alone."

Truth fills the darkness at the same moment something amazing and truly miraculous catches my eye. Ahead of me now is the other bank of the sinkhole and, almost hidden beneath a flat rock, I see a slight green glow in the slanted moonlight. I gasp. It's an emerald, the biggest one I've ever seen. The gem is magnificent, level with the water—as if it's waiting just for me.

Still, I haven't forgotten about the crocodiles. So I pray, begging for the Shepherd God to keep me safe, and after a few moments I have the sense to move on. Stroking slowly, being careful not to splash, I paddle to the muddy edge, reach under the rock, and grab the heavy emerald—it's not stuck at all, or else I would certainly leave it behind. Then I launch myself out of the water and dash up the steep slope, just in case those crocodiles decide to chase me after all.

Papa? I stumble ahead, my mind spinning. My *mtungi* is in one hand, the emerald in the other. Stealing glances at the gem, I quickly put space between me and the swamp. "Papa?" I wonder aloud, "Is this from you?"

Perhaps Papa did hide the gem there, knowing he'd go back for it one day. Or maybe it washed down from the mines a hundred years ago and has been guarded by crocodiles ever since. Regardless, I decide in an instant that this emerald is from him—he and the Shepherd God surely sent me this gift tonight.

"Thank you," I gasp as I break through the last row of trees. The cold night air slaps my wet skin. Shivering from head to toe,

my teeth chattering like a sack of coins, I find myself on top of an open clearing. Staggering, almost tripping, I make my way around tall, jagged rocks, whipped by wind, surrounded by stars.

And even though crocodiles won't follow me up a hill like this, I'm spooked. So I take turns, staring down at the emerald in my hand, then back at that dark spot between the trees where I just climbed out of the swamp. Backing away, I spit on the gem and polish it quick. *And oh!* The way it catches the moonlight! With a flame of gold in the middle—so light it glows. I press the stone to my heart, thinking how happy Mama will be! How we'll buy seeds and meat! How this emerald could even—just maybe—*drill us a well!*

With my eyes back on the trees, I bite a long strip from the hem of my *kitenge* and knot the emerald in tight, criss-crossing loops to tie it around my neck. I've done this so many times with melted glass and shiny rocks—but nothing as heavy as this gem. I press its points with my fingertips and gasp. It's sharp on the top and curved in the middle, like a tiny, green banana.

I tug the knot, thinking of Desta, who taught me this trick, and of Nala and the *Others* and how they're worth more to me than a million heavy emeralds.

A howling wind blows and the swaying trees swish and it's just so noisy all around, but I'm pretty sure I'm laughing because I'm too happy to be crying as I back away from the swamp, *quickly, quickly, quickly* over rocks and brush. Shaking all over, I glance down—in disbelief—at the emerald, then look back up, expecting a crocodile to dart from the trees.

Until I fall. Forgetting the shortness of this cliff, I've lost my footing and am *falling,* crashing through the bushes, rolling through a milky-white bank of fog, which in spite of its dense-ness doesn't slow me down a bit. Fortunately, a tree growing sideways from the steep hill's crinkled face kicks me and whips me around. I land hard, flat on my back—all alone—at the edge of a grassy meadow.

CHAPTER 60

Talitha
the Shepherd

I'VE HAD THE WIND KNOCKED OUT of me before, but had forgotten its bite. Unable to breathe, I lie perfectly still with pain searing out from the spot beneath my breastbone in fiery rays.

In spite of my beaten-down state, the sweet taste of survival slows my pounding heart. I touch my necklace, relieved it's still there. Then I stare up at the treetops that line the hill above me, watching them dip and sway. They saw my last struggle. Their swishing *wooshes* excite me because never before have I felt this happy to be alive. To breathe in the cold night air. To kick my legs up to the sky, to wiggle my toes. In my heart, I'm flying up there with the stars. I reach out with both hands and I bless them.

Frogs croak, an owl *hoo hoo hoots*, and it's as if all of creation is crying out to me: *You're alive, Talitha! You're alive! You swam with a crocodile. You looked it in the eye, but you're alive!*

Still, a sharp pain fills my lungs. I turn my cheek and let long strings of onion grass tickle my ear. It's the kind that our goat loves to chew, but that makes her milk bitter.

The noise of faraway voices catches my attention. And there, off in the distance, bobbing up and down, are three glowing suns. They're torches carried by my people as they gather water at the spring. I want to run to them. I want to tell them about the crocodiles. I want to show them the emerald. Pride wells in my heart as I watch the outlines of their bodies running back and forth from our village. They're gathering water for the *Others—* *"for the least of these brothers."* Papa would be proud.

But since I can't even sit up, I look back at the brilliant night sky, at the mountains and valleys of the moon. The thrill of survival is suddenly threatened by a crushing sense of loneliness, by my own smallness in this world.

"Don't look for Him in the stars," Papa always said when we'd lie with the roof thatched open, *"b-because God is* here," he'd say, with a hand on his heart, *"inside you."*

And as I lie all alone, I sense the One Papa spoke of so often in a way I never have before. It's as if I can feel Him approaching me, the warmth of His presence, the sound of His white *kitenge* brushing the grass. I think back over this endless day, and suddenly my longing for Papa is raw, roaring like an overfed fire.

I understand! I want to tell him as my eyes map out the starry constellations that he first pointed out to me years ago. It's as if everything he ever said during our talks in our wheat plot and the swamp have been saved up here in my heart, distilling like a vapor that's now raining down in my soul. All at once, I simply *know* this Shepherd—this Goodness that made the world. And Papa was right—He's not out there with the stars, but everywhere…*even in me.*

And He's bigger than my pain or my jealousy or my anger.

My eyes burn, but still, they're dry.

"Damn it!" I whine, wanting so badly to cry. Because I can handle it all: Desta being taken, Moses betraying her, even the *Others* getting sick. But I can't handle the fact anymore—not for one second more—that my father has died. I want to talk to him. I want to feel his arms around me. I want to hear him laugh and catch the scent of him at the end of the day—that mixture of marula nuts and mine soot and sweat and the aftershave he'd pluck from aid packages. None of the other men used this lotion because it was too Western. But Mama liked the way it smelled, so Papa would slap it on his neck after he rinsed off in the river. Peter and I would sit on the floor, playing a game of *mancala*, and Papa would smile back at us through the foggy mirror—the mirror with a crack down its center that hung on the wall in the hut we shared *when we were a family. A family!* I don't want to be an *Other* anymore. I want to be a *daughter.* I want to be my *father's daughter!*

A wren's cackle interrupts my thoughts as it's stirred from its nest by some nighttime hunter on the prowl. For a second, it sounds like baby Brave. The birdcall snaps me back from my sorrow. Feeling guilty that I've lost so much time when Brave and the *Others* need water, I catch the thought of the small boy in my praying hands.

"Please," is all I say, lifting my request toward the sky. And as I do, I get the very real sense that our Shepherd God is receiving the sick child from my hands into His own.

For a second, it feels as if Brave himself has been lifted off my chest. I'm lighter. My lungs don't hurt anymore. My hands ripple over the prickly grass at my sides. I rip out two fistfuls and lift them to my nose. Their roots crumble damp soil on my cheeks.

And as I inhale the earthy smell of onion grass, a tingling feeling scatters across my sinuses. Then, a single tear, so fat it reflects the moon's light, drips slowly down the side of my nose. Tilting my head, I catch it in my hand and watch with wonder as it splashes a clean circle in the center of my dirty palm.

"He restores my soul."

Papa's voice—the sound is so clear, I roll sideways, face first, onto the cushiony meadow. The floodgates of my heart lift as what feels like a warm summer's rain drives down, pounding over the length and width of me, quenching every dry creek bed, overflowing every cracked cistern.

I cry and I cry.

Then I crawl over to a boulder, lean on it, and cry some more. Behind me, although invisible to the eye, the Shepherd approaches. He covers my shivering arms with the corner of his robe. He cups His hands and He catches all my tears.

Then, ever so gently, He leads me to the spring.

CHAPTER 61

Flora
Timkat

"WILL YOU HAVE DAMIEN OFFICIALLY christened by a priest?" Clara asks in a quiet moment.

Since Flora woke up, the conversation has flowed like one between old friends. At first Clara was horrified when she realized she'd been caught baptizing the baby.

"Something just came over me!" she said. "I don't even think I did it right!"

Once Flora convinced Clara that no offense was taken, subjects spilled back and forth between them, meandering like a river carving out a new path. Lucian had left them puzzled, but rather than discuss his strange behavior, Clara had launched into a series of questions. She then spent the evening contorting her wrinkled face into expressions of awe as she listened to the story of a city girl who moved out to the bush for love.

Baptize. The word, the question—it meets Flora with the misty spray of *Timkat,* the holy day on which her husband was christened long ago. And even though Talitha and Peter didn't have a public baptism, as Auntie Eshe and many of the tribe's elders could only tolerate Flora and Salim's faith as long as they practiced it quietly, Flora knows the answer to Clara's question immediately.

"Yes," she sighs, looking Clara in the eye. Then she rolls over and back to that feast day long ago. *Timkat.* Celebrated in the New Year, it's remembered in the Church of the Western world as the Epiphany, when the three wise men brought gifts to the Christ Child. In Flora's hometown, as well as in a few other places, it marks the day Jesus was baptized in the Jordan River.

᛫ ᛫ ᛫

Salim was with her for the celebration on his first visit to her city. Because he had been raised in the old Kilokie ways, where the beliefs were in many gods who were powerful and easily angered, the concept of the One True God coming as a tiny baby both baffled and delighted him. So after a week of questioning the priests at Flora's church and being prepared for his desired healing of his stutter, Salim laid his hands on the pilgrimage site nearby. The priest there prayed over him, touching his lips with an oil smelling of honeysuckles.

After the priest anointed him, Salim returned to the nearby church's sanctuary and knelt on the cold stone floor. Flora waited quietly for him at the back, watching him pray. Soon, two rows of darkly-robed men, about eight on each side, slowly processed to the front of the church—it was a Vespers service, their evening prayers.

They were led by a boy shaking a ring of bells and another swinging a golden ball of incense side to side in a wide arc. Sweet-smelling smoke swirled over their heads, taking on a shape, forming a mystical body as they intoned the psalms. Abba *Yosef* was among the men. Flora saw him pause from his sung prayer to whisper in Salim's ear. Then he passed Salim a missal.

Salim took the small black book. Flora wondered how much he could really follow along, as he'd only recently learned how to read. But as the men's voices lifted with a richness that certainly rose beyond the mosaic-domed ceiling, Flora recalled what Salim had told her earlier that day, as they prepared to leave for the church.

"The rites of the K-Kilokie…many of them are b-beautiful. The dances to celebrate a g-good harvest, the songs of mourning as we send off our dead. I have never felt so alive, so c-connected to my people, as when we all share one song of joy or sorrow. B-b-but other traditions of ours…"

He trailed off, at a loss, his fingers absently tracing the scars on his arms—the ones he still hadn't told her the stories behind. Finally, he went on, his voice soft, "I d-don't understand. Why must we live in fear of c-c-curses and make sacrifices to please the gods of our ancestors? Why do they not t-touch my heart the way your Shepherd God does?"

Flora hadn't known what to say to him then. But later, as she watched his bright eyes stray again and again to the gold-leafed icon of Jesus painted high above the altar, she sensed he was close to finding the answers he sought.

He rubbed the ropelike scars marking his skin, seeming captivated by the Man's tender expression, the wounds in His hands and feet. Then, finally, his own hands dropped and the tension left his shoulders. She could almost feel the peace radiating from him as he lifted his voice with the others, the rich bass and baritone chant filling the ancient stone sanctuary.

Long after they all finished singing, long after the black-robed men filed out, Salim remained kneeling on the floor. Finally, Flora went to wait for him outside, watching the crowd that was buzzing with preparations for that night's feast.

After a long time, Salim came out with Abba Yosef. As Flora made her way over to them, she could just hear Salim's response to the priest's words, "Th-th-th-ank y-y-you." He looked away in embarrassment at the sound of his stammering voice, and Flora's heart sank for him. Personally, she didn't mind his stutter in the slightest, but she knew that he'd placed much hope in praying for a cure. His and Abba Yosef's eyes met, both surprised and—it was impossible to hide—disappointed.

"Often, miracles take time," the priest said. "Pray."

Flora and Salim walked away from the church without a word shared between them. She felt that to say anything would inter-rupt the remarkable change that was obviously taking place in Salim's soul. She looked into his eyes. There was a new light there, a new peace.

For months, Salim never said exactly what had happened at Vespers that night. But on the eve of their wedding, he took Flora to kneel before that same icon of Jesus. "He b-bled," Salim whispered, "so that we wouldn't have to...Yes, pain in this life will come. But He has already saved us."

Salim touched the wound on Christ's side as he continued, "So many of our K-Kilokie rites...they are only a shadow of the sacrifice He made long ago." A look of longing crossed his face. Then, his voice filled with urgency: "If my p-people only knew! If they only

*knew the p-price already paid for us!" He wiped his eyes, barely able
to speak, "If they only knew...""*

*Captivated, Flora spoke, cementing their plan without count-
ing the cost: "We'll go to them!" she promised, "If it's the last thing
we do, we'll go!"*

❋ ❋ ❋

Flora kisses the baby's hairline. Her aching body sinks
deeper into the bed as her heart sinks deeper into a past she's
long neglected.

"Damien Salim," she whispers, breathing in his soft scent,
one that's oddly reminiscent of the chrism oil that covered her
husband's brow at the Feast of *Timkat* long ago...

❋ ❋ ❋

*Sundown marked the beginning of the all-night festival.
Crowds took to the narrow city streets, shaking beaded tambourines
and beating tiny drums. Just before dawn, Flora and Salim lost each
other in the crowd. She had stopped to look at a vendor's tray of
shiny saint medals, thinking she'd like to find Father Damien's for
Salim. He'd recently struggled through reading the saint's story, and
his incessant talk about the holy man and his lepers had already
become a private joke between them.*

*"Father Damien this, Father Damien that; what would this priest
think of you trying on a nice button-down shirt?" Flora teased earlier
that morning. Salim's answer was quick and delivered with a smile.*

*"He'd say I should if I were to best love the people of this city.
But since my heart is Kilokie, I will wear my robe."*

When Flora turned from the vendor's table, Salim was gone.

Searching for him through the streets she'd known all her life, surrounded by so many familiar faces, she'd never before felt so alone. She didn't realize it, but Salim was looking for her too. Thinking Flora was beside him, he'd been carried along with the crowd watching ribbon dancers swirl their sashes high into the slowly dawning sky.

Once morning broke, the front doors of the church opened. Three priests wearing colorful vestments moved forward in a solemn procession. Like the Red Sea, the people parted before them and knelt. Then they followed the priests to the river, chanting prayers, throwing confetti, and smashing together tiny brass cymbals.

Flora felt ashamed that her eyes were roving the crowds for Salim rather than watching the priests who stood by the river's edge, blessing the water and flinging it out over the people in a symbolic renewal of baptism. Too distracted to pray, she continued to search for this mysterious man who had eyes so dark and thoughtful that—when he turned them in her direction—they felt like two arrows piercing deep into her soul. She ran through the crowds until she came to an open place where the black asphalt ended. The soil there was soaked, and worshippers dressed in white stretched out in a long, quiet line. These were the ones here for the first time. The ones who couldn't take part in the renewal of the river's spray until they'd first had the River. They were the ones being baptized.

Of course, there were many babies in the line. Most were sound asleep in their mothers' arms. Toddlers hung tiredly on to legs, fussing and rubbing their eyes. A big brother, about eight years old, sat alone a few feet away, gently thumping a drum. Steam rose off the ground behind him and also off everyone's damp shoulders. The air blurred with heat waves as the sun climbed higher. Finches trilled and priests walked among the people, blessing them with great sprinkling arcs of tossed water.

When Flora finally found him, Salim was kneeling at the front of the line. The sun shone down on his brow just as the three priests poured. The first, "I baptize you in the name of the Father." The second, "and of the Son." The third, "and of the Holy Spirit."

Salim then folded his hands over his heart and leaned forward as if he were praying. When he finally looked up, Abba Yosef was there reaching out a hand to him. Pulling Salim up, the priest turned him toward Flora, having spotted her in the crowd. And gently, Abba Yosef pushed Salim in her direction. Flora held out a hand, receiving Salim as one would a blessing—a walking, breathing benediction.

Neither Flora nor Salim spoke, but at the same moment they clasped hands a conclusion was made in each of their hearts— rock solid and unwavering, although neither would speak of it for some time.

※　※　※

"I'll have Damien baptized at the Feast of *Timkat*," Flora says, catching Clara's attention. Again, she longs for her husband. But for the first time in months, a sense of quietness fills her. The roaring pain in her heart has been hushed by the bundle in her arms, this tiny baby who is to her the very essence of hope. She misses Salim, but she also holds next to her heart a new piece of him, a piece the world has never seen before. The feeling of joy surprises her like the coolness of a new day, but not the coolness of any ordinary day. It's the feeling of that sacred day when she walked the streets with her future husband.

"I will journey to my city," she smiles as color returns to her cheeks, "and my baby will be baptized outside in the morning for all to see."

CHAPTER 62

Talitha
sparks and beauty

THIS DAY—THIS DAY EQUALLY CRUEL *as it was magical— it ends much as it began. Good and evil, darkness and light fight until the bitter end, running neck and neck, overlapping in color to form, at times, a murky gray. Because for everything given, something was taken away. The cruelty, the beauty—they were bedfellows, kicking for the biggest spot on the mat.*

When I was a young girl in my family's small hut, Papa would light a candle, hold it high, and say, "See, children? One tiny light always defeats the night."

His smile is still toothy and white in my mind's eye. His voice still melodious as the river. But his absence leaves me to doubt the truth of his claim on that candle.

Does light always conquer darkness? Each and every light? Each and every dark night?

No. If it did, I'd still have a father.

But in spite of my pain, in spite of the tears I—for a time— forgot how to cry, I've seen too much beauty to not believe. I see it everywhere: in Nala's dimpled hands, in the ordinary sky, in a bird's song carried in on the breeze. It's these endless sparks, these landmarks that goad me on, again and again. They take me to the water. They teach me to drink.

And so you understand what I mean by sparks *and* beauty, *I must tell you about the end of this day—but not the end of this story.*

✳ ✳ ✳

All alone in the grassy meadow, I finish my long-awaited cry. By the end of it, I feel like an overripe orange after a hard rain, pressed until the ashy pulp won't offer even one more drop. Then, stumbling on with the spring in sight, I'm light, so light in every way—I think I may float up to dance with the stars.

Moses. The thought of him seeing me like this with swollen eyes and sticks in my hair…*Who cares what he thinks*, I chastise myself. Still, there's comfort in the darkness. I blow my nose on the underside of my *kitenge* and, yes, that feels much better.

The spring and the flat stones all around it are empty. Bobbing torches, looking like so many orange eyes, head away from me up the path. I press my *mtungi* beneath the water's surface, and bubbles *glug glug glug* extra loud in the dark. Once full, I take a quick moment to wash off the worst of the swamp's mud, then hoist the heavy *mtungi* onto the top of my head. Icy sheets stream down my face and neck as I follow along quickly, trying hard to catch up with my people. The cold wind on my soaking wet skin wakes me up. There's a skip in my step. I miss Nala.

But at Weeping Rock, something strange surprises me, stopping me in my tracks.

Light swirls from a torch wedged in the boulder's center crack, and I'm baffled. Deaf Man should be sound asleep. But instead, he's standing on top of the boulder, babbling excitedly, holding out his tiny tin cup in my direction with shaking hands. It's full. Water trickles from its rim. A passing villager must have spared him a few drops.

He places the tiny mug with its skinny curved handle beside the torch and claps at it dramatically. I know right away— he wants me to take his cup to the *Others*.

Tears return to my eyes, blurring everything I see—the torchlight, his shaky hands as they form shapes and make frantic gestures—because everyone knows *this tiny tin cup is all Deaf Man has*.

I set down my *mtungi* and go to him. He's panting because he's so upset. I can tell I'm not the first one he's asked. Surely many have zipped by without hearing his pleas, in a rush to get back with their precious burden of water.

"*Thank you,*" I say, picking up the cup. "This will surely help the *Others*."

Relieved, he climbs down off the boulder to face me. His good eye narrows in on my face. I can tell he knows exactly who I am, even in the dark. I'm sure he's about to make the sign for yeheb nuts or ask about Papa by pressing his hands together in front of his face, as if in prayer.

But then he gasps at my emerald, letting out a strangled little yelp.

"I know," I say, looking down, seeing the gem for the first time by torchlight. It's funny—I'd almost forgotten about it. But now, the emerald looks so dark green around the edges that it's almost black, while in the middle, it's light and shimmery as if it's filled with gold. Lifting the gem to him, I make sure he can see my mouth when I say, "I found this in the swamp."

"Aaaahhh," he squeals, pointing a bony finger for a quick touch, then pulling back as if the emerald were hot. His watery eyes shine. One is foggy and white, but the other eye studies the gem, fascinated. He babbles excitedly, spit flecks collecting on his lips. I back away, my mind flying to the few measly coins we have saved up to drill a well. I think of the time Mama and I walked for days to the aid station with them tied in a leather pouch around her hip.

❊ ❊ ❊

We arrived exhausted. My tongue was so swollen from thirst, I would have been happy to receive even one tiny cup of water. I would have forgotten about drilling us a well if someone, anyone, would have shown us the least bit of kindness.

No one did. In fact, I'll never forget the way the bloated man laughed when Mama dropped our purse on his table. His shiny head was lined with bushy red curls.

"We would like to pay you to drill a well," Mama said, speaking his language.

He picked up Auntie Eshe's emerald, held it up to the light, and turned it over a few times like he was thinking. Then he exploded into laughter.

"I could maybe buy you a bottle of water with this, sweetie," he said, sweeping his hand over her coins, scattering them to the floor. I dove to gather them up, but Mama didn't flinch. The man held on to his sides, laughing and wheezing.

Mama let him finish, her jaw flexed. When the mzungu man realized she was seething, he tried to apologize.

"I, um…I'm sorry, miss," he stammered. "It's just going to take a lot more than a few coins for us to bring our drill way out there to you—a whole lot more."

"I see," she said, standing taller. "Then we will be back."

᭥ ᭥ ᭥

That was years ago, yet our coin purse is still just as empty. Until now.

Deaf Man must be reading my mind, because he's smiling extra wide as he takes his cup back, sets it by the torch, grabs my hands, and tries to dance me around in a circle. He hums a song, swaying his head back and forth—it's a celebration stomp we all know well, one we save for children. I can't help but laugh, letting him lead me around once. But with my heart ever near the *Others,* I pull away and lift my *mtungi* to my head.

"Your cup," I say extra loud as I pick it back up and motion toward the village. "They will be thankful."

He nods quickly, sighing in agreement, making a triumphant sign with a crooked fist. Then his legs fold beneath him as he sinks down, assuming his familiar spot beside Weeping Rock. He looks relieved, but also completely exhausted.

"And this," I say, touching his cup to my necklace, "is for all of us to share."

He grunts in a way that makes me think he understands completely. Actually, the look in his cloudy eyes—I'm pretty sure *he's* dreaming of a well for our village too.

"Beloved is smarter than we think," Papa said often, always calling Deaf Man by his real name. And I wonder as I stare at him looking so crippled and yet so amazingly perfect: *Why don't we all call him Beloved?*

A gust of wind sneaks up from behind, lifting a cloud of dust and leaves. The sudden movement takes him by surprise. He hugs his skinny knees and squeals again, showing off his one-toothed smile, looking old as an uncle and yet young as a baby. His excitement is contagious, fueling my dreams:

"Drill me a well!" I'll slam this heavy emerald down at the aid station and that bloated man will drill it himself, right outside my hut—so we'll *never* have a night like this ever again!

I tap his foot with my toe, my way of saying *goodbye* to Deaf Man—I mean *Beloved.* Then I head for home, my bright thoughts about drilling a well lighting my way—until the bleating begins, snapping me from my lovely dream. I lean into the sound. It starts off small, but then it grows into a haunting cry that means only one thing...

CHAPTER 63

Deaf man
tied in vines

LONG AGO, WHEN HE WAS TWENTY years old but still the size of a child, he tasted what it meant to drown. The terror of darkness, the bursting sizzle of lungs, the eyes so wide they threaten to pop from their sockets...

*   *   *

The river was running high, brown and swollen from the monsoon they'd had the day before. Beloved sat with his mama by the riverbank where it was cool and quiet, a pile of pea pods in front of them. She was giving him a lesson, letting him read her lips as she repeated certain words for him. He learned "green" and "snap" and "pea" in a short span of minutes, brightening under his mama's smile every time he was able to repeat the words back to her.

After a while, when he started getting restless, she motioned for him to take a break while she continued shelling the peas into a bowl. Beloved happily walked along the bank, looking for the tiny frogs he liked to catch in his hands. Then something caught his eye in the river: a white stick being whisked along by the churning waters. As it was sucked under, he leaned over to peer into the current, trying to see where it had gone.

He couldn't hear his mama's panicked voice, calling for him to stay away from the edge, but he saw the movement out of the corner of his eye as she dashed toward him. Startled, he turned toward her, but his feet slipped in the mud. Arms flailing, he tumbled straight into the rushing river.

"Nooo!" she screamed, as his head went under. "Please, someone help!" But there was no one nearby—the uncles had already left for the mines, the aunties for their fields. Beloved's mama was all alone…

Looking up and down the river, she was desperate. She couldn't swim, but was about to jump in anyway when suddenly from the trees, a tiny voice yelled: "Beloved!"

A set of skinny legs ran down the slope and splashed through the water. A fuzzy head and a smooth, bare back dove into the river like a fearless bird of prey.

Beloved's mama wept as time—and far too much of it— passed ever…so…slowly, with no trace of Beloved or his savior in sight. Then two nose tips appeared downstream, breaking the water's dark surface, inhaling sweet, fresh air. Beloved's mama fell to the ground in relief as the two small friends struggled back to the riverbank.

Beloved and his savior were about the same size. They stood on the shore, hugging, the breeze kicking up gooseflesh on their arms. After a few seconds, they pulled back to look at one another.

"Salim," Beloved tilted his head to the side, pressing his hands together in front of his face to signify their closeness, making the sign for his dearest friend.

Salim's lips parted. He commanded his tongue to speak, but something was wrong...

"Be-be-bee..." he shook his head in frustration,"Be-be-bee-lov-ed."

Deeply confused, Salim stuttered for the first time in his life. It was as if his friend's name was trapped on the back of his tongue, or even worse—tied up in vines at the bottom of the river. Because never before had this redeemer's tongue stuck so. And never again would it be loosed.

☀ ☀ ☀

Deaf Man wakes from his nap with a start. He's had the nightmare about murky water again—holding his breath, clinging to Salim as they kick against the underwater vines tangled around his ankles.

"My friend," he mutters, drawing Salim's face in the sand with his finger. And then he gasps, scratches his head, and leans forward.

"Where have you been?" he asks in his own way.

He recalls Salim's last visit as if it were yesterday, but it's been at least six months since they last sat together in this spot, feasting on gooey rice balls cooked in coconut milk. Deaf Man licks his lips, recalling the rare taste of sugar. He claps to the dark sky, celebrating the memory again and again. Joy fills his heart, but then loneliness follows, stark and stifling.

With his one good eye, he studies the drawing once more. His foot must have smudged half of Salim's face away. Deaf Man gasps, taking the smudge as a sign, a confirmation that his oldest friend won't be coming back again. Groaning softly, he lays his cheek in the dust, beside what's left of the drawing.

But then he remembers Talitha, and the happy feeling he had just a little while ago returns—the hopeful way he felt when he touched her emerald and she ran off with his cup. It's the same feeling he always had when Salim came around, the sense of his soul being more alive in his skin. It was this sensation that let him know, years ago, that Talitha belonged to Salim— his savior who shared everything with him, including this gentle daughter's friendship.

He redraws Salim's face, knowing this is the only way he'll see him now. Deaf Man smiles down, recalling their many good times together. And touching a thumb to the side of his chin, he motions his sign for *thank you* again and again.

CHAPTER 64

Lucian
swept up from the river

HIS MOTHER'S ROOM IS OVERHEATED, smelling of rose talc and stale breath. She opens her eyes at the sound of the door. Lucian hasn't visited in ages, and she's shriveled in his absence. Her cheekbones protrude while the skin around her neck sags. She's tiny as a little girl.

"Mother?"

Squinting in his direction, she clears her throat. The television drones as she studies him with a confused expression.

"Which one are you?"

"Lucian," he whispers, and even though a vanity chair is well within reach, he remains standing, biting his nails, yearning for a hit of junat.

"Ah yes...the smart one." She pushes an avalanche of crumpled tissues off the bed with a swipe of her hand. "I always liked you best," she coughs, and they stare at each other for a while.

"Well…what do you want?"

It takes a few seconds for Lucian to find the words, but when he sees she's turned her head away to stare out the window, he starts mumbling. Finding the chair, he sits awkwardly with his head in his hands, talking more to himself than to her as he explains the situation, working up the nerve to ask her about the wedding ring. The TV stays on the whole time, but it's turned down—a vague background din of soap operas and commercials. Lucian pauses to look up now and then at this woman who is technically his mother but practically a stranger. Her eyes are closed. She's breathing in a steady rhythm like she's fallen back asleep.

When he realizes she's not really listening, something comes over him and Lucian carries on, laying his many sins bare: theft, kidnapping, embezzlement, torture. Murder. They fill the room from top to bottom like so many invisible corpses, spilling out the door, down the hall, and throughout the dazzling white castle his father named Dekadente, an Afrikaans word meaning something like *decadence*.

When Lucian is finally done, an infomercial for face cream blares on.

"Where's that clicker?" His mother startles and shuffles the blankets on her lap. Not able to find the remote control, she looks up at him. "You there," she says. "Who are you again? Would you mind turning this up?" She motions to the television. "I want to order this cream. This 'Silk Cream.' Now, where's that clicker…"

Lucian grabs the remote control off the floor and hands it to her.

"Did you hear anything I just said?" he asks softly, suddenly embarrassed.

She stares at her lavender lily-patterned quilt without acknowledging him. Finding a loose thread, she tugs it.

"Mother, don't you understand? This life, this palace…it's a deck of cards. And we're sitting on top, but it's crumbling down all around us."

She's wound the thread so tight that her fingertip bulges with blood. Staring at her fat pinky, she pokes it with her fingernail. Some of Lucian's story did penetrate her foggy mind, because it's now full of vivid scenes from her childhood—of bathing with her baby sister in a stream when men with guns came to drag her away. *"Nia!"* She had screamed for her sister, who was left crawling all alone toward the water. *"Did they take her too? Nia!"* She wants to scream now as she did that day when they threw her in a burlap bag and hauled her away. *"Nia! My sister can't swim! Don't leave her all alone!"*

Nia, the name she's muffled with every hit of the junat pipe.

Because speaking of this horror is impossible. She's tried a few times over the years with Clara, even with her husband when things were peaceful between them. She tried to tell him about the family that kept her as a "servant" when he found her, and how the master wouldn't let her leave the compound; how he only finally let her go to sweeten a business transaction. Also, she only remembers the horror of being stolen in her old language—one she hasn't forgotten, but one that would hurt too much to cross her lips.

"Here," she says, catching Lucian's attention as he stands to leave. She holds out her wedding ring—an enormous diamond nestled between two slightly smaller emeralds. He stares as she places the ring in his hand. She then removes a black velvet pouch from the drawer in her bedside table.

"Please," she says quietly, "buy back the girl."

Lucian is speechless. He takes the ring and places it in his pocket, knowing it alone will certainly pay off the loans both he and the poor boy Moses owe Badru. Its heft and sharpness against his thigh, along with the fact that his mother gave it to him before he got a chance to ask...he can breathe again, deeper than he has in years.

"Thank you," he says as she motions him over, her arthritic hands struggling to untie the velvet pouch.

Grabbing his palm, she empties the bag. A puddle of emeralds rattle out as a familiar voice whispers in his ear—

Surely you could afford a tiny bag of junat...

His head flinches sharply when he hears it again—

Come on, just one last smoke...

Forcefully, he exhales, breathing out in a way to rid himself of his old crutch, his old life. But it's been such a long day. The idea of relaxing—even celebrating—one last time would be so...He shakes his head swiftly, like an animal shaking off water.

Misinterpreting the gesture, his mother cries, "*You won't buy her back?*" She grabs his wrist, staring up with urgent eyes. "*Please,* Lucian, buy back the girl! *I beg you, please!*"

"Oh no," he assures her hastily. "I'll buy her back—*I promise.*"

As the words leave his mouth, Lucian suddenly knows exactly what he needs to do. He remembers Nelson saying they were taking the girl to the city on the other side of the mountain tonight. He's still got time—not much, but maybe, *just maybe...* there's a chance to make this right.

Hearing this promise, his mother sees her long-lost sister swept up from the river and laid peacefully back in their mama's arms.

CHAPTER 65

Desta
tiny enough

S HE BOUNCES ON THE FLOOR of the black jeep as it twists and turns, racing up the side of Great Mountain. Desta finally stopped singing hours ago. It wasn't because the filthy bag on her head made it hard to breathe or because her constant "Song of the Birds" infuriated her captors, spurring on their abuse— closed-fist punches to her face, rifle jabs, even a crack to the skull that made Desta sleep for a while.

No, the violence didn't stop Desta from singing. It was her thirst.

She attempts to swallow her spit, but her throat burns like sandpaper.

Should I pray to the god of water? Desta wonders, but she's never seen this done without a sacrifice, an overturned cup poured out on the clay.

Her head injury from a few hours ago has done a bit to buffer the initial terror of being kidnapped. Now there's a blurriness mixed in with her fear, a confusion. Something in her wants to pray, but Desta's at a loss because that's always been something the grown-ups do, the chief and aunties and uncles. She remembers her mama groaning about her headaches, always asking an elder to *"take these herbs to Great Mountain, burn them—beg for my cure,"* or her Uncle Salim, with his Shepherd God who made the world yet also—*somehow*—lives in our hearts. Grown-ups were the ones who prayed. Desta would learn how when she was older.

But now, this Shepherd God has piqued her mind. The other gods live *outside* of you—how could she reach them on the floor of this jeep? The god of *teff*—he's in the fields. The thunder god is high in the sky. *But this Shepherd is* tiny *enough to fit in my heart?*

The idea makes her smile a painful smile. She lays a hand on her chest, imagining His speck of a candle casting its light. She babbles aloud: "Is his hooked staff small enough for a mouse?" She's so confused and thirsty and it feels like the jeep has been swerving and skidding over ruts in the steep dirt road for hours.

She pictures Uncle Salim sitting beside her. He's enjoying this conversation about his tiny, heart-sized God. He's not offended a bit. Rather, he welcomes Desta's questions. She laughs at his smiling face, wondering if this is what it means to pray, while her kidnappers scream at her from the front seat: *"Shut up—or else!"* Suddenly, the hilt of a handgun cracks her head, and Desta is knocked unconscious once more.

CHAPTER 66

Lucian
a tiny spark

EYES WIDE, DRIVING WILD, Lucian's white truck revs and bumps over the rocky road. The black jeep's tire tracks stretch before him, visible in the meager glow of his bouncing headlights, calling to him, propelling him onward.

"I'm sorry, I'm just so sorry!" He beats the steering wheel with his bloody fist, pretty certain he's praying, hoping he's praying. Begging God to answer with a sign, a glimmer of life, the kidnappers' brake lights up ahead—anything. Because saving this stolen girl, fulfilling this promise to his mother, to himself, *right now, this night*, has become his one and only light—a tiny spark in his soul, but he knows…if this spark is extinguished, it will destroy him.

Sweating, praying, speeding, he suddenly sees a spotted hyena appear in his path, its beady eyes perplexed, its tail straight. Lucian swerves and almost hits a tree. But he doesn't slow down, because this tiny light—he can't let it go out. The moon is covered over with misty clouds, making everything so much harder to see. Yet he fans the flame within him, feeding it with his foot pressed to the gas pedal.

"I'm sorry!" he cries as so many faces flash through his mind— miners he's mistreated, girls he's stolen. *"God, I'm so sorry."*

Lucian catches his reflection in the rearview mirror and startles. His father's face is glaring back at him.

He grips the wheel tighter as he whips along, scraggly trees and dark shrubs screaming by in a blur. A glance at his hands, his bloody, chewed fingernails. And again, it happens— he sees them…*healed*…at the very same moment the black jeep comes into sight.

Lucian knows there's only one thing that will make Nelson hand over the kidnapped girl—and it's the not the wedding ring in his pocket. He speeds up, flashing his lights to catch their attention. When they don't slow down, he rams his truck into the back of the black jeep until it finally pulls over. Nelson hops out of the driver's seat and slams the door shut, his face filled with confusion and anger. "What the hell's going on, Rot? Why are you here?"

Lucian stands his ground in the middle of the dirt road, lit from behind by his truck's headlights, while all around skinny clouds of dust snake up into the night. Nelson's furious. He shoves Lucian's chest with both hands, resentment toward this little brother who's always slowing him down and throwing a wrench in his plans bubbling to the surface. That's how it's always been: Nelson, the firstborn son, is stronger, taller, quicker in every way than his younger brother Lucian. But it doesn't matter that he's more charismatic, or that he always got along better with their father. Mr. Kerr left sole control of Dekadente to Lucian long ago for one reason, and one reason alone: Nelson could never learn how to read. No amount of tutors or trying or thwacks on the back of his head from their father could stop words from dancing around on the pages in front of him. So Lucian, the *"smart one,"* received everything, while Nelson was left as his informal "consultant."

Now, as the brothers stand facing each other on the dirt road, Lucian knows this white mansion—and everything it stands for—is the only thing Nelson will accept in exchange for the girl trapped in the back of the jeep idling beside them. Lucian coughs on the acrid exhaust. He looks Nelson in the eye, something he hasn't been able to do in a long time.

"Dekadente belongs to you now."

The statement knocks Nelson off balance. He steps back, as if blown over by a sharp wind. Badru's mercenaries get out to see what's holding them up. As soon as they recognize Lucian from the dormant mine, they start yelling, and one of them points a gun at him. But Nelson's commanding voice rises above the others, *"Give us a second!"*

There's something of their father's authority in his tone, and the men step down uncertainly, glaring at Lucian from behind Nelson's back as they move to guard the jeep. Lucian ignores them, focused solely on his brother.

"The mines, Dekadente—they're all yours. I wrote a signed confession about my crimes and sent it to our lawyer. I've passed all ownership on to you, and I'm turning myself in to the police tomorrow."

A slow grin of pleasant surprise spreads across Nelson's face, but it disappears with Lucian's next statement, "But there's *one* condition…" He gestures to the jeep. "You've got to give me the girl."

Nelson scowls, retorting angrily, "What about the bank? A lot of good Dekadente does me if they seize our holdings. *We need that girl.*"

"Don't worry about the bank or Badru—I found a way to take care of them."

"Why should I believe you?" he sneers suspiciously, waving his arm. "Why should I believe any of this?"

Lucian steps closer to his brother, taking the diamond ring from his pocket and showing it to Nelson where the mercenaries can't see, as these muscle-bound men look starved for a taste of his blood after what Lucian did in the mine a few hours ago and he doesn't want them running off with it. Nelson's eyebrows go up in shock when he recognizes the ring. His voice is barely a whisper, "You *took* Mother's…?" He sounds almost impressed. Lucian shakes his head in disgust at the assumption.

"She *gave* it to me. She asked me to buy back the girl." He re-hides the ring in his pocket, adding, "Call our lawyer if you don't believe me about Dekadente; he'll tell you."

For a long moment, Nelson's eyes search Lucian's, trying to figure out if this is some sort of trick. But Nelson's always been able to tell when his little brother is lying, and he was never much good at it anyway. Nelson nods slowly, making up his mind. "Take her," he says. "I'll tell the guys there's been a change of plan."

Lucian breathes a sigh of relief as Nelson turns away, going to talk to the mercenaries standing by the jeep. He stops after two steps, though, his shoulders taut. "Lucian," he calls. Lucian straightens, surprised—he can't remember the last time his brother used his real name. But Nelson doesn't turn around as he warns, "Badru isn't going to be happy about this. Even with the ring—*watch your back*."

Before Lucian can respond, Nelson strides toward Badru's men. He motions for them to come close and speaks to them quietly. Lucian runs to their jeep before his brother can change his mind, opening the back door and uncovering Desta's head. She's unconscious, her eyes swollen shut, her lower lip split in half.

"*My God!*" Lucian whispers in horror as he cradles the girl in his arms. He needs to get her out of here. He needs to get her home.

Lucian carefully carries Desta to his truck, hearing a furious argument break out among Badru's men. He quickens his pace as someone pulls out a cell phone to check on the story Nelson just fed them. When Lucian reverses to make a U-turn on the road, he tries to meet his brother's eye. But Nelson won't turn around. He won't even glance in his direction. And as Lucian speeds away, thoughts of Nelson keep returning. His brother's face—the look in his eyes when Lucian gave him Dekadente. *Relief* is the word that comes to mind, enormous relief, as if Nelson had finally found something he'd lost long ago.

Lucian gasps, covering his mouth with a battered hand as he realizes he just returned the first big thing he'd ever stolen, even though he hadn't stolen it on purpose. Because Dekadente— the weightiest burden of Lucian's life—has been cut loose. The sense of freedom is exhilarating. No wonder Lucian feels as if he's flying down the mountain.

But even as he puts distance between himself and the mercenaries, he senses Badru's talons closing in on him. "*Watch your back,"* Nelson's final words ring in his ears. His brother knows Badru better than anyone. Lucian has no doubt the warning is real. Yet he has no concern for himself. His only hope is to get this barely breathing girl to the doctor in time—the doctor who is hopefully caring for Flora right now.

CHAPTER 67

Lucian
my fault

CLARA'S ROCKING THE BABY when Lucian rushes into the room with Desta in his arms. It's the same way he carried Flora this morning, only Flora was writhing in pain. Desta, by contrast, is slack, lifeless.

"Help me!" he begs Clara as he lays Desta at the foot of the bed.

Shocked, Flora sits up straight. "Cousin!" she gasps.

Clara passes Damien to his mother and leans in close to the girl's face.

"She breathes," Clara sighs with relief. Then she grabs Desta's wrist to take her pulse as Badru explodes into the room. There are a few men with him. They each carry an automatic rifle. Badru looks like he's about to start shouting, his weapon brandished in the air. But then he sees Clara with Desta and steps back.

His expression changes dramatically—from fury to shame in the blink of an eye. Calmly, Clara smiles at him.

"Well, hello, Bad-*rrr*u," her Spanish accent sneaks in, rolling the *r* in a name she's spoken so many times: at the kitchen table when she fed this same man as a skinny, ravenous teenager, and—of course—in her nightly prayers. She's merely greeted him, but Badru shrinks back as if he's been smacked.

"The power of the Señorita," Mr. Kerr's voice echoes in Lucian's mind from the grave. It was his common sentiment about the beloved housekeeper who struck respect into the hearts of his sons, and apparently into the hearts of their lifelong friends as well—even those who grew up to be mercenaries. Badru himself had folded his hands to say grace many times when he was a teenage boy at their table, but only if Clara made the request. Back then, it wasn't because he feared some sort of punishment from this petite, gray-haired woman. No, he happily gave thanks at her table because she made the best empanadas, which she heaped on his plate, all the time looking him in the eye and listening to him in a way that no one else did—like she really cared. Badru never left the table without a full stomach and a full heart.

Now, Clara fixes him in place with a look, her right eyebrow hitched precariously high. The men's shoulders slump because they can tell—Clara knows *exactly* what's going on. Lucian is the first to speak.

"It's my fault!" he confesses, holding his mother's wedding ring out in a closed fist to Badru. "But this will cover what I owe you—what I *and* Moses owe you, and more."

Without looking up, Badru takes the ring. He knows about Lucian's financial situation and assumes correctly that he's just been handed Lucian's mother's wedding ring, a one-of-a-kind, exquisite diamond. He holds it tightly in his fist and stands still as a statue, his face impossible to read. Lucian feels he's in the presence of a crouching lion that's sizing him up. He knows full well that the mercenary's temper is unpredictable. He once saw Badru freeze this way when one of his underlings accidentally insulted him. There had been a moment of silence. Then Badru shot the man three times in the head, so fast that Lucian hadn't even seen him draw his pistol. But another time a farmer had come to Badru, pleading him to forgive a debt. When Badru measured the man up with that expressionless face, Lucian had been sure the farmer was as good as dead. But after a tense moment, Badru had laughed as though it was nothing. He gave the man a whole extra month to repay him.

Lucian knows he can't stop Badru from ruining him. If the mercenary decides he's gone too far—wedding ring or no—Lucian fully expects his body to be found in the river the next morning. All he can do is pray that Badru is in a forgiving mood, or at least that the diamond is enough to distract Badru from how Lucian had made a fool of him today.

He watches nervously as Badru's hand strays to the gun at his hip. But suddenly, Desta screams, cutting through the tense silence like a knife. She's woken with no one noticing. Terrified, she grabs at the quilt as she looks around the room, frantically taking in one strange face after another. In her struggle, she falls off the high bed loudly, an awkward tumble, a panicked yelp.

"Cousin!" Flora cries, and Desta darts to her auntie's side, trying to climb behind her, sobbing uncontrollably.

"It's okay!" Flora assures her as Desta buries her face in her auntie's neck. "You're safe now…I know, I know, I know…"

For just a second, Lucian looks at the girl he would have sold to pay his debts, the one he would have condemned to a life of prostitution or forced labor. Maybe he deserves whatever Badru will do to him. But as his gaze moves back to the mercenary, Badru slowly takes his hand from the gun, and instead speaks to Lucian in a tone low and threatening, "Cross me again and no diamonds will be enough to save you." Badru slices a finger across his own throat. *"You understand?"*

Lucian nods wordlessly, not sure if it's the sobbing girl or Clara's presence that's changed the man's mind. But whatever the reason is, he's grateful.

Badru glares at him a moment longer with a look of disdain and fury, and for a heartbeat Lucian wonders if he'll shoot him after all. But then Clara clears her throat loudly, a noise that carries over Desta's terrified whimpers. At the sound of it, Badru drops his head, curling his pinky finger through the wedding ring.

"We're done here," he growls, motioning to his men, and they file out of the room one by one. Badru is the last to leave. He casts one final look in Lucian's direction. "In regard to you and me..." He shakes his head in disgust. "We're done too."

Lucian receives Badru's message loud and clear—the mercenary will never loan him money again. Such a threat even a few days ago would have sent him into a panic, as Lucian's relied on Badru for years. But tonight, the idea of being cut off hits him with same emotion he felt when he unloaded Dekadente a little while ago.

Badru slips out of the room, and Lucian exhales, a long, pent-up shiver snaking down his spine.

CHAPTER 68

Talitha
an explosion of voices

MAYBE IT'S NOT A WOMAN *at all who's making that bleating sound, I hope and pray.*

Maybe it's a lost lamb calling for its shepherd.

The wailing swells, becoming its own crushing force, like Great Mountain's outline looming in the darkness before me. It's an explosion of voices I've heard before, one impossible to mistake for another. It's the only reason why I—once again, for the second time in a day, for the second time in my entire life—toss a full *mtungi* of water from my head and run as if I'm being chased by a cheetah.

Faster, faster, faster, legs zipping through the valley. Glancing down at Deaf Man's cup, I notice it's empty, but I hold its handle all the tighter.

Dekadente glows in the corner of my eye, a passing thought. I take no time to miss Mama. Legs flying, lungs burning, my feet snap vines that would have been beans; my fist rips stalks that could have been corn.

All the while the bleating grows, filling the dark purple clouds overhead. Questions explode—*Is it Nala? Or an* Other? The screaming is human, but sheep come to mind, jackals ripping their throats—red blood, white wool.

I land in Papa's plot, *slap slap slapping* his trees. Pebbles rain down as I climb the last cliff home. Grabbing a root, I slice open my hand. Pushing myself up on a rock, I gash my foot, but I don't care because *the mourning cry won't stop now!*

The fire pit is in sight, and the aunties—not only are they wailing, they're wilting into one another.

Impossible, I think. *The retches are never that fast!*

Moses yells my name, running down the slope, a torch held high in his hand. He slows at the sight of me. His stormy eyes take in the giant emerald, confused.

"Talitha, what's—?"

I cut him off.

"*Is it Nala?!*"

He touches my shoulder.

"Brave spit up," Moses says, looking at the ground, "and must have choked…by the time Eshe realized—he was gone."

Jaia's voice rises above all the noise—the women mourning, Moses' heavy breathing, my own heart pounding. Hers is a bouldering cry that leaves a black hole in the sky, a dark sucking vacuum—the sound empty arms make when they reach for a baby who is no more.

I push past Moses and run up the hill. Torches part to let me in. But I hold back, stunned by the scene before me: Jaia cradling Brave while so many *Others* lie curled on their sides, writhing in pain, oblivious to anything but the devil in their bellies. Then there's Auntie Eshe's dark silhouette, hunched over, silent for the first time ever.

A few villagers notice me. They point and gasp at my necklace. Some reach out with trembling hands, and even Peter turns to look, his sad eyes widening in shock at the jewel around my neck. But Jaia only has eyes for the baby boy in her arms, the one Papa loved, the one we all love too.

And as she bathes Brave in tears, I lay the empty cup at his feet.

ONE YEAR LATER
MORNING

CHAPTER 69

Talitha
Brave Water

I STILL WAKE BEFORE THE *OTHERS*. It's a habit Mama struggled to impart, but one I can't stop now no matter how I try— no matter how I'd like just a few more minutes in the dark, sleeping on my side, cuddling Nala.

Let me get a jump on the corn mash, I tell myself as I step over a snoring Desta and walk out into the morning.

❋ ❋ ❋

Mr. Lucian brought her back with Mama and Damien once they had recovered. We'd gotten word she was safe—that he'd rescued her, just as he had rescued Mama. But nothing could have prepared me for the second she stepped out of his truck—her face covered in bruises.

During the time she and Mama rested at Dekadente, I was thrilled my Desta was back with us already when I thought she could be gone forever. But I was also nervous to face her again after how cruel I'd been. After…

Shut up! Shut up! Shut up!!!

But not just that—the words were only one part. There was also the jealousy, the way I had ignored her, the way I had resented her for simply being herself. For months.

I knew I needed to apologize, but I didn't know where to begin. So I laid on my mat at night, practicing my apology again and again:

"I'm sorry, Cousin," I whispered, "I will never curse you again. I will sing with you anytime you want!"

I had a whole speech planned, and that's why I was so surprised when I almost didn't get to say any of it. Because when Desta hobbled out of the truck, she fell into my arms and blubbered her own apology first:

"I'm so sorry, Talitha!" she whimpered. "The way I made you mad…I was peacocky! A show-off! Please for—"

"NO!" I pulled back. That's when I realized everyone was watching us. "I'll tell you later," I said softly, then hugged Mama. Auntie Eshe and Peter were there, and we all laughed and took turns holding the baby. Mr. Lucian backed into his truck and drove away. Once Mama was settled in our hut, I took Desta by the hand.

"I'm the one who should be sorry—not you," I said as we walked to the Spirit Tree. I had to beg her to hear me out.

"You may have been careless," I said as we sat on the cliff, listening to the bells and broken glass lifting on the breeze. "But I was mean on purpose. I'm truly and deeply sorry." Then I told her everything I'd been holding inside for months, starting with my jealousy toward her, and about Moses—the baby birds he sends flying inside of me and what they mean. I told her how much I hate

my scabby knees and skinny legs and how I wish I could be beautiful like her. It all just came pouring out of me like water from the sky during a monsoon.

I couldn't believe it, but I blurted out the part about Moses' role in her kidnapping, and how I tried to rescue her and failed. Then I told Desta what I regretted most of all, more than anything else: my last words to her, shut up, shut up, shut up!

When I finally finished, she looked away. I covered her hand with my own. Wind snuck around the corner, whipping our hair into our eyes, lifting our decorated strings. We sat quietly for a while, watching the white strings fly, listening to the melody of our friendship.

When she finally looked at me again with that sneaky little grin, I saw forgiveness in her eyes. It was a moment I'll never forget. My heart flew out of my chest, high as one of the untethered strings before me—cut free from the weight that had been holding it down.

※   ※   ※

I hear a noise and stick my head back in the hut, thinking Nala has woken and wants to join me at the well. But the rustle was her sneaking over to Desta's mat, because now she's curled up in a ball on top of my cousin's back. I smile, wishing I could sleep as deeply as Desta; wishing…wishing…this time could go on forever. But I know she has to return to the Korins soon. She won't be far, and we've been separated like this before. Still, it will be hard to say goodbye.

A few meters down the path, and I'm the first in line at our new well.

As always, Beloved waits at his new post by the yellow-han-
dled pump. The vibration of feet wakes him the same way it
did at Weeping Rock. He reaches for my pail. I hand it to him
and stretch my arms up to the sky, which is opening slowly like
a violet.

For just a second, I miss my old walk to the spring—my
time alone with Mama. Even though those days feel lost in the
past, I think of them often as a time when we were all so much
younger; when life was innocent, but impossibly *hard*.

Beloved primes the handle, lifting it up and down, again
and again until water gushes against tin, loud and hard. In a
few seconds, my bucket fills with enough clean water, ice cold
and clear as glass, for the morning meal and half a day's cleaning. By the time it's full, I smirk at the thought of missing the
spring. Our newly drilled well makes me feel like royalty. I look
down, remembering the heavy emerald pendant that paid for it,
shimmering like Weeping Rock in the sun.

I take a moment to sit beside my bucket and thumb Papa's
mequeteria, praying, *"Lord have mercy, Lord have mercy, Lord
have mercy..."* I snatched these beads from the Spirit Tree the
morning Desta came back to us, and I'm not afraid to pray
them out in the open. Ever since Mama and I got the well
drilled, everyone is more tolerant of our faith. The chief lets
the traveling priest visit whenever he wants, and the little ones
come to listen when Mama reads from her green Bible at night.
Papa and Uncle Ibrahim would be proud of the way she teaches
them. Some of the aunties and uncles are coming to believe
in our Shepherd God too. They see His hand in everything
that happened on that magical night a year ago, the same way
Mama and I do.

A few members of our tribe have even asked to be baptized, just like baby Damien was a few months ago, when Mama took me, Peter, and the baby into the city for the first time for the feast of *Timkat*. We met Jane, Mama's sister, that day. She gave Mama a bouquet of white roses, a gift from their parents, who could not join us but who sent their best regards. Mama said she didn't think they were ready to see her again just yet. But she hoped one day they would be. I hoped so too. I wanted to meet them.

And the stutter in my soul, the one that made me so afraid... it's gone now. It's been gone ever since the night the Shepherd God touched me. Things have been different since then. It's as if I'm never really alone anymore, because I know *He's with me*.

Still, Mama and I don't see these things completely the same way. While I love her, I like to think these prayer beads help me see life through Papa's eyes. Like the time she raised her fists to the sky, shouting, "It's a triumph!" She was celebrating because the chief bowed before the giant crucifix our priest had pounded into the clay beside the center stump. Before that moment, he'd only ever bowed like that to Great Mountain. Mama said the same thing when I started carrying these beads like this out in the open. And while I'm glad she's happy, to me this *mequeteria* isn't any sort of triumph. To me...I'm just holding hands with Papa.

The familiar whir of a motor and a cloud of red, swirling dust announce Mr. Lucian's arrival. His truck stops a little way down from our well. He hops out and waves at me, then runs quickly up the path. I act like I don't see him. But he knows I did. This kind of thing happens all the time lately. He's always running to talk to Mama about the search for Adia, Shani, and some other Korin girls, as though that could earn her forgiveness. It makes me crazy! I mean, this is the man who made fun of the way Papa talked *to his face!* This is the man who worked Papa like an animal and let Badru blow up the mine with Papa inside it! Yes, he's the same man who saved Mama and Desta; for that, I am truly grateful. It's also true Mr. Lucian turned himself in to the authorities and convinced them to let Moses out of jail by explaining his impossible position in the whole ordeal. Lucian tried to take the blame for everything, but the police put out warrants for Nelson and Badru anyway, sensing that Lucian wasn't the sole mastermind behind Dekadente's corruption. Both men ran, which is why the police didn't arrest Mr. Lucian. They said he'd be more helpful "on the outside" to guide them to Badru's hideouts and search for the lost girls.

Now, Mr. Lucian lives on strict parole, the police monitoring his every move with an electronic ankle bracelet. He stays with his mother and Miss Clara in a small guest house on the grounds of Dekadente, the mansion which is now boarded up but where sprinklers still turn on every day. Only now, instead of merely watering the coconut trees, they water us Kilokie too; the Korins as well. And there's nothing more fun than sneaking off to run through these wide arcs of clean water without fear. Children leap and squeal. Sunlight catches on the droplets, casting rainbows all around. We cool off, darting through the spray, drinking our fill. For a while, some of the boys like Peter—whose knee finally healed—even climbed over the fence to jump in the pool. But that thing's murkier than the swamp now.

Mama stands sideways in front of our hut. She tips her head back, laughing aloud at something Mr. Lucian has said. I grit my teeth, wondering how much more of this I can take...

I know Mama hasn't forgotten what Mr. Lucian did to Papa, but her kindness and sympathy toward him is unbelievable. *"He's miserable with himself,"* she's whispered in my ear when I've cringed at his presence. She always reminds me how his sole mission now is to find Adia and Shani.

I often see her glancing at his hands, the way they tremble uncontrollably. Auntie Eshe says all the shaking, as well as the dark circles beneath his eyes, are signs of junat withdrawal. Perhaps this is why Mama pities and even tries to forgive him.

But for me…forgiveness toward Mr. Lucian is a full-to-the-brim bucket, one very hard to lift. And to be honest, I'd rather ignore this bucket of rocks—I'd even kick it over, but Mama's laughing at him again. So I do what Papa would if he were here. I thumb his *mequeteria*.

☀ ☀ ☀

The other day, I clung to these beads because I caught Mama and Mr. Lucian at the river cooling their feet. She was talking in her excited way about one day opening a school.

"What's going on here?" I demanded. "You're loud enough to wake Deaf Man!"

Clapping my hand over my mouth, I was shocked I'd called Beloved "Deaf Man" by accident. I guess when my heart slips, so does my tongue. Because after our magical night, I demanded everyone call Beloved by his real name—the name his mama gave him, the name Papa always used for his oldest friend. I was bossy and loud, stomping my foot just like Mama does. So now I feel like a fool when I forget.

But I got so angry when I spotted them by the river, I dropped the cloth I'd been dyeing with crushed pomegranate seeds, even though its acidic juice was everywhere, drying my lips, stinging my hangnails, staining my palms. I was working on a new robe for Peter, hoping to have it done in time for his first real hunt with the uncles. But when I heard Mama chatting happily and realized it was Mr. Lucian she was talking to, I ran down the slope. I grabbed her from behind, leaving a purple handprint on her new white kitenge. When she turned to me, I could tell we were both surprised by my strength, but even more by the emotion beneath it.

Mama was holding Damien, and Damien was holding Papa's cross. It dangled on a chain around her neck.

The sight of it—the brassy shine of it—snatched the wind from my lungs like a thief.

"Where did you...?" I reached for the necklace, stunned. I hadn't seen it in years. After Ibrahim and Abba Yosef died, Papa kept it hidden inside his robe. He never took it off, but he didn't dare show it either.

Mama's face softened. She took the cross from the baby.

"I've wanted to tell you," she said, nodding to Mr. Lucian— again, making me furious. He nodded back as if they were speaking some secret language. Mr. Lucian then took my brother in his arms.

Mama lifted the necklace for both of us to see.

"Did you know the medal behind Papa's cross is of Father Damien?" she asked gently.

"Of course I do," I snapped, but then I held it. The feeling of Papa's cross back in my hand..."How did you...?" I coughed through tears. Tears that now—too often—flow freely.

Trembling all over, I kissed the cross Papa had worn faithfully since the day he was baptized. I knew he surely would have had it on the day he died.

"Come, Talitha," Mama whispered. "I have something to show you."

She took my hand and walked me up the path. We stopped into our hut for a burlap sack I'd never seen before. And then quietly, without many words between us, we made our way up to her peak. For a second, I leaned into her arm and imagined we were simply off to the spring as before. She stopped in front of a giant flat rock, the one she leaned on when she was in labor with Damien. She rubbed her hand over a cross chiseled deep into its side.

"Talitha," she said. "Here below this rock…Mr. Lucian has laid your father to rest."

The shock, the dizziness I felt was so strong my knees wobbled. Mama caught me, her arms guiding me down to sit and stare at the carved rock. My fingertips traced the cross' white roughness again and again, and everything I saw became blurry as I stared, refusing to turn my eyes from the mark that now spoke to me, saying Papa. And as my tears splashed dark starbursts on the clay, Mama draped the heavy brass cross and chain around my neck.

"Mr. Lucian didn't tell me until it was done," she said. "He had the mine searched, found Papa, and buried him in the middle of the night. He didn't want the sight of him to upset us. When Mr. Lucian brought me this cross, he thought I'd be mad. But the funny thing is…I wasn't."

"How could you not be?" I whispered, but I couldn't bring myself to look at her. My purple-stained fists squeezed into balls, and I searched my mind for something to say—something hot, something scathing. I wanted to shame her, to scold her for spending time with the enemy. But as I struggled, as my eyes pondered the clay beneath me, the realization that Papa was here met me with a comfort as real as Mama's arms around me, holding me tight.

"The Lord is my Shepherd," she said softly, looking out over her valley, "I shall not want. He makes me lie down in green pastures. He leads me beside still waters. He restores my soul…"

Mama reached into the burlap sack and pulled out Papa's thick black Bible, the one he'd read by the fire at night, full of underlined verses and all his handwritten letters. "Mr. Lucian found this too. Your papa had it in his knapsack when he died," she said, rubbing her hand softly over its cover. "I've been wanting to give it to you so badly, but didn't know how."

I took the Bible from her and hugged it to my chest. As we wept together, I pictured Papa sleeping peacefully in the ground below us. And at that moment, something in my heart gave up. My soul seemed to hush my mind, saying, "Quiet now, let him rest in peace. Let us all rest in peace."

᛭   ᛭   ᛭

"Talitha! *Talitha!*" Mama runs down the slope. Sunlight dances through the dust behind her head, a constant blossom high in the sky. Damien's on her hip, wearing nothing but a swaddling wrap. Nala trails behind sleepily, rubbing her eyes. Mr. Lucian hovers over Nala attentively as she picks her way down the slope. Little does he know my girl could fly up and down this hill with her eyes closed.

"We've found Adia!" Mama yells. "We're sure this time!"

Mr. Lucian and the police have traced many leads to cities on the other side of Great Mountain. Last month, they returned a Korin girl who was forced into prostitution before being sold to a factory owner in the city. She'd been there for years without ever leaving the same building and was even made to sleep under her sewing machine with her leg chained to the floor. But no one has ever found a trace of *our* girls. Until now.

Water sloshes from my pail, soaking my legs, and I suddenly need to sit down. I'm prickled all over with goose flesh. Nala hops on my lap, oblivious to my shock.

"How do you know it's Adia?" I ask Mr. Lucian, looking him square in the face for the first time.

His eyes brighten at my attention.

"The girl they've found has an injured tongue and is fair skinned," he says. "She also arrived in the city shortly after Adia was kidnapped."

Nala splashes her hands in my bucket. Ordinarily, I'd make her stop, but Mr. Lucian's news has stunned me. All at once, I hear Adia's clumsy voice and her laughter is everywhere, in the cool breeze and especially in the warmth of the sun on my face.

Just then, Moses slides down the slope on his heels, his traveling pack slung over his shoulder.

"Azizi and I are going along with Mr. Lucian. The police want someone Adia knows to be there when we get her out."

I lift my hand to him. He looks into my eyes, smiling tenderly. He pulls me up, whispering in my ear, warm and close so no one else can hear:

"Hello, my Beauty."

It's the name he's called me ever since I was finally able to forgive him for betraying Desta—forgiveness that took a very long time, even though I was aware of his horrible position that day; he wept giant tears when he got out of jail, apologizing to Desta and me and Mama and anyone else who would listen to him again and again and again. But I couldn't listen to him. I couldn't even look at him. The funny thing is—Desta forgave him quickly, almost right away.

So when I first raised my eyes in Moses' direction a few months ago, rather than staring at the clay by his feet, he gasped *my Beauty* ever so softly. Now, the name is a secret—like our swimming lessons—only better. And each time he says it, the tiny birds swoop in, fluttering up and down, perching all over me with their pin-prickly claws.

All of a sudden, I'm dizzy, because everything everywhere is too much, too good to be true—Adia returning to us and *my Beauty* and the bright blue sky and Beloved clapping like he knows exactly what's going on.

My heart soars as I watch Moses and Mr. Lucian climb the slope. It's a feeling like the first time our new well gushed water into my very own tin pail. I'll never forget that day, the feeling and the noisiness of it all. It's a feeling and a day and a sound I'd call *joy*.

I squeeze Nala and say a prayer for her mama—*Dear God, bring Shani back too!* The joy travels from my heart down my legs and explodes in sparks under my toes.

Mama senses my song. Papa's cross swings from her neck—worn always now on the outside of her *kitenge*. Damien bounces in her arms, their matching smiles widening as we all hold hands, circle-stepping to a happy rhythm saved just for the babies. Nala reaches into the bucket and splashes us cool. We laugh, and Beloved must feel the celebration too because he beams, showing off his one-toothed smile. And releasing his hand from its faithful grip on the yellow pump handle, he reveals for a moment the name we christened our well:

A name carved with Papa's knife so we'll never forget the son we lost while we receive so much life every day in our buckets and bins, our plastic bottles and our metal drums.

It's my turn to lead the dance, so I wipe happy tears from my eyes and throw them up to the sky and to the red clay. They go out from me to Papa, to Uncle Ibrahim, to Brave, and to all the ones who left us too soon. They spin into silk and wrap those I love in a heavy-laden, soaked *kitenge*. Its fibers are drenched to the core with every tear I've ever cried. And right now, as I hold hands with Mama and Nala, as we sing and dance a circle stomp, this prayer shawl is being twisted, wrung over me like a driving summer's rain. My cisterns pour out, my cup overflows, and my tears—they've turned to dancing.

AUTHOR'S NOTE

I'm an unlikely person to have written a story set in eastern Africa, as I am not from the region. I can only say *Brave Water*—like so many other precious things in my life—*came to me*. I never searched for Talitha on her dusty red trail. Rather, a pamphlet arrived in the mail one day describing the need for clean drinking water in certain regions around the world, and I was captivated by the bright-eyed girl on its cover. Suddenly, telling Talitha's story became imperative to me. I'd watch water gushing from my kitchen faucet, and I couldn't get her voice out of my head. "Turn that off!" she'd tisk just about every night after supper. "I'd have to walk five kilometers with a bucket on my head, just for that one sink load!" I'd scrub pots and pans with her story running through my mind, dry my hands, and go to put pen to paper.

All the while, I knew that if I didn't tell the tale rattling around in my skull, one that I realized could shed light on some really important issues, how could I be certain that someone else, perhaps someone with more cultural acumen, *would*? It was a tale that needed to be told. Because of my trepidation, I reached out for lots of help and tried to be as respectful and sensitive to cultural details as possible.

Lastly, I must explain the special role Mother Josephine Bakhita had in the writing of this novel. I read and re-read her biography when I felt stuck in the writing process—particularly when an editor pushed me outside my comfort zone, asking me to cut a favorite chapter or character or to create a new one. Very often, I'd learn something new about Bakhita that informed a choice I made with the narrative, particularly in regard to the character of Desta.

Interestingly, the name "Bakhita" means "fortunate," and that's how I feel to have been the author of *Brave Water*—thankful for the opportunity and very fortunate indeed.

APPENDIX I: HUMAN TRAFFICKING

WHAT IS IT?

Human trafficking involves the use of force, coercion, or fraud to exploit a person into labor or sexual acts. It is a form of slavery. There are two main types of human trafficking: forced labor and sex trafficking. Victims of either type may be in debt bondage (forced to work to pay off a debt).

WHY IS IT WRONG?

It is a violation of human rights and a serious crime. It is an offense against the sacredness and dignity of the human person.

WHERE DOES IT HAPPEN?

Human trafficking is prevalent throughout the entire world. In areas of Africa that experience poverty, conflict, or cultural acceptance of child labor, young people are particularly vulnerable to human trafficking. Strong trafficking circles also exist in many other parts of the world, including the North American countries of the United States and Canada. According to the United States Department of State, it is estimated that there are almost twenty-five million victims of human trafficking worldwide at any given time.

WHO ARE THE VICTIMS?

Victims and survivors of this modern-day slavery are often young women. However, people of both genders and all ages and cultural backgrounds are victims of human trafficking, including children. Because they frequently face fear of their traffickers and of law enforcement, or have language barriers, victims are often unable to seek help on their own. Poverty, inadequate housing, and lack of opportunity can contribute to vulnerability.

HOW DOES IT HAPPEN?

Some victims are kidnapped by strangers, like Adia and Shani in this novel. Some traffickers are known to the victims and use their relationship to trick their victims. Desta's traffickers relied on the help of Moses, someone Desta and Talitha knew and trusted. Traffickers may also employ a ruse such as promising a job or an educational opportunity to draw victims in. Psychological manipulation is the most common way for traffickers to control their victims. They might threaten harm to family members, humiliate and blackmail their victims, or confiscate their passports or legal documents. Sometimes, as in *Brave Water*, physical force is used.

KEY INDICATORS OF HUMAN TRAFFICKING:

A POTENTIAL VICTIM MAY BE...

- someone with a vulnerability such as being lonely, depressed, emotionally isolated, or having low self-esteem; traffickers exploit this by posing as friends or mentors
- contacted in person or through the internet by a stranger or new acquaintance who asks to meet at a private location
- offered a highly desirable job, or offered bribes or money in exchange for sex or manual labor

A VICTIM MAY...

- be rarely alone without his or her guardian, who is vigilant and controlling
- have a "boyfriend" or "girlfriend" who is noticeably older

- avoid eye contact and appear shy
- not speak the language of his or her given locale and could be discouraged from learning this language
- not perform well in school
- not have access to his or her identification papers or money
- show signs of physical and/or sexual abuse, physical restraint, confinement, or other serious pain or suffering
- be working long hours with no days off, and possibly living at his or her place of employment
- show signs of physical neglect such as being deprived of food, water, sleep, or medical care
- have new branding or tattoos

IF YOU OR SOMEONE YOU KNOW MAY BE THE TARGET OR VICTIM OF HUMAN TRAFFICKING:

- **In the United States,** call the National Human Trafficking Hotline, (888) 373-7888.
- **In Canada,** call (833) 900-1010.

TO LEARN MORE ABOUT HUMAN TRAFFICKING:

- www.usccb.org/offices/migration-refugee-services/ human-trafficking
- www.talithakum.info
- www.humantraffickinghotline.org
- www.canadianhumantraffickinghotline.ca

*Source: US Department of Homeland Security—www.dhs.gov

NOTE: All the web addresses provided in the appendices are for general information only. If you or someone you know is in danger, please contact one of the hotlines listed above or the proper authorities. At the time of initial publication, the URLs listed here are accurate, but website information changes often. No guarantee can be made concerning the accuracy, reliability, or completeness of the information and opinions on the websites referenced.

APPENDIX II: WATER SCARCITY

KNOW THE FACTS:

- Millions of people around the world rely on inadequate sources of drinking water——even today.
- Young women like Talitha and Desta in *Brave Water* spend hours, often walking several kilometers in the hot sun, fetching drinking water. Sometimes they must make this trip several times a day.
- The World Health Organization estimates that 40 percent of the sub-Saharan African population is without easy access to safe drinking water.
- Drought exacerbates the problem, causing loss of livelihoods, displacement, increased food prices, and the death of livestock, especially in agricultural communities.
- Access to clean water makes a significant difference. When a well is drilled near one's home:
  - the frequency of bacteria-borne disease is lessened or eradicated
  - water gatherers are able to spend their time in other ways such as getting an education or seeking employment
  - radical improvements are made to the health and economic prosperity of individuals and the community

*Source: The Challenge: Clean and Safe Water—www.africa.com

TO LEARN MORE ABOUT WATER SCARCITY:

- ▣ www.CRS.org/our-work-overseas
- ▣ www.foodforthepoor.org
- ▣ www.ChurchInNeed.org
- ▣ www.CrossCatholic.org

APPENDIX III: QUESTIONS FOR DISCUSSION, REFLECTION, OR JOURNALING

PART 1: PSALM 23

Psalm 23: a special prayer of Talitha's family:

THE LORD, SHEPHERD AND HOST

¹ The LORD is my shepherd;
   there is nothing I lack.
² In green pastures he makes me lie down;
   to still waters he leads me;
³   he restores my soul.
  He guides me along right paths
   for the sake of his name.
⁴ Even though I walk through the valley of the shadow of death,
   I will fear no evil, for you are with me;
   your rod and your staff comfort me.

⁵ You set a table before me
   in front of my enemies;
  You anoint my head with oil;
   my cup overflows.
⁶ Indeed, goodness and mercy will pursue me
   all the days of my life;

I will dwell in the house of the LORD
for endless days.

1. **How do the words of Psalm 23 reflect the experiences of the characters in Brave Water, literally or figuratively?**
   - Does anyone in *Brave Water* ever have his/her head anointed with oil?
   - Who has his/her "cup overflow"?

2. **How do the words in Psalm 23 relate to your own life?**
   - Have you ever sensed yourself being guided by a power greater than yourself?
   - As for Flora in Noon, Chapter 8, have you ever had "a table set before you in the presence of your enemies"?
   - Talitha has the wind knocked out of her in Night, Chapter 7. Have you had such an experience, where you were literally "made to lie down in green pastures"? Perhaps an illness, where you were forced to ponder life a bit more?

3. **Some characters in Brave Water walk "through the valley of the shadow of death." For example: Talitha struggles in the swamp; Moses hangs from his feet in a pit; Desta is beaten by her kidnappers.**
   - Imagine yourself in one of those dark moments. What thought, prayer, or hope would sustain you?

PART 2: FATHER DAMIEN OF MOLOKAI

In *Brave Water*, Talitha's parents are greatly inspired by the story of the real-life priest, Father Damien of Molokai. This missionary of Belgian descent ministered to the lepers on the

Hawaiian island of Molokai for sixteen years. He died in 1889 after having contracted the disease of those he loved and served: leprosy, also known today as Hansen's disease.

Before Father Damien came, the sick people of Molokai had been on their own for many years. Leprosy was feared because it was a contagious disease with no known cure. Those who had it were exiled to a remote leper colony on the island of Molokai. They remained there until they died, often suffering the pain of separation from their families as well as the ravages of leprosy. Father Damien heard of the lepers' plight and sought permission to move to the island of Molokai and minister to them.

On Molokai he spent his days teaching the Christian faith, building homes and a chapel, and providing comfort and medical care for the sick and dying. Father Damien transformed Molokai from a place of despair into one of faith, hope, and peace.

After years of tireless labor, Father Damien faced his parishioners after Mass one Sunday to inform them that he had contracted the disease himself. But far from being bitter, Father Damien echoed the words of the Apostle Paul, who once said, "I have become all things to all, to save at least some" (1 Corinthians 9:19). Father Damien bravely declared, "I make myself a leper with the lepers to gain all to Jesus Christ."

Father Damien died at age forty-nine surrounded by those he loved the most: the lepers. He is the patron saint in the Catholic tradition of those with leprosy and HIV/AIDS. His feast day is May 10.

1. **Think of a person** or a group of people in your life who is treated as an outcast. Perhaps it is someone at your school who is simply shy or lonely.

- How can you befriend and care for the outcast in the spirit of Salim and Father Damien?
- In what situation(s) are you the outcast?
- Who is your Father Damien?

2. **Father Damien** was known for overcoming obstacles. For example, because of the fear of leprosy, the only way he could go to confession was by rowing out to sea and screaming his sins to a priest in another boat.
- What obstacles get in the way of you living out your beliefs?
- In what creative ways can you overcome these obstacles?

3. **Father Damien's** superiors claimed he wasn't educated enough to be a missionary priest. Salim spoke with a debilitating stutter. Each, in his own way, was considered "not good enough."
- Where and when are you "not enough"?
- What "shortcoming" do you need your faith in order to be "bigger than"?

PART 3: MORNING, NOON, AND NIGHT—PONDERING THE JOURNEY

1. **MORNING:** Fear is a powerful emotion that often directs a person's choices—sometimes effectively, sometimes ineffectively. In the Morning section of this book, many characters make choices motivated by fear. Reflect on those decisions.
- **Talitha yells at Desta**—Was this a good decision? What could Talitha have done differently?
- **Moses directs the masked men to Desta**—Was this a good decision? Did Moses have a choice? What might he have done instead?

- **Lucian acquiesces to another kidnapping**—Was this a good decision? How could Lucian have responded differently?

2. **NOON:** Love, rather than fear, is a more trustworthy motivator when it comes to making life decisions. In the Noon section of this novel, there are many situations in which the characters are motivated by selfless love, rather than fear. Reflect on these examples.

   - **Talitha decides to rescue her mother and Desta**—What situation in your life is calling for such fearless heroism?

   - **Flora marries Salim and moves out to the bush**—Do you sense that you are called to do something out of the ordinary for the love of another? (Romantic love is not the only kind of love that can be selfless.)

   - **Salim denies the comforts of city life to take his newfound beliefs to the Kilokie**—Are you called to deny yourself something right now for the sake of others? What is your own personal idea of service? Could you be called to something more than sharing mere words?

   - **Lucian rescues Moses and his uncle in the mine**—Is there anyone you should go out on a limb for right now? Lucian chose to do the right thing without letting fear of the consequences affect his actions. Are you, or have you ever been, in a similar situation?

   - **Which character's choices** do you admire the most? Which character can you relate to the most? Which character has qualities that you would like to emulate? What are those qualities?

3. **NIGHT AND ONE YEAR LATER:** Love and fear, as well as other emotions such as anger, jealousy, and pride, are a powerful part of the human experience. In the third and fourth sections of the book there are moments when the characters rise above their situations. They refuse to be swallowed by the emotions of the moment, acting out of their will rather than their feelings.

- **In the swamp scene, Talitha stares the crocodile in the eye and refuses to thrash around. She "becomes the monsoon. Only contained."** How did this work for her? Is there a situation in your life where you need to contain an emotional monsoon?

- **Flora makes peace in the end with Lucian, the man who ordered the death of her husband yet repented in word and action.** Have you ever experienced the freeing power of letting go of anger? Is anger or resentment in your life weighing you down? Would you be better off letting it go? Who in your life needs a second chance?

- **In the book's final scene, we see that the characters' "tears have been turned into dancing." They are happy about finding Adia, but forgiveness for past offenses is certainly part of their joy.** Can such transformations happen in real life? Is it possible in your life today?

PART 4: MOTHER JOSEPHINE BAKHITA OF SUDAN

In the process of creating *Brave Water,* the author was inspired greatly by the story of Mother Josephine Margaret Bakhita. Bakhita is a survivor of slavery. She was born around 1869 in the Darfur region of Sudan.

When Bakhita was about eight years old, she was kidnapped by Arab slave traders. The trauma caused her to forget her real name. "Bakhita," meaning "lucky" or "fortunate," was a nickname given to her by her kidnappers, an ironic title for a girl who would go on to receive many scars at the cruel hands of her owners.

Eventually, Bakhita was sold to a member of the Italian Consulate who left her with the Canossian Sisters in Venice when he travelled abroad. It was in the convent that Bakhita formally learned about Christianity. Bakhita expressed that she had always intuitively known about God, the Creator of all things. She was delighted, however, to learn that God loved her and wanted to have a personal relationship with her in prayer. Bakhita asked the sisters many questions and decided to be baptized.

When Bakhita's master returned from his trip, she refused to leave the convent. Her case was brought to the Italian authorities, who declared that Bakhita had been made a slave illegally. Thus, Bakhita won her freedom.

For the first time since she was a child, Bakhita was free to pick her own path in life. She chose to dedicate herself totally to Jesus as a religious sister. For the next forty-two years, she worked in the Canossian Convent and was known for her gentle voice and bright smile. In the Catholic tradition, Bakhita is known as the patron saint of Sudan and the victims of human trafficking. Her feast day is February 8.

APPENDIX IV: BRAVE WATER'S CHARITABLE DONATIONS

The author has committed to donate 25% of all her personal proceeds from the sale of *Brave Water* (in any form) to those in need around the world. At the time of publication, she has chosen

Cross Catholic Outreach to be the recipient of these donations, but she reserves the right in the future to extend the charitable work to a different organization or to split it between several organizations. (Cross Catholic Outreach | Vatican-Approved Catholic Nonprofit | Delivering food, shelter, and hope to the poorest of the poor)

GLOSSARY

ABBA: "Father" in Hebrew; title of respect conferred on priests in the Eastern Rite Catholic Church and the Orthodox Church in some African countries

ACACIA TREE: genus of tree with a distinctive umbrellalike shape that grows in dry, sandy soil and desert climates

BAOBAB TREE: unusual looking tree native to Madagascar, mainland Africa, and Australia; often called the upside-down tree as its branches look like skinny roots; stores a high amount of water in its trunk and produces citrus-like fruits

BARN SWALLOW: small blue bird with a long, forked tail

CASSAVA: dense root vegetable often eaten like a potato; native to South America but increasingly grown in many African countries

CHRISM OIL: consecrated oil used in administering the sacraments of Baptism, Confirmation, and Holy Orders, as well as for the dedication of churches

DIVINE LITURGY: name for the Eucharistic celebration (Mass) for Eastern Rite churches such as Byzantine and Ethiopian Catholic; Orthodox Christians also use the term. In some Eastern Rite churches Communion is received by intinction (the consecrated bread is soaked in the consecrated wine and received on a tiny spoon).

GERENUK: tall, slender antelope that resembles a gazelle

GURSHA: traditional way of feeding someone else during a meal as a sign of love and respect

ICON: religious image typically painted on a wooden panel; holds a special significance in Eastern Christian tradition

JACKAL: small, fox-like animal with large ears, long legs, and a bushy tail

JACKALBERRY TREE: tall tree common in tropical areas, near riverbanks, and in low-lying areas; produces small, tart fruit edible for humans and many other animals, including jackals; also known as the African ebony

JUNAT: fictional drug based on several addictive plants

KAMBU: Swahili term for the lilac-breasted roller, a colorful bird present in much of sub-Saharan Africa; considered to be the national bird of Kenya

KITENGE: article of clothing common in many countries across Africa; often colorful piece of fabric wrapped around the chest or waist; can also be used as a baby sling or headscarf

LAHOH: flat, pancake-like bread made of wheat; used to scoop up food

LIP PLATE: round ornamental plate used to pierce and stretch the upper or lower lip; historically traditional in parts of Africa and still practiced by some today

MANCALA: type of game played with a wooden board and stones or beads; dates back to the seventh century

MARULA TREE: large deciduous tree that grows in many African regions; produces edible fruit and oil that can be used to moisturize skin

MEERKAT: small mongoose; characterized by a wide head, round eyes, and a pointed snout

MEQUETERIA: prayer rope similar to the rosary; often used by Eastern Rite Catholics and Orthodox Christians to say the Jesus Prayer ("Lord Jesus Christ, Son of God, have mercy on me, a sinner"), which is sometimes shortened to, "Lord, have mercy"

MSHIRIKINA: Swahili term; person who practices traditional medicine along with witchcraft

MTUNGI (PLURAL: MITUNGI): Swahili term; large plastic container used to store or carry water; similar to a keg or bucket

MZUNGU (PLURAL: WAZUNGU): term common in many Swahili-speaking nations; person with white skin; can have positive or negative connotations depending on the area and context

NETELA: colorful head wrap; usually made from cotton

ORYX: genus of antelope with three species native to Africa, two of which are endangered; both sexes grow horns

TAMBOTI TREE: medium height tree; grows primarily in southern Africa; exudes a milky latex that can irritate the skin and eyes; wood is valued for making furniture

TEFF: grain native to several eastern African countries; similar to rice or millet; important crop in some countries for both people and livestock

TIMKAT: Eastern Church feast day that especially celebrates the day Jesus was baptized in the Jordan River; coincides with the Western feast day of Epiphany; has Orthodox Christian origins; now a celebration in some countries for religious and nonreligious alike

TURACO BIRD: one of the few bird families endemic to Africa; medium-sized; often have brightly colored feathers; generally better at running or moving in trees than flying

TYPHOID: acute bacteria-borne illness that spreads through direct contact with an infected person or contaminated food or water; patient often develops a rash of red spots on the skin and suffers from a fever and vomiting

WARKA TREE: dense, shady fig tree that grows in many parts of eastern Africa

WAT: also known as *wot* or *tsebhi;* eastern African stew usually made with meat and vegetables

WATERBERRY TREE: shady forest tree; often grows near rivers in many areas of Africa; leaves and fruit are edible

WAZUNGU: plural of *mzungu,* common term for a white person

WEAVERBIRD: family of birds native mainly to Africa; many species have brightly colored feathers and are known for weaving large, intricate nests

WET-NURSE: woman who breastfeeds children who are not her own

YEHEB BUSH: woody bush; produces protein-rich legumes (or "nuts") that taste sweet when roasted and can be eaten raw, boiled, or mashed

THE AUTHOR WISHES TO ACKNOWLEDGE:

MY DEEPEST THANKS to the people who made this book a reality…

Philip Kosloski and Michael LaVoy, of Voyage Comics and Publishing: THANK YOU for believing in this project, generously adopting it as your own, and seeing it through to completion.

Dr. Annie Hounsokou-Lefler for providing key insights about eastern Africa, as well as guidance and light and laughter with the manuscript.

Dr. Molefki Asante, from my alma mater Temple University, for your help with the tiny, last-minute details.

Father Timothy Coday, C.PP.S., a longtime missionary in Tanzania who serves on the Board of Directors for the Tanzanian Unbound Project (unbound.org), for your insights and personal expertise in offering feedback on the manuscript.

Mr. Radoslaw Malinowski, the director of Awareness Against Human Trafficking (HAART) Kenya (haartkenya.org), and the members of HAART who helped critique Brave Water before its final revisions.

Jane Meyer and friends at Ancient Faith Publishing for offering generous feedback on several early manuscripts.

Tom Hoopes and friends at Aleteia.org for their support and offering their keen eyes on early revisions.

Sarah Davies at Greenhouse Literary Agency—your "wish list" was unlike all the others and arrived just in time.

Cadence Purdy and Lan Gao for your amazing contribution to the artwork.

Greg Lloyd, the director of the National Coalition of Clergy & Laity (NCCL), for the work you've done to restore health and dignity to survivors of human trafficking; thanks for sharing your experiences with me.

Lisa Ottaviani and the many other volunteers at Project Have Hope (projecthavehope.org) who work to empower female artisans in Uganda. Thanks for your many creative insights.

Rev. Barnabas Shayo, A.J. of St. Patrick's Parish in Pottsville, PA—thanks for bringing the Gospel to me all the way from Tanzania and for the many nuances you added to Talitha's story.

Anssumanne Silla—thanks for adding your voice to this project, especially in regard to cultural details about food and dance.

Susie Lloyd—you're an inspiration; thanks for your encouragement and guidance with this project.

Sean Fitzpatrick—your keen eye on those final final final revisions were priceless; I hope to return the favor one day.

Many thanks to my well-read parents, Rob and Shelley Evans; grammarian grandmothers, Chloe Oliver and June Russ; and insightful friends Amber LoPresti, Charlotte Kriley, Irene Hudock, and Chris Becker—your feedback was enormously helpful and on par with the professionals. Thanks to my brothers and sisters (including the ones that have married into the family)—your unending support means the world to me. Steph Melber—thanks for simply being alive and living on my street when I needed you most.

A final cartwheel-off-the-high-dive for my husband, Pete, and our seven sons—I love you. I love you. I love you.

SARAH ROBSDOTTIR is a homeschooling mom to seven growing sons. One day a flyer arrived in her mailbox describing
the dire need for clean drinking water in developing nations.
Sarah locked eyes with the teenage girl on the cover and knew
she had to tell her story. Visit Sarah at www.sarahrobsdottir.com.

Made in the USA
Columbia, SC
31 October 2022

70268556R00221